"Hold on   both to sh

She slipped.

"I can't!" hollered Sarah, crying, bringing up her other hand to obtain a better grip. "I can't keep hold. It's too slippery!"

"*Nyoh*, you can! You must!"

"I'm trying to, but—"

"She's slipping away from me!" It was Marisa.

"I've got you!" Black Eagle yelled at her. "Keep hold! Keep hold!"

But Sarah's hands were too wet, as were Marisa's. Though Sarah tried with all her might, her grip was loosening. Meanwhile, Black Eagle was pitching them toward shore with all his might, but Sarah's strength was failing. She was crying.

However, Marisa wouldn't let go. "Sarah! Keep hold!"

It was not to be. With a deafening scream, Sarah's grip broke and she fell, her screams echoing over the rushing water, drowning out for the moment the sounds of the pounding weight of the falls.

The last thought she had as she swooped down into the water was that she had failed in her duty—she would not be there to chaperone Marisa and Black Eagle. Indeed, her fate now lay elsewhere.

Praise for *Black Eagle*

"Engaging . . . Fans of Cassie Edwards will enjoy."
—*Genre Go Round*

Berkley Sensation Books by Gen Bailey

SENECA SURRENDER
BLACK EAGLE

SENECA SURRENDER

GEN BAILEY

BERKLEY SENSATION, NEW YORK

THE BERKLEY PUBLISHING GROUP
Published by the Penguin Group
Penguin Group (USA) Inc.
375 Hudson Street, New York, New York 10014, USA

Penguin Group (Canada), 90 Eglinton Avenue East, Suite 700, Toronto, Ontario M4P 2Y3, Canada
(a division of Pearson Penguin Canada Inc.)
Penguin Books Ltd., 80 Strand, London WC2R 0RL, England
Penguin Group Ireland, 25 St. Stephen's Green, Dublin 2, Ireland (a division of Penguin Books Ltd.)
Penguin Group (Australia), 250 Camberwell Road, Camberwell, Victoria 3124, Australia
(a division of Pearson Australia Group Pty. Ltd.)
Penguin Books India Pvt. Ltd., 11 Community Centre, Panchsheel Park, New Delhi—110 017, India
Penguin Group (NZ), 67 Apollo Drive, Rosedale, North Shore 0632, New Zealand
(a division of Pearson New Zealand Ltd.)
Penguin Books (South Africa) (Pty.) Ltd., 24 Sturdee Avenue, Rosebank, Johannesburg 2196,
South Africa

Penguin Books Ltd., Registered Offices: 80 Strand, London WC2R 0RL, England

This is a work of fiction. Names, characters, places, and incidents either are the product of the author's
imagination or are used fictitiously, and any resemblance to actual persons, living or dead, business
establishments, events, or locales is entirely coincidental. The publisher does not have any control
over and does not assume any responsibility for author or third-party websites or their content.

SENECA SURRENDER

A Berkley Sensation Book / published by arrangement with the author

PRINTING HISTORY
Berkley Sensation mass-market edition / April 2010

Copyright © 2010 by Karen Kay Elstner-Bailey
Cover design by George Long
Front cover art by Gregg Gulbronson
Handlettering by Ron Zinn
Book design by Kristin del Rosario

ISBN: 978-0-425-23384-9

BERKLEY® SENSATION
Berkley Sensation Books are published by The Berkley Publishing Group,
a division of Penguin Group (USA) Inc.,
375 Hudson Street, New York, New York 10014.
BERKLEY® SENSATION is a registered trademark of Penguin Group (USA) Inc.
The "B" design is a trademark of Penguin Group (USA) Inc.

PRINTED IN THE UNITED STATES OF AMERICA

10 9 8 7 6 5 4 3 2 1

Acknowledgments

A special thanks goes out to the following who are Gen Bailey's Warriorettes. You have not only my appreciation, but my utmost respect.

Frances Miller	Debra Guyette
Cathie Morton	Lori Barnes
Janet Hughes	June Phyllis Baker
Diana Tidlund	Rebekah Elrod
Jane Squires	Heather Bennet
Sheila Lawson	Diane Dicke
Sharon Crumper	Tami Bates
Katherine M. Kakegamic	Melinda Elmore
Dena Walton	Jennifer Johnson
Beth Reimer	Deanna Fullbright
Terry Stuart	Sonja Dimitrovski
Emma L. Metz	Dianne Westbrook
Kristy Centeno	Malana Whited
Catherine Abernathy	Linda Barnes
Denell Wieczorek	Monica M. Carter
Melissa Keith	Kathy Lynn Reed
Amy Lytle	Jean Paquin
Raeann Williams	Robin Priddy
Arlene Jones	Debbie Mercer
Marilyn Wigglesworth	Tressa Thorp
Jenny Cooper	Donna Bratton
Kimberly Roulean	Deidre Durance
Katherine Edgar	Carla Corless

Lillian Gilliers

Vickie Batten

Kristen Waxler

Sarah Wendt

Heather Wentz

Paula Willhoite

Pepper Cash

Michele Rose Sonnenberg

Debbie Cosentino

Tamara Miranda

Charlotte Everhart

Author's Note

I would like to acknowledge the following sources of reference:

The book *White Savage* by Fintan O'Toole. It was in this book where I first learned the story of how the white race came to America, and learned more of the Condolence Ceremony.

And the book *The Code of Handsome Lake, the Seneca Prophet* by Arthur C. Parker, 1913.

Both of these books reference the story of how the white race came to America.

Also, the book *Roots of the Iroquois* by Tehanetorens. It was in this book where I learned the early history of the Iroquois.

SENECA
SURRENDER

One

It is a time of unrest. Both the English and the French are battling for control of the North American continent. Both seek the support of the united and strong Iroquois Confederation. Deprivations are extant on both sides of the quarrel, the French and Indians of Canada against the English, the Mohawk and Seneca of the Americas.

As always, in any time of dissension, there are those who seek to profit from the ruin of others.

The Territory of the Iroquois Indians
Lake George area in what is now upstate New York State
By the Lake-That-Turns-to-Rapids
Saskekowa Moon, September 1755

There were eight enemy warriors paddling their two canoes on the lake. One canoe held four of the Ottawa warriors. The other carried two Frenchmen and two more of the Ottawa. At the sight, Sarah's stomach twisted. They were all heavily armed with guns, tomahawks, hatchets and knives, some carrying two muskets. Sarah's guide, on the other hand, possessed only one musket, a hatchet, a tomahawk and perhaps several knives. And he was only one against eight.

Sarah bit her lip and placed her arm around Marisa, a younger woman who was under Sarah's charge. Although Marisa was now full-grown, Sarah, at twenty and nine, was the elder by ten years. Plus, Sarah was Marisa's confidant

and companion, as well as her maid. She was also Marisa's
tutor, and most probably her best friend. So it had been for
most of Marisa's life, and fourteen years of Sarah's.

"They have seen it," whispered Black Eagle.

"What?" muttered Marisa.

"The silver dish. They will come here. And when they
discover it, they will find us. Go to the horses now, mount
them and ride away from here. Go now! Go fast! Ride to
Albany. That will be safest."

"And leave you?" It was Marisa speaking.

Sarah watched as Black Eagle looked long and hard
at Marisa, his glance emanating a love so deep, it caused
Sarah to sigh. In truth, for a moment she wondered if she
might ever be on the receiving end of such attention from a
man, one who was so deeply in love with you that he was
willing to give his life to protect you.

Sarah shook her head and gazed away. She might never
know. Indeed, if circumstances continued in the same vein
as they had begun this day, this might very well be her last
day upon this earth.

At last Black Eagle yanked his gaze away from Marisa
and said, "Yes, you are to leave me, and at once. I will hold
the enemy off for as long as I can."

As he spoke, he turned his attention to his weapons,
whereupon he proceeded to load his musket with powder
and lead. "Go! Now!" He waved them away.

Sarah watched as Marisa hesitated. But then, as though
compelled, she inched toward Black Eagle and laid her
hand on his arm. She said, "I cannot leave you."

Sarah would have spoken up in denial, for it was her
duty to protect her charge. But she was spared the opportunity.

"You must," responded Black Eagle gently. "If you
stay, you might be killed accidentally. Now go! Both of
you, go!"

Sarah was already backing away. Grabbing a handful

of the material of Marisa's dress, she urged the woman to crawl backward along with her. But Marisa broke free of Sarah's hold and again scooted up close to Black Eagle. Placing her fingers over Black Eagle's hand, she massaged it gently before she said, "I want you to know that I love you."

He was quiet, but for a moment only. At last he replied simply, "I know. Now go!"

Unfortunately for Marisa, there was little more to be said. As Sarah watched the two lovers exchange a look, she backed away, and this time Marisa followed.

The horses were already saddled. Both women were good riders, and though Sarah offered a hand to help Marisa into her seat, Marisa waved her away. Sarah wasted no time, and ran to the other mount, but had no more than placed her foot into the stirrup when Thompson appeared out of the woods, running toward them. He was a big man, unclean; plus, in Sarah's opinion, despite the fact that he was supposed to be their real guide, he was a bully. Lucklessly for them, he had his sights set on Marisa and was shooting toward her like a well-aimed bullet.

"Yaw!" he shouted as he ran. "Where do ye think ye are a-goin'?"

Neither Sarah nor Marisa had a chance to utter a word. In an instant, Thompson had laid siege upon the two women, attacking Marisa first, pulling her off her seat. Instinctively a scream formed in Sarah's throat, but more than aware of the enemy about them, she contained it. Whisking her foot out of the stirrup, she came down, landing on both feet. Immediately, she pulled two pistols from their cases on her mount, pushing the guns into the pockets of her dress, and rushed toward Marisa. Thompson held Marisa in his grip, but by sheer willpower alone, Sarah snatched her out of their tormentor's clutches.

But Thompson was a persistent bully, and bringing up his flintlock, he took aim at Marisa. However, luck was on their side; his gun wasn't primed.

Both Sarah and Marisa ran for cover. Extracting one of the weapons from her pocket, Sarah handed it to Marisa, keeping the other gun for herself.

Fortunately, Thompson's shot never materialized. Perhaps the brute was well aware of the threesome's precarious situation. Mayhap he was cognizant that the three of them—Black Eagle and the two women—might never escape.

Whatever the reason, instead of loading the weapon and taking aim, Thompson merely grinned toward the spot where the women had disappeared. Then, clutching hold of both of the horses, Thompson fled back into the woods. But not before he said, "I leave ye to yer fate."

"Pray," Marisa mumbled softly, "Black Eagle was right. It was Thompson who was causing our troubles."

"Aye," agreed Sarah, "so it was."

"Well," said Marisa, "there's little we can do now. Let us return to the shore and help Black Eagle as best we can."

"Yes," whispered Sarah. But exactly what help they could be to him remained to be seen. They needed Black Eagle's protection much more than he required theirs. Still, both women bent down to hands and knees, and pushing their skirts out of the way, they scooted back toward Black Eagle.

They found Black Eagle in the same spot where they had left him, and Sarah was quick to note that one of the canoes, the one carrying the two Frenchmen, was continuing on forward on the lake. However, the enemy's other canoe—the one carrying the four Ottawa warriors—had turned to shore. Sarah glanced at Black Eagle. This was it. It was only she, Marisa and he against a well-armed enemy. What was Black Eagle thinking? she wondered. Was he preparing himself mentally and physically for what was to come?

But what if the confrontation never came? After all, it was possible that the enemy might examine the silver cup that lay next to the shore, the one that had obviously caught their attention, and do no more than be happy with the treasure.

But even as she thought it, Sarah knew it would not be so. The obviously seasoned warriors were Indian; they would take witness of the tracks both she and Marisa had made when they had been washing up after their noonday meal. Indeed, with all the impressions that she and Marisa had left on the shoreline, their prints would lead the Ottawa warriors to them, and neither she, Black Eagle nor Marisa would be spared.

Meanwhile, Black Eagle was alert to the enemy.

"Sir Eagle!" It was Marisa speaking.

Briefly, Black Eagle swung around to look at her. Obviously he had not been expecting this turn of events. He looked incredulous. "Why are you not gone?" he asked in a whisper. "I told you to leave."

"I'm sorry, sir, but we cannot do so," Marisa muttered, her voice quiet. "I fear that Mr. Thompson overpowered us before we had even attained our seats on the horses."

"Where is Thompson now?"

"He rode away, taking the horses with him. But before he left, Sarah was able to secure these." She held up her pistol. Sarah did the same.

"Do you know how to use those weapons?" he asked her.

Sarah and Marisa nodded in unison.

After a moment, Black Eagle ordered beneath his breath, "Both of you, move back behind me. Stay down. Fire only if you get a good shot, otherwise, do no more than watch. If I go down, do not fight the enemy. Yield to them. It is doubtful that they will kill you. Do you understand? Do nothing."

Sarah nodded. Marisa did the same, and following Black Eagle's orders, they each one backed away.

Panic was mounting within her, but oddly, now that the moment of confrontation had arrived, Sarah felt a strange calm come over her. She positioned herself for a good shot, checked her powder and took aim.

Meanwhile, the canoe slid silently to shore. Sarah watched as the warriors disembarked in the water, keeping themselves low. Slowly, quietly, they brought their canoe farther inland, anchoring it on the rocks lining the shore.

Stepping onto the ground, one of the warriors bent down, examining the tracks over the rocks. Another warrior crept forward toward the bushes, where Black Eagle, Sarah and Marisa were hiding. The two other warriors were sneaking toward the item that had gained their attention: the silver dish. Black Eagle waited with what appeared to be great patience, until the warrior who was stealing toward the bushes was almost upon him. Then crying out, he jumped up, the savage attack and the element of surprise in his favor. The ploy worked, but only for a fraction of a second. Still it was enough: Black Eagle thrust his tomahawk into the warrior's neck.

However, with the first war cry, the three other Ottawa warriors went instantly into action. Black Eagle was ready for them. With musket in his left hand, he fired a shot toward one of them. An almost instant scream followed, and another warrior hit the ground.

Without pause, Black Eagle shot forward toward the other two warriors. They were prepared, muskets ready.

What they didn't know was that Sarah had taken aim toward them. She dare not miss. She fired. It was a good shot. Another one of the warriors fell.

Unfortunately, Black Eagle hadn't waited to see if the shot made its mark. Instead, he hurled himself toward the remaining warrior. The Ottawa was ready for him, and thrust out at Black Eagle with his tomahawk.

Marisa gasped, for it was a deadly joust but Black Eagle was agile and quick. He threw himself down, turning a somersault underneath the man's arm. Coming up on the other side of the man, and with a backhand, Black Eagle rammed his tomahawk into the back of his opponent. The warrior was thrown off balance. Regaining his feet, Black Eagle finished the job. Using his hatchet, he landed a disabling blow into the warrior's arm.

Still, the Ottawa was standing; taking hold of his tomahawk, Black Eagle dealt the man a clean blow to his chest. That finished it. The Ottawa went down.

But it seemed the ordeal wasn't over. Already, Black Eagle was shouting at the two women.

"Come!" He pointed toward the lake. "Do you see? Their friends have come back to investigate. Hurry to the canoe. We'll take our chances on the water."

Both Sarah and Marisa jumped instantly to their feet. Springing out of the bushes, they made a line to the canoe. Black Eagle had already set the boat out into the lake and both women hurriedly splashed toward it.

By this time, Black Eagle was waist deep in the water and shouting, "Get in. Pick up a paddle."

Already, shots from the oncoming canoe were hitting the water around them, the barrage a deadly reminder of what was to be if they three didn't escape. Sarah plopped herself into a seat and reached out to help Marisa. But Marisa needed little assistance. She, too, was already seated. Quickly they each picked up a paddle and had no more than set them in the water when the oddest thing happened.

Thompson suddenly reappeared, splashing his way toward them. Sarah reached toward Marisa's weapon, for Sarah had already fired off her one shot.

But Marisa stayed her hand. She said, "Maybe he has come to his senses and will help us."

"I fear your heart is too kind!" exclaimed Sarah over

the noise of the water and the oncoming enemy. However, Sarah hesitated.

Meanwhile, Thompson had pulled himself up alongside the canoe, and he plopped himself into it. He even picked up a paddle. Maybe she was wrong, thought Sarah. Amidst all the adversity, perhaps the man had changed the color of his stripes.

"Let's get out of here!" Thompson yelled, and Black Eagle didn't argue. Hoisting himself up into the boat and settling his paddle into the water, Black Eagle guided the boat out into the deepest part of the lake, heading west, away from the enemy, but in the direction of a sound that had Sarah's heartbeat picking up such speed that she could feel it in her throat.

It was a waterfall, and from the sound of it, a large one. Was this their only advantage?

Perhaps it was so, for they were outnumbered. In a fight, it would be the two men against four of the enemy, two French, two Ottawa. Worse, Thompson was an obvious traitor whose actions could not be trusted. Still, now that he was back among them, it was Thompson's neck as well as their own.

"Faster!" yelled Black Eagle.

Arrows, aimed at their speeding canoe, hit the water beside them with deadly force. Marisa's paddle hit the water at an angle, causing her to tip dangerously toward the water. Sarah threw down her paddle and pulled Marisa back against her with one arm while she gripped the side of wet canoe with her other; though her fingers slipped, Sarah held on fast.

As she nestled Marisa into her arms, the two women sat silently in the canoe, riding out the jerks and sways of the boat.

The scent of Thompson's unwashed body assailed Sarah, causing her to wonder that a human being could emit such odor. Why was Mr. Thompson back? she wondered.

And though she feared it was for no good, Sarah held her tongue.

"Faster!" Black Eagle yelled again.

Behind them the French and Ottawa kept up a steady stream of fire, the arrows landing dangerously close. It was impossible. The odds were against Black Eagle. And yet, he must escape. They all must. If they didn't get away . . .

How had they gotten themselves into this? Suddenly the idea of journeying to New Hampshire to visit friends seemed a bad idea indeed. Was it only minutes ago— perhaps no more than thirty—when Sarah and her ward had been seated beside the lake, calmly washing up after their noonday meal? It seemed hours ago.

But that was when they had first caught a glimpse of the enemy. Had it not been for the silver dish that she had left at the water's edge, the enemy might have passed them by. But it was not to be.

The Ottawa *had* spotted the dish. They *had* investigated. And now, because of her own error, she had taken another's life.

The killing of another human being was not an action to be entered into lightly. But it had been kill or be killed. Ultimately for her, there was no going back now.

The sound of rushing water, of the pounding roar of the waterfall, drowned out her thoughts. Indeed, she could now see the danger. Rapids. Surely Black Eagle wasn't thinking of braving the rapids, was he?

Instinctively, Sarah leaned toward the shoreline, as though by sheer inclination alone she might steer the boat in that direction. An arrow hit at the water, scraping her hand. Close; much too close. Perhaps the rapids were their only means of escape after all. Black Eagle must be thinking so, for he was steering their canoe directly toward the source of that noise.

Again Sarah's heart jumped into her throat.

Meanwhile the canoe picked up speed, heading toward

the waterfall at a pace Sarah knew was deadly. Marisa was still leaning back into Sarah's arms, and Sarah instinctively tightened her hold on her friend. There was no changing course now. The speed of the water had them within its grips.

Sarah threw a look over her shoulder. Even now the enemy was almost upon them.

Truly it was a test. Which would come first: the watery death on the rapids, or the sure hand of the Ottawas?

The velocity of the current pushed at them and thrust them one way and then the other, taking them into an ever faster speed toward the noise that signified the end: the waterfall.

Another well-aimed arrow knocked against the canoe's lining, barely missing Sarah's shoulder. Was the enemy, too, chancing the rapids? Sarah glanced back again, this time hurriedly. No, the French and Ottawa were turning back, paddling their boat toward the southern shore of the lake. Sarah inhaled deeply. But her relief was short-lived.

Before them lay perhaps a greater danger and surely as deadly a hazard as the Ottawa.

Sarah watched as Black Eagle struggled to turn their canoe toward the northern shoreline, away from the enemy, but the currents pulled him back.

"Damn!" Black Eagle muttered. The curse word seemed unusual coming from his lips. In all their adventures so far on the trail, Sarah had never heard him utter anything but the more formal speech. She watched helplessly as Black Eagle set his paddle into the water once again, struggling toward the northern shoreline. But he had no more than set his course when a hidden eddy took hold of their canoe and swung it round and round.

Then the worst happened: The canoe rocked back and forth unnaturally, and Sarah, looking back over her shoulder, was startled that Thompson had come up onto his knees and was struggling forward. Then it came. Reaching down, he grabbed Marisa out of Sarah's grasp.

Instinctively, Sarah tugged at Marisa, trying to keep hold of her. When that failed, she used all her strength to pummel Thompson with her fists, but he was much too big and strong, and he kept a grasp on Marisa despite all of Sarah's attempts to thwart him. It looked bad. He raised Marisa up high, to his shoulder level, and would have thrown her from the canoe, into the lethal undercurrents of the eddy had Sarah not bitten his arm.

Thompson and Marisa screamed at the same time, but Sarah clutched at Marisa and Marisa fell back into the canoe, guided by Sarah's hand. But Thompson didn't give up. He grabbed hold of Marisa again.

At last Black Eagle, who seemed to have had been centering his effort in the struggle to save their canoe, became aware of the fight. Throwing down his paddle, he surged back toward the skirmish to confront Thompson.

Thompson had no choice now but to let Marisa go, and the two men, fighting in an upright position, sent the boat rocking so greatly that Sarah feared it would tip over and throw them all into the tumultuous water.

By the good luck of the Lord, it didn't happen. However, their fate appeared to hang on the ability of a single man, Black Eagle, to best a man who was both bigger and stronger than he.

Thompson raised a knife; Black Eagle blocked Thompson's hand, thrusting the man's arm high in the air. Each struggled for supremacy. The canoe lurched precariously against the currents, and both Sarah and Marisa used their energy to keep the boat afloat.

The struggle pitched the canoe out of the eddy. However, the forceful motion hurled the boat more furiously than ever into the rushing current, washing the canoe steadily toward the thundering sound of the rapids. Just how high was this waterfall?

The two men didn't notice, locked as they were in their own deadly struggle. Thompson launched out at Black

Eagle, socking him in the jaw. The blow knocked Black
Eagle backward, but he recovered easily and shot forward,
catching hold of Thompson's arm and raising it again high
in the air.

Both men fell down into the canoe, Thompson looked
up, and Sarah was witness to the horror that came instantly
onto his face. Without further pretense at the fight, Thompson let go of Black Eagle. Immediately, he dived over the
edge of the canoe, disappearing into swirling streams of
water.

Black Eagle, who was still obviously in the throes of
battle, must have briefly felt the urge to do the same—to
take the conflict into the water's fatal depths. But with a
quick look about him, sanity must have returned to him.

Glancing forward, Sarah beheld the look of dread that
fell over Black Eagle's features. It was obvious: Their boat
was on a one-way path to the falls.

They were doomed.

Sarah watched as Black Eagle knelt down beside
Marisa. Within his gaze was so much love and admiration
that Sarah felt as though she were an intruder in something utterly private. It was as if Black Eagle were saying
to Marisa that were this to be his last moment on earth, by
looks alone, he would shower her with adoration.

And Marisa appeared to be of a similar frame of mind.
Her look matched his. Sarah glanced away, feeling as if she
were trespassing.

It couldn't last, however. Time wouldn't allow it. When
Black Eagle at last jerked his gaze away, Sarah watched as
he scanned the scene in front of the group. Instantly he sat
up, alert.

"Take Sarah's arm!" he yelled to Marisa. "Don't let go!"
He stood to his feet.

Marisa and Sarah exchanged a gaze. They immediately
took hold of each other.

Then it happened. Sarah watched as Black Eagle grasped

hold of Marisa's arm. "Hold tight to me!" he ordered. "Use all your strength, both of you. Use everything in you, but don't let go!"

Marisa and Sarah nodded.

Meanwhile, their boat, caught in the currents, tipped over the edge of the falls. Both Marisa and Sarah screamed. But it wasn't over, not yet.

There was a branch that Sarah hadn't noticed. It was a strong and sturdy part of a mighty oak tree. The branch had extended out over the falls. If Black Eagle could but hold of it with his arm . . .

He did it. Black Eagle seized hold of the tree limb at the same moment their canoe would have carried them past it.

The force of the motion jerked all three from the canoe, and there they hung, each one dangling from the other's grasp. Were they saved? Sarah couldn't say with certainty. She was holding on precariously to Marisa, who was, in turn, grasping Black Eagle. But the force of the movement out of the canoe swung both the women back and forth, causing Sarah's grip to slacken.

There they hung. Thank goodness Indians were conditioned to carry heavy loads, for Black Eagle held them both with only one arm. Then, using their natural momentum, Black Eagle began to swing them both toward the shore. Sarah looked. It wasn't that far away.

"Hold on!" Black Eagle shouted. "I'm going to sweep you both to shore!"

She slipped.

"I can't!" hollered Sarah, crying, bringing up her other hand to obtain a better grip. "I can't keep hold. It's too slippery!"

"*Nyoh*, you can! You must!"

"I'm trying to, but—"

"She's slipping away from me!" It was Marisa.

"I've got you!" Black Eagle yelled at her. "Keep hold! Keep hold!"

But Sarah's hands were too wet, as were Marisa's. Though Sarah tried with all her might, her grip was loosening. Meanwhile, Black Eagle was pitching them toward shore with all his might, but Sarah's strength was failing. She was crying.

However, Marisa wouldn't let go. "Sarah! Keep hold!"

It was not to be. With a deafening scream, Sarah's grip broke and she fell, her screams echoing over the rushing water, drowning out for the moment the sounds of the pounding weight of the falls.

The last thought she had as she swooped down into the water was that she had failed in her duty—she would not be there to chaperone Marisa and Black Eagle. Indeed, her fate now lay elsewhere.

Two

The sun was a low, pinkish-orange orb in the sky, announcing its departure from the day in glorious streaks of multicolored sunlight. Shafts of light, streaming from the clouds, beamed down to the earth, looking as though heaven itself smiled kindly upon the land. And what a magnificent land it was. The birch trees were yellow, the maples red, and the oaks announced their descent into a long, winter's sleep with multicolored oranges and golds. The hills were alive with autumn hues, while the air was filled with the rich, musky scent of falling leaves.

Into this world of beauty came the delicate and pale figure of a woman, looking as though she had been plopped down on a large, flat rock. To a casual eye, it might have appeared as though she were engaged in nothing as untoward as taking in the sun. However, closer inspection would have shown that she had only recently been washed to shore.

Soon, the lone figure of a man emerged from the

forest. Buckskin clad, he was tall, black-haired and brown-skinned, with a mohawk hairstyle that hung long and well past his shoulders in back. He'd been hunting this day, very far from his home. From deep within the forest, he'd felt the breeze and heard the rustle of the water. These things had called to him.

Stepping quietly toward the lake, he looked up, his gaze one of admiration for the splendor of the woodlands. Squatting down and setting his musket onto his lap, he bent over to partake of a drink from the water's cool depths.

Instantly he sat up, alert. From out the corner of his eye he'd caught the movement of something, and glancing toward it, he recognized a piece of clothing; it was a woman's skirt. Rising up, he stepped toward it to get a better look, if only to satisfy his curiosity.

That's when he saw her. She was a white woman, blond-haired and slim.

Was she alive?

Hauling himself up onto the rock where she lay, he stepped toward her and bent to look at her. He placed his fingers against her neck, feeling for a pulse. Her body was so very, very cold, and he was more than a little surprised when he felt the sure sign of life within her.

The pulse was weak, but it was still there.

Turning her slightly, he was surprised at her pale beauty. Of course, being Seneca and from the Ohio Valley, he'd had opportunity to witness the unusual skin color of the white people. But it wasn't as familiar a sight to him as one might reckon.

Who was she? How had she gotten here? And what had happened to her?

Glancing in all directions, he took in the spectacular sights of the forest. Where did she belong? Who did she belong to?

There was nothing here to answer him; nothing to be

seen, no other human presence to be felt. There was nothing but the ever expansive rhythm of nature.

Using his right hand to brush her hair back from her face, he noted again how cold she was, however, he couldn't help but be aware of how soft her skin was, as well. Putting his fingers against her nostrils, he could feel the weak intake and outflow of breath. She was alive, barely.

Did he dare take her away from here? A white woman?

He hesitated and waited. He watched. *Nyoh*, he was the only one here, the only one to settle her fate.

That decided him. If she were to live through the night, he had best take care of her. She needed warmth, nourishment and a chance to heal.

Bending down, he spread his hands over her torso. Depending on the type of injury he might discover, he would either nurse her here or take her to a more protected spot. He ran his hands gently down each of her arms, including her hands and fingers. He felt for anything broken but found nothing.

Spreading his fingers wide, he sent his touch down the sides of her ribs, ignoring her ample breasts. Though his scrutiny was fast, it was thorough. Were there any bruises? Was anything broken? Amazingly, he found nothing.

He continued his search down each of her legs. Surely, he thought, there must be some clue that would tell of her recent history. Perhaps she had broken her neck or back? Gently, he tested the theory, sending his fingertips down over the muscles and bone structure of her neck. Nothing. Nothing substantial to indicate a problem that would claim her life. Turning her lightly onto her side, he felt along her spinal column. Several bones were out of place, but nothing was broken. Her body seemed intact.

He frowned. Again, he wondered what had happened to her.

Was it the spirits of the water? The falls? This was a

dangerous area. Had the force of the rapids claimed another victim?

But why would she have been near the falls? A white woman in the woods alone? His jaw clenched. There had to be someone close by. But, glancing up and looking askance again, he realized that the puzzle of her appearance would not be solved here. His examination of her had at least established one fact: She was fit to travel.

Taking her into his arms, he was more than aware that she felt light in his grasp. Quickly, he stepped down off the rock. Not knowing exactly how she had come to be here, he kept his attention attuned to the environment, listening for a sign of other life . . . anything to indicate the presence of another in the surroundings. She was a beautiful woman; surely whomever she belonged to would miss her.

But again, he could sense nothing unusual. Not a thing that would give him a clue as to what had happened.

Enough. She required care.

Quickly he rushed toward the security of the woods. If someone were here watching, the trees and bushes offered sanctuary. At least they would hide the direction of his path. But where would he take her? He hadn't yet constructed his own shelter for the night, and it was already late in the day.

Perhaps . . . if his memory served him correctly, there was a cave nearby that might lend itself well for their purposes, provided of course that a bear or other animal hadn't already laid claim to it. It was a quiet place, if he remembered rightly, away from the all-seeing eyes of the forest. Plus, it was little known by his own and other tribes. Long ago, his grandfather had shown it to him, indicating that it might serve well if ever he were in trouble.

As White Thunder hurried toward that spot, he gazed down into the pleasing features of the woman, realizing that his curiosity about her hadn't abated. However, there would be time enough to discover who she was once they were safely sheltered. For now he had best hurry to see if the cave were occupied or vacant.

Balancing her weight and his musket into more secure positions, he darted through the forest, disappearing into it.

"Wah-ha, *young beauty,*
sleep well into the night.
The Creator shall take pity
so fear thee not.
Wah-ha, *young beauty,*
sleep well into the night.
The Creator shall take pity
so fear thee not."

White Thunder's deep voice echoed off the walls of the cave, giving the song an eerie quality, as though it might have been a ghost, instead of a man, repeating the lyrics. Carefully, White Thunder sprinkled water over the woman's forehead, enough to keep her fever low but not so much as to kill it altogether.

White Thunder could almost hear his grandmother speaking to him, as if she were standing at his shoulder now, telling him what to do. What was it she had once said to him? That a fever is not always a thing to fear; if kept to a minimum, a fever had the power to drive away the evil spirits from within the body.

White Thunder laid his hands on the woman's forehead, then he moved his touch down slowly to her cheeks, on down to her neck, then one hand down each arm. He repeated the action, once, again, over and over, gently singing the song he had composed.

"Marisa!" The cry of the woman's voice was choked, barely a sob.

He placed a finger over her lips.

But she squirmed beneath his touch, and rocked her head back and forth. "Marisa! Beware!"

He understood her words well. Having lived among the white people for three years, White Thunder had grown used to the strange language and ways of the missionaries who had come to bring their beliefs and their God to the Seneca.

He didn't regret the time he'd spent with them, for they had taught him much about a people who seemed to be swarming the countryside. But not all the English and the French were as honest and intent as those missionaries had been. Indeed, strange were these English and French who were invading the territory of the Seneca, and as they came, they brought their conflicts and wars with each other into Seneca country.

"Always they want something," his grandmother Evening Song had said to the council of sachems. White Thunder had been present, listening. "Always they ask for Seneca boys and men to fight their wars. 'Come and die for us,' they say. 'Come and die for us and we will ensure you keep the land you have always owned.' Beware, I say. He who gives a man what is already his is not to be trusted."

Silence had followed her speech.

At last a chief of the third party of the sachems rose up to speak. He said, "Your words are wise, Grandmother. Have you said all that you wish to say?"

Evening Song had nodded.

"Oyendere, good. But I will say this. Do you forget that a council was held on this matter and that the outcome has already been decided? We of the Seneca Nation objected to siding with the English in this fight, but as is the law of the Confederate Council, the mat-

ter was referred to the Firekeepers, the Onondagas. As you well know, their decision is final.

"Let me repeat in my own words their resolution: Long it is that we have been tied to the English, even before William Johnson, who represents them, came to be a member of our Nation. As you might well know at the time of the Firekeepers' decision, the Mohawk were already fighting the war alongside William Johnson, and as we have been cautioned by the Peacemaker, if we of the League are to remain strong, we must be united. Besides, when have either the English or the League broken the Covenant Chain, a silver chain that was forged long ago, and which binds us to the English? Never have they broken that chain. Never have we. It ties us to them, and they to us.

"Has not William Johnson shown us how the English will debate and discuss our problems as though they were their own? And if he is our brother, are we to ignore him in his time of need?"

There was silence in the hall as the wise sachems listened and nodded their approval.

Yet Evening Song rose up again to address the council, and she said, "Have you spoken all that you wish to say?"

"I have."

"Oyendere, very good. Your words are true. William Johnson has done much for the Mohawk. But beware. He is English though he presents himself as Mohawk. And now he attempts to speak for all the people of the Six Nations, and place himself as one of our wisest sachems. But William Johnson is not Seneca. He does not know our sons and daughters, and thus, not knowing, how can he provide for their needs?

"But do not think, because I say this about William Johnson, that the French are any better. Have you not noticed that whenever the French trader Joncaire, comes to our country, that he talks a crooked talk? And the English are no better. With their talk, they each try to incite our people to hatred for one or the other of them. Do you not recall how last summer Joncaire spread stories of fear and hatred of the English? Did he not say that the English desired to kill us and take our lands? That both the French and the English were planning to attack the Six Nations and drive us from the face of this land, Turtle Island? Yet, we found these tales to be lies.

"Save for William Johnson, have not the English done the same? Overstating a half-truth so as to incite our men and women to hatred of the French? And what is it that they want, that they all say? 'Fight for us,' 'Send your best into battle for us.' I ask this about that: What is wrong with the English and the French that they cannot fight their own wars?

"Harken, ye wise sachems. He who would once lie to you about a thing will do so again. As a lion cannot change his ways of stealth, so, too, this sort of man cannot change habits. Have not our wise fathers told us that he who lies even once will always in the end revert to telling false truths? I say to you, by the truth or not of his words, we can know him, and so knowing, can disgrace him for the rest of his life.

"This is how it should be. Are we then to send our sons and husbands to fight the wars of liars? I say 'no,' I am against this."

Strong words. True words. Words that had influenced him, though as a youth he had sought the ways of war.

But long ago White Thunder had determined to ignore the French and English war and all its influence on his people. He had to. Indeed, he would go about his life as he always had. Besides, it was White Thunder's opinion that it mattered little who won this conflict, since both the English and the French had their eye on the same objective: taking control of the country . . . Indian country.

Though once a warrior of repute, White Thunder knew he would never again go to war. There was the matter of his oath to consider, his duty and pledge to Wild Mint . . .

White Thunder knelt next to Wild Mint, his wife. Her breathing was strained, coming in short gasps. Tears streamed down White Thunder's face as he watched her, felt for her, wished it were he, not she, who had been in the village to confront the enemy. He had faced death many times—it was an expected trait of a Seneca warrior—but never had he thought he would bear witness to Wild Mint's death, even before his own. Picking up her bloodied hand and bringing it to his face, he cried into it.

"Who did this to you?" he asked. White Thunder had been away from the village when the raid had happened. He had been hunting.

"An evil man." She coughed, the action bringing up blood, which spilled down over her chin. Gently, he wiped it from her face.

She was dying. He knew it. She knew it. Worse, there was nothing to be done. Their baby had been cut from her body, leaving their child, in its eighth month, dead, and his wife dying.

Who would do a thing so wicked?

It was not that he was unaware of torture. Many tribes—his own included—persecuted prisoners who had been caught in war.

But this rarely extended to women, and never to an unborn child. Most tribes prized the gift of a woman prisoner, and particularly one with child. Didn't they desire the prisoners as replacements for those loved

ones lost in war? Didn't his people usually treat the
prisoners well, making them part of the tribe?

"Find him," Wild Mint managed to say. "Do not
spare him."

"I will find him and I will kill him" said White Thun-
der. It was a promise. If need be, he would spend his
life fulfilling that oath.

"I cannot rest 'til it is done," she choked out. "My
blood, the blood of our child is on his hands. Find him.
Seek revenge, but kill no other in his place. He alone
must pay. I will wait . . ." She coughed again, took a
deep breath, which rattled deeply in her throat. In an
instant, she was gone.

"I will kill him," said White Thunder. "I will."

Tears fell down White Thunder's face as he cried
openly, unashamed of the emotion. He loved Wild
Mint, had loved her since they were children. In truth,
it seemed as though he had loved her all his life and
always would. He would find this man who had done
this to her and to his unborn child. He would find him
and he would exact his revenge.

Yet, this matter, sworn to so easily, had not proved a
simple task. Though White Thunder had spent fifteen long
years searching for this man, his duty to Wild Mint was
still unfulfilled.

It should have been easy. On the day of the raid, the
attacking party had been Huron. Under normal circumstances, he would have found the murderer and quickly
brought about well-deserved justice.

But it was not to be.

No one fit the description of this man; no Huron
seemed to know who this man was, and although the
Huron might lie to him about this thing, it had proved to
be true. Worse, White Thunder had no other option but

to find this exact man; he could not kill another Huron in the murderer's place, a remedy often sought by the Seneca. By his oath, only this one man would pay for the crimes committed. Wild Mint would not rest until this was a fact.

And so he searched. It had proved to be a lonely business, also. So many villages scrutinized, even those that were not Huron; so many people questioned, so many disappointments. Yet in all this time, with all this investigation, White Thunder was no closer to finding the culprit than he had been at the beginning of his quest, except for one fact: Recently he had discovered that the raiders had been Huron *and French.*

Was the murderer a Frenchman? To satisfy this new clue, White Thunder had journeyed to the north, seeking out the villages of Quebec and Montreal. It had been a long trip, an intense search. But it had ended in the same way as all the others, with nothing to show for his efforts but the passage of time.

He was only now returning from that quest.

"No, do not leave me! Do not go in there!" The delicate woman with soft ringlets of yellow sat up all at once. Her eyes were wide, yet unseeing. "Mother! Stay with me! Do not leave me!"

White Thunder took the woman in his arms and held her, simply held her. Bending his head toward her, he endeavored to take her pain upon himself. But it was not possible. Her misery came from something he knew not of. Still, he tried.

"Mother! No! Don't go! Stay with me!"

Her tears fell to his shoulder. And though he knew he shouldn't feel as he did, he gloried in the warmth of having a woman in his arms. She was soft, she was sweet and her scent was delicately feminine, a heady perfume for an unattached male. He had forgotten.

Her hair was fragrant now with the aroma of the smoke from their fire and the herbs he had used to rub into her scalp. That one injury had been the only scrape he could find upon her. Luckily, the abrasion was little more than a finger-long scratch.

Its discovery had caused him to wonder again what had happened to bring this woman to the brink of death.

One fact was certain, however. Duty to his beloved, which was keeping him celibate, was not a sound frame of mind for a healthy male.

"No! Not my mother, not my father! No, it cannot be!"

Her pain sent shivers up and down his spine. This woman had known real torment. It was there in her voice, in her words. The knowledge drew him closer to her, and as her tears became more profound, he rocked back and forth, his arms still wrapped firmly around her.

There was nothing for him to say. Instead he held her until the last her tears became a mere hiccup. Even then he didn't release her.

Tentatively, he massaged her spine. And it wasn't until her breathing was free and her eyes were once again closed that he laid her back against his blanket. Beneath it were fragrant, cushy boughs of pine branches, enough so that her body did not repose upon the hard floor of the cave.

Quietly, he exhaled. He didn't want to admit it, but he was drawn to her. Or perhaps, he conjectured, it was simply that he hadn't held a flesh-and-blood woman in his arms for too many years.

Finishing on a snort, he realized there was yet work to be done. The fire required stoking and if he were to nurse this woman back to complete health, additional sustenance had to be found at once. While his meager diet of dried meat, corn and berries might satisfy him, she would require the healing properties of fresh meat to restore her vigor, and it needed to be in a liquid form since she was not conscious enough to eat on her own.

Dutifully, he rose up to begin his work, though he couldn't help but wish for his grandmother's presence beside him, speaking words of wisdom to him. An herbalist, she would have known the exact plants and foods that would bring this woman back to health. Unfortunately White Thunder's skills in this realm were rudimentary; he had never harbored an interest in learning the craft.

"No! Do not ever touch me again! My body is my own! Get back away from me!"

Again, White Thunder fell to his knees beside the woman, taking her up in his arms to give comfort.

"I will repay my parents' debt to you, but I swear it shall not be in this manner!"

Her words made White Thunder want to weep, for he did not misunderstand. Did the Englishmen misuse even their own kind?

As the woman's tears fell, White Thunder found that his own grief, though of fifteen years in length, mingled with hers.

"No! No!"

Gently he rocked her back and forth, until at last her fears again quieted.

But it was not so for White Thunder's. Even though he would never act on such a thing, his body was ready and willing for the ultimate action between a man and a woman. The reaction surprised him; it also caused him to consider a truth: Man lives best with a flesh and blood woman, not her mere image. And when absent . . .

He sighed against the fragrance of the English woman's hair. He had best not like it too readily. Until Wild Mint's murderer was found and justice served at last, there could be no other woman in his life.

Perhaps, like the white man's double-edged knife, this

was a test of him, of his strength and devotion, for no matter which way the knife was thrust, it cut.

But enough. The woman in his arms needed special sustenance and attention. He would give her both.

Three

The delicious aroma of meat and vegetables awakened Sarah. Was that a soup she smelled?

She opened her eyes and looked up at the dark ceiling of . . . where was she?

Were those stalactites hanging from a ceiling about ten feet above her? She narrowed her eyes so as to obtain a better look at them. And if these massive columns were stalactites, what were they doing here in her bedroom? Weren't these icicle-like projections of rock, formed by the action of water and corrosion, normally to be found in caves and caverns? She was in her bedroom—wasn't she?

Carefully, slowly, she took in the dark terrain of her surroundings. Except for the dim light of a flickering fire at her feet, she was surrounded by a murkiness so dense, it was like staring into the starless black of night. There was a chill in the air, though luckily the warmth from the fire presented her with a means to keep in her body heat. Moisture filled the air. Was it raining outside? If so, that would

explain the sound of dripping water that seemed to come
from somewhere close by to her. Was she in a cave?

And if she were in a cave, *why* was she here? Sarah
searched her memory. Unfortunately she could recall only
rudimentary details . . . but that didn't include her name . . .

Closing her eyes, she endeavored to remember what had
happened. But there was nothing there to present itself to
her, no memory, nothing to answer her questions.

Returning her attention to the environment, she discovered a feeling of warmth beneath her, like the flannel of a
blanket, and there was some indefinable softness wrapped
around her. Miserably, that's when she became aware of
her situation: She was naked beneath this blanket.

Where was she? Why was she naked? What had happened to her?

All at once, a tantalizing scent of pine added its fragrance to the aroma of food, and she wondered at its source
until she moved slightly and realized she was sleeping atop
pine boughs. She was definitely not in her bedroom.

She exhaled and slowly moved her head so as to take
in more of the features of her surroundings. Perhaps if she
could see a little bit of it, she might recall what had happened to her and why she was here. Her name would be a
good place to start.

Turning her vision to the right, she soon realized there
was little to see except the blackness that seemed to pen-
etrate this place. However, in the flickering light off the
cave wall, she made out the silhouette of a man. Firelight
seemed to paint his shadowy image in glimmering flashes
of light and dark.

She could tell very little about him, save that he appeared
to be as big as a bear. If she shifted just so—not so much as
to draw his attention, but enough to look toward the fire—
she could see him in the flesh.

For a long moment, she studied him. Then she lay back.

He wasn't so big after all, though he did look to be tall, perhaps six foot or more. He was an Indian, also. Odd that she should know that detail about him, but not remember her own name.

He wore his hair like the Mohawk did. Except for a section of longer hair styled atop his head, he fashioned his hair clipped close to the head. However, a section of his mane was allowed to grow to great lengths in back, and tied to this longish hair were what appeared to be eagle feathers.

Her gaze ranged down over his body and she noted that, excluding several tattoos covering his arms, his chest and arms were bare. He wore necklaces of stones and beads around his neck and the ever present breechcloth that the Indian male seemed to favor was tied around his waist. There was also a red cloth sash fashioned around that slim waist, and leggings that came up high on his legs outlined the muscles of his thighs. Undecorated moccasins covered his feet.

Was the man a Mohawk warrior? Perhaps. But Sarah knew there were six tribes that made up the Iroquois Nation, though how she knew this piece of knowledge when she couldn't recall who she was, was not quite clear. However, she decided that this man might originate from a different one of the tribes that made up the Iroquois Nation, since his hairstyle mimicked the Mohawk, but was not exactly the same.

Hopefully he was not Ottawa.

Sarah frowned. Why would she hope he was not Ottawa?

Again she tried to concentrate. But her mind seemed to draw nothing but blanks.

The man was handsome, she decided, and Sarah allowed herself several more glimpses, admiring the clean look of bare chest and that strange mixture of short and long hair. Odd, too, that she wasn't afraid of him.

Shouldn't she be?

It did strike her as peculiar that a man so muscular, so incredibly male and so obviously fitted for manly tasks was at work over a fire, doing chores considered feminine. He was cooking a meal. Despite herself, his image made her smile.

But why should she smile? She was naked beneath this blanket and couldn't remember the most elementary things about her life. Logic alone would dictate that she should be afraid.

But she wasn't.

Did she know this man? Was that why she wasn't frightened? Frustrated, Sarah let out a soft moan, and returned to her assessment.

He was young, perhaps younger than she. There was also something about him that stirred her curiosity. His demeanor was very sexual, although why she should think so, she didn't understand, unless . . . perhaps he was her husband? Or maybe it was his attire—or lack thereof—that caused the consideration.

Unfortunately that thought had the effect of reminding her that she was scantily dressed. Had this man taken advantage of her? Now came the fear, and a sensation of vulnerability swept over her.

Again she wondered, who was this man? Who was she?

Wretchedly she realized that there was nothing else for it but to find out what was going on, and after chasing the knot that seemed to have collected in her throat, she asked, "Excuse me, sir, but have I had an accident?"

The man looked up from his work and glanced askance at her. He said, "You are awake at last."

He spoke English. Sarah frowned at the thought, marveling again at how much she "knew" without knowing. However, he hadn't answered her question, and she tried again, "Yes, sir, I am. But please, I beg you to tell me, have I had an accident?"

"You have," he said simply.

"Do you know what happened? And if you do, sir, could you please relate it to me?"

"I do not know exactly what happened to you," he replied. "I was hoping that you might be able to explain the story to me."

"Oh." Gazing quietly toward her hands, she found them to be nervously clutching her blanket. Their color was pale, she noted, at least when compared to the sight of this man's hands, which were brown. Perhaps her next question wasn't the right query to ask, given their circumstances, but she couldn't help herself as she probed, "Sir, are you my husband?"

He hesitated a moment as his gaze scanned her features. "I am not," he said at length.

Sarah took in his reply with some bit of shock, again more than aware of her state of undress beneath the blanket. She said without thinking, "I am deeply unhappy to hear that, sir."

He frowned. Seeing his reaction, she asked, "Sir, please excuse my coming directly to the point, but I would know immediately, if you please, if it is your intention to torture or rape me." She stopped and cleared her throat, realizing she was more than a little afraid of his reply.

But he answered her readily. "That is not my intention."

Sarah paused as she let out a breath. "I am very happy to hear that."

He nodded and returned to his work next to the fire, presenting her with his back.

"Pardon me, again, sir, but I feel I must bring your attention to the fact that I am in quite an ill state of dress beneath this blanket, and I was wondering—"

"It was necessary to remove your things after I brought you here," he explained, interrupting her. "Your clothes were wet and you were very warm with fever. It was done to tend to you, and for no other reason."

"Ah," she said, and she paused while she sought to test her failing memory. Once again there was nothing there to steer her in any direction. It was as though her memory had been wiped clean.

He continued, "I little understand the English woman's style of dressing, nor did I recall which piece of cloth went where, and so I did not attempt to re-dress you once your fever had abated."

"Oh, yes, of course."

The man turned to regard her. It was the first time she had looked upon his face in full. It would have been most reassuring had a memory of recognition stirred to tell her something about him, or about herself. But it was not to be.

Again, not able to help herself, she asked, "Do I know you well, sir?"

"*Neh*, no."

She took in this fact well enough, then asked, "Do I know you at all?"

"We have never met." So saying, he presented his back to her.

Sarah remained silent, unsure of how next to proceed. If this man didn't know who she was, how then was she to discover it herself?

In the end, she decided to change the subject and commented, "That smells delicious." She came up onto her elbows to see if she could discover what it was he was cooking. "I think I'm hungry."

"That is to be expected."

He didn't turn around or say anything further, not even to indicate when she might eat, and so after a while, Sarah lay back against the soft bed of blankets and pine boughs that cradled her. Somehow, she didn't feel strong enough to make a point of it. If he didn't desire to share his meal with her, it was beyond her to do anything about it.

But she had reckoned too soon. Within moments, he had

moved to kneel beside her. Sarah shivered. Up close, he looked formidable, dangerous, alien and alas, handsome.

It seemed, however, that he had nothing more in mind than feeding her. In his hands, he held a large shell. Its contents were steaming . . . and smelled like heaven.

He said, "I will require you to sit up if you can. Since it is soup, it is best eaten in an upright position."

Sarah gazed up at him, noting several things that she had missed when he'd been sitting next to the fire: the proud tilt of his head; the healthy look of his skin tone, even though its color was a few shades darker than her own; the long fingers that looked capable enough to snap her in half, if he desired. As she gazed up into his eyes, she beheld a gentle look about him as well, and it was toward that spark of kindness that she responded. "I think that I can sit up. Shall I try?"

He nodded and waited.

She struggled to do it. But to her chagrin, she was too weak to accomplish more than coming up onto her elbows. Moreover, even that small movement sent her heart to beating heavily in her chest. Her breathing quickened as a result, which caused her some anxiety. Not knowing him, fearing he might be untruthful about his intentions toward her, she was afraid the movement of her chest might attract his attention toward her bosom, a thing she wished to avoid.

But it didn't. His eyes seemed focused on her facial features alone. However, he made no move to help her sit into a better position, either.

At last, casting him what was probably an irritated glance, she said, "I fear 'tis as far as I can come."

Again, he nodded, and setting the shell carefully to the side, he placed an arm around her back, bringing her up into a full sitting position. Only then did he say, "It is good that you tried to rise up on your own. There is no other way to regain your strength."

His voice was low and pleasant, a deep baritone, and his face was so close to hers, the intake and exhale of his mint-scented breath was soft upon her.

However, it caused her to wonder at the odor of her own mouth, and she closed her lips, as if that might keep any offending smell at length.

Keeping one arm wrapped firmly around her, he picked up the shell that contained the delicious smelling liquid, and brought the concoction, to her lips.

"It is hot," he warned. "Beware. Do not drink too much at first."

Eyes wide, taking in his image, she obeyed, for there was no reason not to. She took a tentative sip of the brew and decided at once that it was good. Indeed, in her state of mind, it tasted as if it might be the nectar of the gods.

"Hmm . . ." Briefly she closed her eyes. "'Tis an excellent cook, you are, sir."

A simple nod of his head acknowledged her compliment.

"I'd like some more, if you please," she said.

He accommodated her, bringing the shell once more to her lips. But he said very little to her, making her wonder if there were a reason why he was niggardly with his words. She brought her hands up to his, helping him to guide the shell toward her, and every now and again she gazed up at him. His features remained handsome even so close up, she noted, though she was amazed to discover there was not even a hint of a beard on his countenance. Did he shave it, or did he honestly not have one?

She tried to recall what she might know of the Indians, but unless her mind volunteered the information, there was little for her to gain from her memory.

As she stared directly at him, she noticed that his eyes were dark, almost black in hue, and as he stared back at her and their gazes met, she recognized a strength of spirit that was at odds with her impression of what the Indians were about.

But what impression was this? Was it a memory?

Sarah tried to bring the recollection back to mind, though it was impossible to keep it from fleeing. Her brow knitted in a frown.

"Do not worry," he said as he reached out to smooth the lines between her brows. "You will regain your strength. Here, eat more. If you are to recover, you will need to nourish your body."

"Aye, yes, of course you are right," she said. "Thank you for helping me, and for this meal. It must be vexing for you to have to prepare it."

"It is nothing," he said. "A man learns enough about cooking to do it a little, since he is often away from his home." He offered her more of the soup, which she was quick to accept, and it wasn't long before the entire amount of the liquid in the shell was gone.

He asked, "Would you like some more?"

She nodded.

"Good." He set the shell to the side, then laying her back on her bed, he rose up gracefully and stepped back to the fire.

Sarah continued to study him. His was a tall figure, slim and well built. He was young, good-looking and probably had a dozen young maidens awaiting a proposal from him.

As he gathered up more of the food into the shell, he asked matter-of-factly, "Do you remember who you are?" He returned to her at once, though he didn't look at her directly, and taking her again into the warmth of his arms, he brought her back into a sitting position.

Although he had probably already guessed what her answer might be, Sarah didn't reply all at once. In fact, she was afraid to. Even though his mild manner was allaying her fears, she was wary—perhaps she had been taught to be so. After all, she didn't know him. If he thought she had no one looking out for her, would it change his intentions toward her?

He continued, "If you will tell me where you are from and who is your family, I will return you to them." Then, as though he were aware of her thoughts, he added, "It is the only reason I ask."

Something about the look in his eyes caused her to believe him, and she said, "I . . . I recall nothing."

"Nothing?"

"Aye, sir." Nervously she waited. What was going to be his response? When he didn't answer at once, she went on to say, "What I do know, or what I can recall, seems to come to me in odd ways, for I remember much, but the details I recall are all of them unimportant." She cast him an anxious glance, and fearful, pulled back away from him.

But if he was affected by her fear, he didn't show it. He simply nodded. "Perhaps it is to be expected, since you have witnessed much trauma. Do not fear, however. Your memory will return in time. More rest and nourishment will aid in your recovery."

"I hope you are right. But I have another question I must ask you, sir. Do you know how I came to be here?"

"I brought you to this cave to provide a place where you could recover, although why you were in the forest alone and unconscious remains a mystery to me."

"Oh." Again she frowned. "I was unconscious? How did you find me, then?"

"You were lying atop a large, flat rock. I assume that you had been washed ashore by the waves of the Lake-That-Turns-to-Rapids. You were alive, but barely."

"Oh, I see." She bit her lip. "The Lake-That-Turns-to-Rapids. I don't recall it. But if what you say is true, then you have most probably saved my life." She had meant it to be a question, but it came out matter-of-factly. Suddenly, Sarah was struck more forcefully by fear. Did this man want something in return for his kindness? Something she might be unwilling to give?

All at once, the enormity of her vulnerability and dependence on this man became too real for her. He could do almost anything to her, for she would be unable to rebuff any slight whim that might take hold of him.

Sarah swallowed noisily, and as panic coiled like a serpent within her, she was more than aware of the state of her nudity. Under the possibility of threat, her femininity reacted in an age-old, womanly fashion, perhaps in preparation for the worst. It was not a pleasant feeling, however. Far from it.

So it was that with wide eyes, she stared up into the dark, dark gaze of her "protector." Nervously, she swallowed.

Four

They stared at one another, as though both were taking in the measure of the other. At length, Sarah roused up her courage, and clearing her throat, she asked, "May I ask, sir, if it is you who has been nursing me back to health?"

"It is," he replied. "It was not my desire to see you die if I could do something about it."

She paused. "Again," she said, "I admit that I must give you my solemn thanks."

He nodded.

"But, sir, I fear I have another concern that I would voice, if I may."

"I am listening."

The muscles in her throat convulsed as Sarah tried to gather her courage. She was already much too aware of this man's touch upon her. The fact that he was very close—so close that she could breathe in his scent—was not helping to ease her mind. Oddly, though her anxiety was almost palpable, she found his fragrance pleasant. Manly and musky . . . but pleasant.

She didn't know how to ask the next question. But because her alarm would not abate, there was nothing else for it but to blurt it out. "Have we . . . have I . . . in my stupor . . . did we . . . engage in . . . I mean to say . . ."

"On this day," he interrupted her, "you are as intact and whole as you were before I found you. You have asked for nothing from me and we are still strangers to each other in all ways except one . . . I have been feeding you each day and caring for you in your fever, hoping it would soon reduce and that you would awaken. I believe there is a fairy tale in your world about a princess who was awakened by a kiss." There was the hint of a smile within his words and upon his lips.

"Did we kiss, then?"

"*Neh*, we did not, though I was tempted to test the fairy tale to see if it be true."

Sarah settled back with a sigh as her apprehension began to ebb. But it was another thing altogether that calmed her: her recognition that he was trying to soothe her disquiet, not heighten it. Innately she realized that this was the action of a good man, and it drew her to him, if only minutely.

However, she was curious and she asked, "How is it, sir, that you are familiar with European fairy tales?"

"I spent more than three years with missionaries."

"Yes, of course. That accounts for your command of the English language, also, does it not?"

"I believe that it does." He smiled, but it was brief, a half-smile at best.

Shyly, she returned the gesture, then blushed and turned away. After a while, she said, "I can see that I have been a burden to you, and for that I apologize."

"You are no burden," he assured her.

"Am I not? I thank you for trying to ease my mind, yet if it be true that you saved me, I am certain you are not pleased with my many questions."

He shrugged. "Your questions are natural, since you have awakened to find yourself in the hands of a man you do not know. It is not a bad trait to be leery of a stranger. Trust is a thing earned, not given without cause."

"But perhaps there is cause."

"Maybe. You will have to determine that yourself. But if I can put your mind at ease, I will try."

"Do you know how far away we are from a white man's town?"

"Many days' ride by the white man's horse, or longer by foot and canoe."

"Much too far for us to go."

"I fear it is true."

"Then if I recover, or when, I will owe it to you."

He shrugged.

"And what is it that you would like from me in return?"

"Perhaps the return of your memory."

"Is that all?" Even she could hear the doubt in her voice. "There are some men who would ask for much more from a woman."

"Not a Seneca man," he said, squaring back his shoulders.

"Oh?"

"Only a beast," he continued, "who is more decayed flesh than human being, would ask for more from a woman than she is willing to give. Furthermore, only a fool, tied to nothing but the physical, would take what *Hawenio* has brought to him and destroy it." He paused. "I hope that I am neither kind of those men."

"Yes, I hope so, too," she agreed. "Tell me, what does *Hawenio* mean?"

"The Creator," he said. "He who made this world and who placed us here in it."

"Ah. That is a beautiful word."

He nodded. "So it is. Now, when you are able to sit up," he went on, changing the subject, "and can do the deed for yourself, your clothes are dry, and you will be able to dress yourself. I have placed them in a stack by the fire."

She glanced toward the place where he indicated. "I . . . yes, I see them."

She started to return her gaze to him, but then as though her skin were highly sensitized, she became more than unusually aware of this man's arms wrapped tightly around her. Suddenly, her skin felt heated by his touch, and she averted her gaze. To her shame, she realized that she liked the feel of his hands upon her.

The recognition startled her because a fleeting memory reminded her that she didn't like to be touched. Not usually. She hadn't liked it since . . .

It was on that note that the recollection ended, leaving her feeling more than a little frustrated. How on earth was she to ever remember who she was or where she was from if memories came and went with such speed?

As though he, too, were aware of her disappointment, he said, "Let me help you to lie back. You should rest now, and you should seek to sleep often. Gradually, you will remember more and more periods of your life. Until then, do not worry."

"Yes, thank you. I will try to keep from worrying. But it is hard to hold back my discouragement. What if no recollections ever return?"

"They will."

She sighed. "Oh, if only I had your certainty. Before I lie down to rest, I would like to ask if you might be so kind as to bring my clothes close to me so that I might dress myself as soon as I am able. Though you have been the utmost in gentlemanlike conduct, I am nervous about my state of undress."

"At once," he said as he set her back against the blanket and placed down the shell holding the soup. Speedily, he retrieved her clothing and returned to her side.

"Thank you, sir," she said as he again took her in his arms, and bringing her up, he offered her more of the broth. Before partaking of the soup, she added, "You have greatly aided me. And I believe there is no human being alive that would doubt that you are a man of ethical quality."

"*Nyah-weh.*" He nodded. "Thank you for the compliment, but do not give me your trust so easily. Be skeptical, doubt me, test me, before you pass judgment."

"Sir, are you saying in a more covert way that you might, after all, be inclined to force me to . . . to . . ."

"*Neh*, no. Were that the case, I believe we would not be discussing it. But since you are obviously nervous and question whether or not you will remain a maiden under my care, let me try to reassure you. Though words are often hollow, I tell you this, I give you my promise that I will not take from you that which you are unwilling to give. The fact that we are alone, that I am physically stronger than you, will not move me to change my mind. I pledge my word of honor that your feminine beauty and privacy are safe with me so long as you wish them to be. Honor alone will keep you safe, for in my society, a decent man takes his pleasure only from the one he aims to make his own. At least, a man who is my age does." Again, there was a detection of humor in his voice as he continued, saying, "In a man's youth, it is not unusual for him to accept whatever a woman is willing to give, even if there is no intent to marry."

"Indeed!"

"But time and age can work on a man to make him wiser, I think."

An uncomfortable silence followed this declaration. And though Sarah realized it was kind of him to do his best to settle her mind, in truth, she had no idea how to respond to him. Indeed, thus far in her life, she'd had little

experience in confronting such brutal honesty from someone, especially a person of the opposite sex. The world in
which she moved never discussed such concepts—at least
not in social settings.

There it was again—a reference to her past. How did
she know these things? More to the point, were there other
memories attached to this one that she might recall?

Frowning, she touched her forehead, as though that
action alone might release the floodgates.

"Did you remember something?"

Sarah shook her head. "No, I thought that perhaps I had,
but, pray, I am still as unaware of my past as you are."

"Do not alarm yourself," he said reassuringly. "In time,
your memory will return."

"I do hope you are right. I sincerely pray it will be so.
But tell me," she uttered, curious again as she asked, "you
said something a moment ago that caught my attention and
I fear I must ask you about it. You said, 'a man of my age.'
Surely, sir, you are not so very old?"

"I am thirty and five summers."

So he was older than she was after all. Why, she was
only . . . Sarah furrowed her brow. Dear Lord, even the
knowledge of her age escaped her. Sighing hard, she said,
"And are you married, sir?"

"Nyoh. Neh."

"What does that mean?"

"Yes and no."

"I fear I do not understand. Yes and no?"

"My wife is dead," he explained. "But she still lives on,
deep within my heart."

"Ah," Sarah said. "Now I think I understand." And so
she did, though why she shared such empathy with him
was not completely clear to her. She continued, "How long
ago did she die?"

"It has been fifteen summers since she walked this earth
in the flesh."

"Fifteen summers," Sarah repeated. "I am sorry for your loss. 'Twas fifteen years ago? She must have been little more than a woman in her teens. May I ask what took her away from you at so young an age? Was it childbirth?"

He shook his head. "*Neh*, no. And I mean no offense to you, so please do not take one. I do not speak of her death."

Sarah gazed away from him. "I understand."

"I know you do."

"Do you?"

He said merely, "You spoke often of people you love."

Sarah frowned.

"In your sleep," he explained. "In some ways, we are alike, you and I. We both love people who can no longer be with us in the flesh."

"Yes," she said, but she was embarrassed. Though she couldn't bring back to mind the memories she'd told him, apparently in her stupor she had related her deepest thoughts and perhaps her most intimate secrets. Alas, the fact was disconcerting. She said, "I am very sorry to hear that I spoke out as I did. Had I been awake and in my senses I would have never burdened you with my memories."

"Do not be sorry. Your pain has endeared you to me."

"Oh? Endeared?" Again Sarah was caught off guard. She simply didn't know what to expect of a man who was so utterly forthright in his words. Indeed, it seemed to be out of her realm of experience.

So as to steer the subject back toward something more easily spoken about in a polite society, she said, "I am frustrated. I have awakened only to find that I do not know who I am, where I am from or even who are my friends."

"It is true, and what you feel is to be understood, but with time, it will come to you," he assured her. "You have only awakened this very first day. Do not expect too much too soon. One begins a long journey by first taking a single step. Yet, if he keeps onward, placing one footfall after another, he will eventually arrive at his destination. Rest, sleep, eat well. You will remember. And when you at last recall the details most important to you, upon your request, I will return you to those who are your people."

"Yes," said Sarah, "I would like that."

But did she really like the idea of that? Some innate warning caused her to doubt the sincerity of those words even as she spoke them. If that were true, why did she not feel more elation at the prospect returning home?

"Come," he said, "we have talked enough. It is time for you to rest again. We will have time aplenty for talk later."

Sarah might have remarked on his presumption, for she was uncertain she could go back to sleep simply because he required it of her, but she held back any criticism. Instead, when he gently lowered her back against her bed, she murmured, "Thank you again, sir. You have been most kind. May I ask the name of my benefactor, please?"

He didn't utter a sound. Instead, as though she had suddenly grown hot to his touch, he laid her down and ended their embrace quickly, albeit too quickly. In truth, the action was so suddenly done that it drew Sarah's attention away from herself, and onto him. Odd. He acted as though he couldn't get away from her fast enough.

He stood up to his feet. Only then did he say, "A man does not speak his own name. To do so is dishonorable."

"Oh?" As Sarah settled in against the cushion of pine boughs and soft blanket, she studied this man before her and commented, "Then what shall I call you, sir?"

He smiled, and Sarah thought the world might have suddenly turned brighter. If it be true that some people's smiles grace the world around them, and that a single grin might be sufficient to cause others to smile, too, then this man certainly possessed that gift. Indeed Sarah discovered the impulse was more than she could resist, and the corners of her mouth twitched upward.

But he was continuing to speak, and she gave him her

full attention as he said, "You state a good point and so I think I might make an exception with you since there is no other way for you to discover who I am."

"Yes, it would be most kind of you to tell me, sir."

"*He-noh*, White Thunder," he said. "I am known as White Thunder."

Sarah breathed in deeply before saying, "*He-noh*. It is a good name, Mr. Thunder. A good name, indeed. Is there a reason?"

White Thunder didn't pretend to misunderstand her question. Coming down to kneel again at her side, he said, "It is well known among my people that the thunder is a kind god, for he accompanies the rain which nourishes the earth. But he is also a lonely god, for his wife, the earth, is ever separate from him. Sometimes, he cannot contain his loneliness and we oftentimes witness what happens when this is so, for the lightning kisses the ground. You have seen this?"

"Aye."

"Because my wife is ever separate from me, I am called Thunder. Because she is amongst the Sky People, I am named White for the clouds."

Sarah was quiet for the beat of a moment while she registered all he had said. Then, softly, she uttered, "You must miss your wife very much."

He didn't respond to her by word. Instead, he drew away from her, as though she had trampled upon forbidden territory. "Sleep now," he said. "Food to nourish you and uninterrupted rest will see that you regain your strength."

Thus spoken, he rose up, and before she could say another word, he turned his back on her and stepped away, leaving Sarah alone to watch his retreating backside.

Indeed, he was gone so quickly and so fast that his reaction might have seemed strange to another, but not so to Sarah. Sarah well understood the ill effect that a great loss can hold over a person.

She might not remember exactly why she knew or how she had come to know it, she realized only that it was. Perhaps, she thought, when it involves matters of the heart, instinct alone is all one needs.

Five

Gradually, the darkness that accompanies the return of dawn became the shadowy silver of early morning. Dew clung to every leaf and blade of grass as the world around White Thunder awakened. The trees, the shrubs, the bushes were bursting with the colors of gold, red and orange as they announced their departure from this world into a wintery sleep. Even without the sun, thought White Thunder, the landscape's brightness lit up the land as though each living thing contained the mystical powers of the sun.

Interestingly, here and there, White Thunder spotted the pigment of yellow, placed in amongst the greens, reds and golds of the forest. The color reminded him of the hue of the English woman's hair.

White Thunder shook his head. He was beginning to think he was besotted with this woman who had literally been dumped into his life. Indeed, if he were honest, he would admit that he was drawn to her. But there was not a thing he would do about it. Not only were the two of them from different worlds—giving him no reason to flirt with her—his heart, his very life, belonged to another, to Wild Mint.

Spreading out his arms toward the eternity of the skies above him, he prayed as he sang:

"Howenio, Creator, I greet the morning with the happiness of a new day.
"Howenio, Creator, I thank you for what you have brought me.
"But, Howenio, Creator, I do not understand.
"Is there a reason this gift has come into my life?
"Howenio, Creator, my heart belongs to another, will always belong to another.
"Howenio, Creator, though I thank you for what you have brought to me, I wonder.
"Do you test me?
"Howenio, Creator, I will do all within my power to remain faithful to the one who will always hold my heart.
"But, Howenio, Creator, a man is but a man, and this woman you have brought to me is beautiful.
"Howenio, Creator, I do not understand.
"Howenio, Creator, thank you for your gift."
"Howenio, Creator, I greet the morning with the happiness of a new day."

White Thunder lowered his arms to his side and turned away from the east, where the sun was only now beginning its artistry, painting the skies with pinks, blues and golds. Soon the world would be bright with the radiance of autumn and sunlight.

As White Thunder stepped away from the large rock

where he had recited his morning prayer, he felt a cold touch upon his shoulder. There was no one there, and no reason to turn around, save one. It was Wild Mint.

He smiled. Wild Mint was here with him. Hadn't she avowed that she would be—at least until his task was completed?

Alas, so heinous had the crime been against her, he understood that she could not, she must not, pass into the realm of the Sky People, even though a ceremony had been performed to release her. Not until true justice had been served, regardless of how long that took, would she be able to travel into the next realm of existence.

On a brighter note, he was happy she was here with him. Her touch was always welcome; it was her way of reassuring him that she was here, on his side, keeping him firmly grounded in his purpose.

But he did wonder: Was it her voice or was it the wind that whispered to him? *"Do not forget your duty."*

"Never!" he cried.

Oh, to hold her in his arms again, to hear her laughter, to touch her, to make love to her.

But no sooner had these thoughts begun, when, unbidden, the image of another woman filled his vision. She was delicate, with a small bone structure and a shortish stature, a woman who would probably come no higher than his shoulders were she to stand upright. With natural ringlets of blond hair and deep, trusting blue eyes, she had managed to become a part of his musings.

The English woman. What was he to do with her?

His life held no place for her, though he admitted that if he were free to woo her, he might try to persuade her into his arms. He might even attempt to coax her into his life. In truth, the mere idea of wedding her and bedding her encouraged such instant changes to his body that his mind spun with the possibilities. It was a shock. He'd thought such cravings were long dead within him.

Staring down, he was not happy to witness the effects mere thoughts about her had on him. Indeed, he realized that although his body's reaction affirmed that he was still a healthy male, this state was a complication he could ill afford.

White Thunder sighed. Were cold-water swims, taken during any part of the day, to become a regular habit with him?

He hoped it would not be. Unfortunately for him, he feared many a cold bath might lurk in his future. For days and days now, he had held her in his arms as he'd nursed her and fed her and coaxed life back into her. And if he were honest, he would admit to experiencing more than one moment when he had wished she were his.

But even then, his body hadn't reacted like this.

What would it feel like, he wondered, to experience her surrender? If he were to kiss her, what would she taste like? If he were to enfold her body within his in a most natural and elemental way, what would be her response?

But even as he fantasized, he knew it could never be. For these last fifteen years he had lived with a mission—which was as yet unfulfilled. He had also lived his life as though there would never be another woman but Wild Mint for him.

Perhaps it was true. Maybe there never would be someone to take that hallowed spot.

But maybe there was still love to be found in this oft-times broken-hearted world. Mayhap if he reached out . . .

No. It could not be. Not with a woman who was English.

Still, he was not dead. Not yet. Perhaps when he reached his village again, he might look to see if there were a pleasing face who might wish to spend her life with him.

But not until his duty to Wild Mint was fulfilled. He must never forget.

Pivoting, he retraced his steps toward the Lake-That-Turns-to-Rapids, astonished that even now, with nothing but the mere thought of the English woman, his body was still firm, alert, ready . . .

A few days turned into a week. Aided by a diet of nourishing soups and fresh meat, Sarah's strength gradually improved until she was able to sit up on her own.

As the need for sleep became less and she was awake more often, one of the first details Sarah noted was that White Thunder was frequently gone from the early hours of the morning 'til dusk. At first she had done little more than sleep while he was away from her, but as she grew better physically, she began to realize that she desired his company.

Certainly Mr. Thunder took pains to ensure her comfort before he left and when he returned, but Sarah was becoming aware that she had an emotional need for the company of others. She desired conversation; she wanted to laugh and to exchange confidences. Indeed, she needed a friend.

She had even broached the subject with White Thunder once, and he had listened very intently to her. But in the end, nothing had changed between them, and she was beginning to wonder what it was that an Indian gentlemen did all day.

She was not left long in pondering the puzzle. Every day he returned to the cave with some form of nourishment. Often he brought a deer or other meat to the cave. Other times, he returned with his bags crammed full of wild vegetables, berries and fruit.

Sarah helped him sort through the vegetables from the comfort of her bed whenever she could. However, that was often strained due to her inability to walk about freely. Although her strength was returning, she had yet to take any of her weight upon her feet.

She could crawl, however. That first day when she had

discovered her hands and knees as a means of movement had been a joy. The first deed she had accomplished— after dressing herself in at least her chemise, corset and underskirt—was to crawl to the fire and prepare herself a drink.

That had been several days ago, and it had become an everyday habit. However, she still refrained from dressing herself fully, since crawling wreaked havoc on one's clothes. Thus she would save her open gown for the day when she returned to her people.

But who were her people? Sarah dropped her head into her hands as if the action might cause the memories to return. Straining her mind, as she was doing now more times than not, brought about nothing but a headache.

She heard a rummaging in the corner; raising her head, she saw that it was Miss Squirrel, an animal that had taken an interest in the goings on in the cave. Miss Squirrel had become a daily visitor and Sarah had taken to talking to it, if only to ease her need for conversation.

"Well, there you are," she said to it. "You know that you could come even closer to me and I would feed you without trying to make a soup out of you."

The squirrel looked at her as if to say, "I don't believe you."

"It's true," Sarah ventured. "You've become my friend and I wouldn't make a meal out of a friend."

The squirrel picked up a plum, which Sarah had deliberately left in a corner of the cave, and the animal stared back at Sarah as it began to munch.

"It's good, isn't it?"

When the squirrel didn't answer, Sarah sighed, and said, "Do you know that seven days have passed since I awoke here, and still I can't remember my name or who I am or where I come from?"

The squirrel chomped happily on the plum, staring at

Sarah as though it truly were her friend and would listen to her troubles.

"Nor can I recall why I am here, or why I was in the woods, or if I were with someone or alone. But if I were alone, how had I come to be there?"

The squirrel threw down the plum and looked up at her as though it might answer. But instead of speaking, it picked up one of the berries that Sarah had also left, and it began to chew on it.

"And what am I to do about Mr. Thunder?"

The squirrel stared at her as though to say it had no idea what she was talking about.

"Who is he? Can I trust him? I certainly want to. Without him, I am doubtful that I would now be alive. So of course I want to like him. He is alien to me, though I must admit that I find him handsome. Do you know, Miss Squirrel, that if you promise to keep a secret, I'll tell you that I find my gaze drawn to the look of the man's chest more times than I ought." Sarah smiled. "Indeed so much is this so, that had I the cloth, I would make the man a shirt simply to keep myself from wondering what it would be like if . . ." She paused. "Well, never mind."

The squirrel finished the berries and picked up another plum.

"Dear Miss Squirrel," Sarah said, "speaking of Mr. Thunder, I do believe that I have come to the decision that he is trustworthy. He certainly is kind, and is helpful to me. Nor does he offer criticism as a means to 'assist' me. He is the utmost in decorum and gentlemanlike behavior. Pray, I fear that from a woman's perspective, her heart might be in danger with this man, for these qualities are said to be rare, indeed."

The squirrel shifted its head to the side, as if to get a better image of this person who spoke to it, and Sarah went on to say, "But there are problems, of course. He's Indian. I'm not. But this I can understand and appreciate. What I don't comprehend is why he appears to be . . . cold toward me. There are times when I fear he must be made of snow and I of fire, for he is always cautious when he touches me, even when he must do so in order to help me."

The squirrel sat down on her haunches, looking for all the world like she were more than a little interested in the conversation. She even offered some advice, chattering to Sarah in squirrel.

"What was that you said?" Sarah asked. "That perhaps I make more of this than I should because he is the only human being in my vicinity? Maybe you're right, because it does seem to me that he is faithful to the image of his deceased wife, to a fault. Indeed, I am left with the impression that Mr. Thunder might never be unfettered of his former wife's hold over him until . . . well, I little know until what. Perhaps he might never be free of her influence over him a'tall.

"But this speculation could be the frivolous wonderings of a feminine mind. After all, I am in a position where he—and you, of course—are my whole world. I know more about him than I know of myself.

"I have wondered: What if I am married? I could be."

"Do you speak to a ghost?"

Sarah jumped and her heartbeat leaped into her throat. She turned quickly toward the cave's entrance.

In a moment, however, the racing of her heart settled back to its normal pace. "Oh, Mr. Thunder," she said, "I didn't hear you enter. I'm afraid you startled me." She placed her hand on her chest, not for theatrics, but because she had been truly startled. "I fear that you so rarely return before evening that I had let down my guard. I was not expecting you."

"Forgive me," he said. "It was not my intention to startle you. I heard talking and was wondering if someone had come to visit."

"And so someone has," Sarah replied. "'Tis Miss

Squirrel, who visits with me most every day. However, she is no longer here. I fear she ran away when you entered."

"As well she should," he commented. "I might take it into my mind to have her for a meal."

"Oh, no," replied Sarah at once. "I specifically told her that she is my friend and that I would not eat her."

White Thunder crossed the room to the fireplace, where Sarah was reposing. She still held a shell full of pine-needle tea at her side, but he seemed not to notice. He said, "Then I shall not place an arrow in Miss Squirrel's side." He knelt down on one knee beside Sarah. "Usually when I return, you are asleep, but I see that you have managed to make your way to the fire."

"Yes," she replied.

"This is good," he said. "Did you walk?"

"No," replied Sarah. "I am still crawling. I fear my legs will not hold me yet."

"Still, you are gaining back your strength and soon you will be walking about. I have been thinking about what we might do when you do come to remember your former life. And I concluded that it would be best that I should take you back to your family, who will be happy to know that you are still alive, I think."

Sarah bit her lip. "And if I don't remember anything? 'Tis hard for me, for I recall nothing."

White Thunder placed a hand on her shoulder, and said, "You will remember. Be at your ease. It will come."

Sarah gazed toward his hand, where it lay so close to her breast. He meant it as comfort. She said, "And if my memory doesn't return?"

"Then I will take you to my home, where you will be welcomed as a guest until a new home can be found for you. My mother will be happy to have you."

And you? Would you be happy to have me? She wanted to ask the question, but knew she dare not. Not only was she uncertain of him, she was also uncertain of herself.

"I have brought you something," he said.

Sarah's eyes lit up. "Have you, now?"

"It is not much." He presented her with a stick. But to call it such was to do it a disservice. Indeed, it was a work of art, for the rod had been carefully carved into the shape of a cane. "It is to aid you in walking. You must try to stand and take a few steps every day, I think, for it may require some time for your leg muscles to remember again that their duty is to take you from one place to another."

Sarah smiled up at him. "It is a beautiful present and I will cherish it and use it, indeed," she said. "Did you make it yourself?"

He looked sheepish as he said, "I did."

"Thank you. I will prize it all the more. It might help, too, the muscle spasms that almost cripple me at times, for the pain is almost unbearable."

He frowned at her. "This should not be."

His voice was so firm that Sarah sent him a wide-eyed stare.

"I will have to sit and contemplate and try to call back to mind the knowledge that my grandmother endeavored to teach me when I was a child. If I recall correctly, she used to say that most physical problems come from something missing in the food that a person eats. Though she tried to instruct me in specific cures, I fear I do not remember them."

"Is your grandmother still living?"

"*Neh*, no, she passed into the next world many years ago, and unluckily for me, the knowledge that she possessed died with her. I was not apt at learning the wisdom of her years; at the time, I thought of little more than the glory of the war path."

"Indeed?"

"It is so, for only as a warrior could I win the hand of Wild Mint, she who had hold of my heart from the first moment I ever beheld her."

Sarah was silent. At length, however, she proffered, "Again, I am sorry for your loss."

"Nyah-weh." He, too, sat in silence. "Of course, now I wish I had listened more intently to my grandmother. But this I know: The broth I brew should contain foodstuffs found only in the bones of animals. Perhaps I am not boiling the bones long enough to ensure the marrow's healing ingredients are in the broth."

"It could be," suggested Sarah. "At home, we often boil the broth for one or more days. It takes that long for the nourishment to leak out of the bones and into the liquid."

He nodded. *"Nyoh*, I will try that, and we shall see if the cramps in your legs become less. But for now, if you would seek your bed and lie down, I will rub your legs—"

"Oh, no," Sarah interrupted, and she noted that he seemed almost as relieved at her refusal as she was to give it.

But he said, "Do not fear me. I will take no advantage of you. I wish only to help take away the pain."

"I thank you and I understand that well," she replied, "but I grasp, too, your hesitation. After all, we are alone, and . . ."

"You are safe with me."

She brought up her gaze to stare at him. "Truly?"

"Truly. Do not think, however, that because I have given you my word I do not find you desirable."

If possible, Sarah's eyes widened further as she regarded him. *Was it true?*

He continued, "But as you know I am committed to she who can no longer be with me in the flesh. Besides, you have my word that nothing shall pass between us that you do not wish to experience, and a Seneca Indian's word of honor, once pledged, is sacred."

Sarah could barely credit what she did next; perhaps his words triggered a challenge. Whatever the cause—and unable to look him directly in the eye as she said it—she whispered, "But, Mr. Thunder, what would you do if I were willing to . . . to . . ."

She thought she heard him groan, and she raised up her glance quickly to see if he were in pain. "Sir?"

He seemed to be all right, at least physically so, but she watched as his Adam's apple bobbed up and down. Was he reacting to what she said?

At last he appeared to come to grips with the constriction in his throat, and he said, "And are you considering testing the pleasures that can be found between a man and a woman? Is that where your thoughts are tending?"

"I—I . . . no, I think not."

Though Sarah's gaze could still not quite meet his, she watched him beneath her lashes, and when he appeared to settle down, she said, "It is only that you are . . . male . . . and I am . . . female . . . and if you touch me . . . there might be a complication."

"Only if you desire it," he said, his voice low as he repeated, "Do you?"

"I . . . no . . ."

"Then there is no danger." His manner and his voice appeared to be normal again, and he continued, saying, "Come, lie down. I will rub your legs so that the pain goes away. And as I do so, I will tell you a story to take our attention away from the pleasures that men and women can experience with one another. Would you like that?"

"I . . ." She still couldn't quite look him in the eye, but at last, gazing up at him quickly, she said, "Yes, please. I believe that I would enjoy your touch upon me very much."

His response was a stunned silence, then an involuntary growl followed; it was low, soft and utterly masculine. Unwittingly, something very feminine in her responded to him, but she was quick to say, "My legs, I should have said. Please excuse me. I meant that I would enjoy your massage, since, when my leg muscles spasm, they hurt to the point of crippling me."

"I understood your intent," he said, and they stared at one another for so many moments, Sarah was left almost breathless.

What was happening to her?

Sarah wasn't certain, but whatever it was, it felt wonderful. She warned herself that she dare not like the feeling too greatly. After all, he was already committed, even though that commitment was to a woman who was no longer alive in the flesh.

Besides, she thought, for all her knowledge, she might be pledged to another, too.

Six

"This is a story often told by the old men of our Nation," he began, his voice soft.

"I am honored to hear it," said Sarah.

"Very well. Once, not so long ago, a great Seneca sachem was visited by three spirits." White Thunder's voice was low, almost a whisper. "These spirits showed themselves to this great man so that they might tell him the story of how the white man came to this land that we Seneca call Turtle Island . . ." White Thunder, who was kneeling beside her, paused as he shifted his massage from one of her legs to the other. "Is it the lower muscles of your legs alone that spasm when you try to walk?"

"Yes, sir, it is," she whispered. "And they convulse even when I am resting."

Sarah was lying facedown on her soft bed of blanket and pine boughs. Interestingly, though it would never do to possess such a berth in a stately home, this makeshift bed was unusually comfortable.

He asked, "Your legs convulse even when you are resting?"

"Aye, sir. Sometimes that is when it is the worst."

White Thunder frowned, looking as though his thoughts might be weighty. He continued to knead the painful muscles in her legs, absentmindedly. Meanwhile, Sarah settled down to enjoy the simple pleasure of being cared for. There was a risk, of course. She liked White Thunder, and with their situation—the fact that they were alone—anything might happen.

Still, the massage did ease the pain in her body. Indeed, it seemed to her that this man's graze was a little like stumbling onto a bit of heaven.

So perhaps it was worth whatever risk she took in allowing it. Besides, having dressed herself in her chemise, stays and underskirt, Sarah felt secure in the fact that there were enough layers of clothing beneath this thin covering of blanket to provide adequate defense. Not that there was a need for one.

That was another important factor to consider: She trusted him. Even though beneath her skirt, she was quite bare—as was the fashion of the day—she trusted him with what was probably her most precious gift.

Sarah had never given the form of feminine clothing much consideration, since it was the general mode by which all women of quality dressed. But when White Thunder's touch ventured up toward her knee—a scant few inches away from an area of Sarah's body that was most private—she was dismayed to discover that his touch felt erotic.

"I fear that I must find a way to present more foodstuffs in your diet," he said, "if you are suffering from this pain even when at rest."

"Aye, sir, that would be most beneficial." Sarah gasped silently, for his touch had ventured upward over her knees. Her body's instant response was quite carnal. Indeed, at the moment, were he to venture even farther upward, toward her femininity, she might like it very well. It was a sobering realization.

To cover over her response, she said, "Were you not going to tell me a story?"

"*Nyoh,* yes, I was. Forgive me, for I was considering how best to obtain the nourishment you need."

"The bone broths might help."

"*Nyoh.* That they might."

"And I should like to hear that story, very much, I think."

"*Nyoh,* I will begin. This is the story that the spirits told one of our wise sachems, and it has been repeated often since then." White Thunder's voice was deep and soothing. When combined with his gentle touch, it was more than any feminine heart could easily reject, and she felt herself respond.

"Long ago," he continued, "at a place across the great salt water, was a land that was ruled by a queen. There was trouble in this land, for the people there had hunted out most of the game and they were hungry. It happened that the queen had a servant who was a preacher, who was told to dust some old books. When no one was looking, this servant boy read one of these books, and he learned many things that prior to this, he hadn't known. He began to dream."

"Hmm . . ." Sarah winced beneath his massage. One of her muscles convulsed.

"Did I hurt you?"

"No, sir," she replied, "you did not. 'Tis only the contraction of my muscles. Sometimes it feels as if the muscle is pulling away from the bone, for the pain is that intense."

He said nothing, but his touch on her became softer, and he asked, "Is that better?"

"Indeed," she said, "'tis so. But please do continue the story. What did the boy dream?"

"Before I tell you, I would like to ask you a question."
She nodded.

"Are you aware that to the Indian, some dreams are sacred? That some dreams are a communication from the Creator?"

"No, I didn't realize that."

"I thought it might be so. It is, however, important to understand this fact; otherwise, the story might not be grasped in its magnitude."

"Yes," she said. "I believe I understand."

"Very well, then," and he continued. "In the servant's dream, he beheld an island he'd never seen before, and on this island was a castle made of gold. There was also a bridge leading from where he was to the island.

"This young servant could not contain his curiosity and so he crossed that bridge. There he met a handsome, young man who was brown-skinned and dark-headed. The handsome man complimented the servant and told him that since he had ventured across the bridge, he was a fearless man. Because of this, he told the servant that he would divulge a secret that would make the young man very rich.

"This was very pleasing to the servant, and the handsome stranger went on to say that across the great salt water was a land where a whole people was virtuous, where honesty and integrity to oneself, to one's family and to one's tribe and to his Creator was without fault. 'They have no evil inclinations,' said this handsome man, 'and because of this, you can become very rich if you do as I say.' "

As he spoke, White Thunder's hands ranged up to her knee and again a little higher. Sarah shivered under titillating sensation; mere inches separated his kneading from the most feminine part of her body. Yet Sarah wouldn't have stopped him had she desired to do so, which she didn't.

White Thunder was carrying on with his tale, and said, "The servant listened intently to what this strange man had to say, which was this: 'There are five things that all men and all women take pleasure in,' said the stranger, 'and I will give you a bundle that contains what these five things are. But before I give them to you, you must promise me that you will do all you can to ensure that these things are taken across the great water and are taken to the people there.'

"The boy hesitated but when the handsome stranger reinforced his demand by stating that the boy would be amply repaid for his efforts, the servant agreed."

"What were the five items?" Sarah asked, interrupting. All at once, she sighed. White Thunder had removed her slippers and had set to work rubbing each one of her feet. Softly, she moaned, "That feels quite heavenly."

"I am happy to hear it," he replied. "And the muscle spasms? Have they ceased?"

"They are less, sir."

"Good," he said. "I will continue to massage you until they stop altogether."

"Do you think they will go away completely?"

"I think they might," he said.

"That would be a most pleasant state of affairs." Sarah breathed in deeply and relaxed. At length, she asked, "But tell me, for you have piqued my curiosity. What were the five things that all men and women desire?"

"*Ah, nyoh*, the five things that all men and women desire. I will tell you soon, but you must be patient for I have not yet come to that part of the story."

"Hmm," she murmured again. "'Tis a shame, for I am quite inquisitive."

"I have hoped that you would be," he said. "Now to the young servant, the handsome man said, 'Take this bundle and study it well and ensure that these things are transported across the water. If you do this, much wealth will be yours.'

"Suddenly the young servant awoke, and when he did, he discovered that he held a bundle in his hands. Had it

been only a dream? he wondered. It is hard to say this was
so, for the items were real.

"At first, the boy was frightened because it appeared
that whatever this was held magic. But soon his desire to
see what was inside overcame his fear and he opened the
bundle. Here is what he found inside: There were playing
cards, a bottle of rum, a few of the white man's gold coins,
a fiddle and a leg bone that was so old that it barely held
together without breaking in two."

"That's odd," she commented. "Such strange things."

"*Nyoh*, it is so. When the boy saw what was inside, he
felt much as you, for these were unusual items to give to a
person, and he couldn't conceive of bringing them to a people across a great body of salt water. Yet, the boy remembered his promise to the stranger, as well as the vision of
the riches he would acquire if he did exactly as he was told
to do. And so the servant boy sought out another man and
told his story to this man, who was an adventurer. From that
moment on, this man and all the other people who followed
him carried these five things with them when they came to
Turtle Island."

"And what were those things again?" she asked.

"They were playing cards, a bottle of rum, a few of the
white man's gold coins, a fiddle and a leg bone that was so
old that it barely held together."

"But I don't see—"

"Be patient, for I have not finished the story yet. Now,
these gifts soon spread throughout this new land, Turtle
Island, for these items were, indeed, things that all people
took pleasure in. Now do you remember what I told you
about dreams and about the Creator?"

"Yes."

"Good, because this handsome stranger was a man we
of the Iroquois Nation call *Hanisse'ono*, the evil twin of the
Creator of this world. *Hanisse'ono* laughed at the mischief
he had caused and said to himself, 'The cards will cause

the people to gamble away all their property, and will make them fight amongst themselves; the bottle of rum, when drunk, will make the people indulge in the evils of their bad mind until they will fight and kill each other and become fools who will sign away their country; the coins will bring about dishonesty amongst the people and will make them lustful of others' property and they will forget the teachings of the Peacemaker and Hiawatha; the fiddle will cause the men to dance with women of easy virtue and cause gossip and the tattling of tongues, tearing down the reputations of good people; all of these things will bring about the ruin of the people and they will lose all sense of who they are, thus the gift of the bone that withers away.' "

"But your Nation has not withered away," Sarah objected. "I may not remember much of my past, but I do know that the Iroquois Nation still exists. It is strong, united, invincible."

"So it is. Now. But if my people do not hearken to these warnings from our great sachem, we might become a people who were only once mighty. Think of what has happened in a mere few years: My people have become reliant on English trade goods, the blanket, the iron pots and pans, the gun. Where before we were the creators of all things that we needed, we now make almost none of those goods that keep our society together."

"But isn't that the way of all great civilizations?" Sarah asked. "For instance, I have no desire to weave the cloth that I use to make my dresses, but someone else does, so I buy it from him, but he might not be able to make the style of dress that I create and so he then buys a dress from me."

"True," White Thunder said. "But you are English. You will still find cloth even if your governor argues with the French. It will still be there because there are those among you who know how to weave the cloth and sell it to you. But imagine if no one among your nation knew how to weave this cloth, nor even desired to do so, and that only the French knew this skill. Imagine now that if your governor argued with the French, so that the French became upset and stopped trading with you, what would you do? Go naked?"

"We would probably take war into their country."

"You might if you were united and strong. But now let's observe that others come into your camp and try to divide you. Some want you to fight the French and take their cloth from them, but others want you to trade only with the Dutch, who also have a cloth, though perhaps of lower quality. You cannot muster a force of arms, because you are not united in your cause, but have become scattered, like seeds, to the winds. Indeed, you have sold the soul of your nation for want of being able to make the things you now need amongst yourselves."

"But," Sarah interrupted, rising up onto her forearms and casting him a speculative glance, "you carry a gun, and your shirt is made of cloth. Even this blanket that has become my bed is European made. How can you be honestly critical of something, when you engage in buying those things from the people you criticize?"

"A man must purchase from whatever source he can garner the things he needs to clothe himself, and since the Seneca no longer make these things, we are left with no choice but to buy what we can where we can. In the past, we used the skins of animals to make and sew our clothing; even this skill is disappearing. Consider also that in the not-too-distant past, these things were free to the man who could trap and kill the animal.

"Now we must buy the cloth from the English if we are to clothe ourselves," he continued. "And with what exchange do we purchase it?"

"With gold or with silver?"

"It could be," he said, "or the skins of animals that we little value, but that the English seem to esteem beyond even gold. And when the animals are gone, what will we use then? Gold? Silver? And where shall we obtain those metals?"

"From the English?"

"Perhaps. But recall that these things were once free to us before the English invaded our country."

"But isn't your society better for all these things?"

"Better? How do you mean better?"

"I little know, since I have never been among your people. But I think that perhaps your women might not have to work so hard. That would be an advantage. Maybe these pots and pans and cloth make their lives a little easier so that they have more time to spend with their family?"

"Ah, but do they spend more time with their families, or do they spend the time they save by arguing over the iron pot that their neighbor has?"

As he spoke, his touch quickened over her and Sarah winced under the accidental pressure. Seeing her reaction, however, he gentled his massage, and she again relaxed, putting herself willingly into his care.

"Our lives were not so bad in the past," he went on to say. "While we did not have the guns or steel of the English or French, we had one valuable the Englishman has want of."

"Oh? What is that?"

"Harmony in our villages and between each other, and an independent spirit. What need did a mother have to spend more time with her children, when her children were beside her in the fields?"

"But," said Sarah, "if a person had more conveniences and life wasn't so hard—she had more leisure—then she could spend that time thinking, considering ways to make life even better, couldn't she? After all, as human beings, aren't we always striving to better conditions for ourselves and our children?"

"True. What you say is so; and in a perfect world, it would be this way. But what if these comforts were used, not to better a person or his family, but rather to chain them to another? And what if those chains were forged, not to fashion a tie of goodwill toward one another, but rather to hold one back?"

"Then that is not progress."

"No, it is not, and so it is not for the Indian, I think. We have these new things, but what has been the result of having them?"

"I don't know."

"War. We have constant war in a land that was set into motion to be a nation of peace. Since the English and French have been among us, we have war among ourselves over mere triflings. Then we are persuaded to go to war for the English against the French or for the French against the English. Since the English and French and Dutch have come to our shores, bringing with them their many and varied things, we have been involved in more war than is within the living minds of our elders."

Sarah lay still in silence, not knowing what to say, for she recognized some truth to his words. Indeed, White Thunder had made a rather convincing point.

When it appeared that he had little more to say on the matter, she asked, "Then you're saying that these things that the European brings are evil?"

"Perhaps these 'conveniences' are not themselves evil, but they bring an evil with them that is unparalleled to the Indian mind. If we could make these things ourselves, if we weren't dependent on the English or French, we would have a chance, I think, to remain united and be a force to be reckoned with. Without this, it is only a matter of time before we are run over by the English or the French for want of their things."

"But, sir, if you were to have your way, you would remain living in poverty."

"Poverty? We had no poverty before the Englishman came to our shores. There are three things a human being requires in order live: food and water, shelter and clothing. All were free to us before the coming of the English and French. All that we required was made from the earth by our own hands. If a man was ambitious enough, he might hunt better than another and make a name for himself. A woman, too. Poverty was unknown because all that the earth produced was free to take, to harvest, to make, to produce. Only since the coming of the English and French have we had to pay for the requirements that a human being needs to simply live. Is that the action of a friend?"

"No," she was quick to say, "but by the same argument, in order for all to be free, all people then would have to engage in the same occupation, all would need to be farmers or hunters or workers. And there are careers beyond these to which a human being also aspires; those things that if a man is without or if they are withheld, he will deteriorate."

"Such as?"

"The arts," she said. "Music, literature, painting, creativity."

He nodded.

"If one had to till the soil and work the fields, when would he have the time to write a great work of music, or paint the great pictures or build the awe-inspiring architecture?"

"And within your society, there is room for this?"

"There is," she said. "It took a bit of leisure time to think of and invent the gun, to make the iron pots, to put together the little trinkets that make life tolerable."

"And these people who do this, how do they pay for their necessities?"

"From the profits they make by selling their works."

"And do they live easily and free?"

"I . . ." Sarah stopped. No, they rarely did. Unless they were taken under the wing of some monarch, they usually experienced poverty and hardship.

He was continuing to speak, however, and he said, "If the English had come here and let us remain free to make our own goods and harvest our own food and build our houses, and brought us things that would make our lives easier within our own idea of how life should be lived, that is the action of a friend. We, too, could have expanded our society to include music and much, much more. But to bring with him a means to exact a payment to him for items needed to do nothing more than live, is to enslave a man, for who then can be free but he who holds the most wealth?"

Sarah didn't know what to say to this piece of logic, and so she simply asked, "Was your grandmother happy, then?"

"It was so. If she were alive and you were to ask my grandmother if she lived a hard life, filled with poverty, she would have laughed at you, for her life was happy. Yes, she worked the fields, she made the meals, she clothed the children, but she did so with the help of her mothers, her sisters, her aunts and grandmothers. A day spent sewing was a day spent socializing. A day when she worked the fields was a day she played games with her children, chased off crows, climbed high posts, looked for far-away enemies."

"It does sound almost . . . ideal."

"I think it was. Now with these new inventions of the English, we need each other less, and so our socializing is less. We even go to war and act on our own, instead of staying together as a united whole."

Sarah paused while she contemplated what he said. At last she responded, saying, "Although I understand what you say and can appreciate it, you must realize that one cannot live forever in the past. New inventions are a part of life, if only for the reason that the young will always try to find new ways to do old things. There must be a happy medium."

He nodded. "And so there must be. For my part, I believe we Seneca should learn to make those things the trader brings us. Either that or do without them."

"Perhaps you are right," she said. Then, changing the subject, she uttered, "Hmm . . . after this massage, I am thinking that I might obtain a good night's sleep."

"Have the cramps awakened you from your sleep at night?"

"They have, indeed."

"I was unaware of that. Usually I awaken easily, but I have not heard your plight."

"That is because I have not given one. I have done all I can to remain quiet."

"But if you are in pain, then you should tell me so that I may help. It is not in my mind that you should grieve."

"I will remember that."

"And now, if your pain is less, I think that I might bring in the fresh meat that I hunted this day. I believe we can make dry meat with it and some soup to help you on the path back to health. If you can, try rolling over and standing."

She did as he asked and came onto her back, so that she lay faceup, but she said, "I fear, sir, that I might still be too weak to stand. When I am on my own and have tried it before, I seem to do nothing but collapse."

"But I am here now and if your legs cannot hold you, I will catch you."

"Very well, then. I will try. Perhaps you could assist me to stand?"

She sat up and as she did so, his arms came around her. It was nothing unusual, nothing to set off a spark within her. After all, he had been assisting her and holding her for days and days now.

But at this particular time, there was something differ- ent about him. This day, when he helped her rise, and they stood chest to chest within each other's embrace, there was a seductive pull that Sarah would have been hard-pressed to ignore. Indeed, she swooned in toward him.

It was a tense moment as he caught her, made more acute by his gentle breath upon her hair.

She looked up at the same time he glanced down at her, and they stared at one another until at last, he said, "You are most beautiful."

"I? Beautiful? After being almost drowned and lying here with a raging fever?"

"Indeed, I think you are beautiful."

Then he kissed her on the cheek. Perhaps it was meant to be no more than a light peck, a gesture given to bring comfort. But something went wrong with it.

She turned her face into his so that all he had to do was move his head ever so slightly, and . . . He seized the opportunity and kissed her, this time on the lips, fully, completely and without restraint.

Although Sarah little understood what drove her, this she did grasp, she wanted more. She wanted to be held closer, loved and cherished. Little able to stop herself, she swooned in toward him. It was a mistake. She knew it at once.

However, it felt so incredibly good . . .

Seven

It was a moment of rapture. It was a moment set out of time, reminiscent of the Englishman's heaven. But it was wrong—the wrong time, the wrong place, the wrong woman. Yet contradictorily, something about her was right, and White Thunder felt himself surrender to the softness of her curves, her scent, her taste.

However, it had to end. It should have never begun. After all, he had his duty, and she . . . she couldn't even remember who she was. Might she not belong to another?

Common sense demanded he withdraw. Instinct, however, saw him reaching down and pulling her buttocks in even closer toward him.

She didn't object. This was his downfall.

He thought he might go mad with desire. He deepened the kiss, opening his lips so that he might explore the warm inner recess of her mouth.

He groaned. She sighed and fell in toward him. So close was she, he guessed that he could feel every feminine hill

and valley of her form. The knowledge sent his mind spin-
ning, and his body reacted with all the pent-up frustra-
tion of an aroused male. His heartbeat raced and he could
barely catch his breath.

In the end, he had to breathe, and he ended the kiss, but
not so the embrace. In fact, he pulled her in even closer.
They both gasped for air.

He should say something. But what? At last, all he could
think to utter was, "I am sorry."

She didn't respond, not by word or by action. Indeed,
she remained fixed in his arms.

After a brief hesitation, he decided he should explain
himself, and he said, "I am sorry because I, who have told
you that you are safe with me, have yet taken you in my
arms." He shook his head against hers, but he didn't release
her. In essence, she was still so close that he figured he
could commit her physical form to memory.

At last she spoke, her voice soft and breathless as she
said, "You have nothing to be sorry for, sir. If I remember
correctly, you promised that as long as I didn't desire your
attention, you would not give it."

He nodded. "That I did."

"However, sir, I fear that I am as much to blame as you
are." She paused. "You see, I wanted to be kissed."

She stared up at him, and he pulled away from her
to glance down at her, though his arms remained firmly
locked around her. Surveying the look in her eyes, he realized at once the truth of her words, plus he recognized
something else . . . something more profound. Passion, amorous and sensual, stared back at him from the depths of her
gaze.

His heartbeat leaped into furious action, and blood
surged through him with alarming speed. At once, his
body was ready for her. He feared she could feel it.

He uttered, "Do not tell me these things if you do not
mean them, for I fear it encourages me very much. I have

taken it on myself to care for you, which does not and must not include making love to you."

"That's not necessarily true. In this instance—"

"Do you tease me?" he interrupted her. "You must know that I am already thinking I will not let you go until we have explored one another as a man and a woman might."

"As a man and a woman might? Of what are you speaking, sir?"

He didn't answer.

"In my society," she continued, "men do not speak such words to a woman unless that man is contemplating marriage, for to do so is unseemly. And yet I can hardly believe that this is your intention . . ."

He gulped. Marriage? His heartbeat stilled. Even his arms loosened from around her. Luckily, with that distance came a ray of sanity.

How could the conversation have progressed so far in only a few minutes? He realized he had to tell her. He had to be truthful.

However, there was a problem. How does a man explain the truth of his life to a woman who is as sweet and desirable as this one? How does he tell her what's in his heart without tearing out hers by doing so?

He breathed in deeply, then took the plunge, his voice barely a whisper as he confessed, "Know this, I would make love to you and give you all that I could that is within me to give, but I cannot ever marry again. At least not until my duty to my deceased wife is fulfilled."

She was silent for so long, he almost wished he hadn't spoken.

"To Wild Mint?"

"*Nyoh*, yes."

"Oh." It was all she said before she backed away from him, her countenance gradually mirroring her understanding. She said, "I fear this conversation has gone too far, much too quickly."

He agreed, yet he felt bereft without the warmth of her body next to his. However, in this case distance was not to be so easily gained. While it might have been a good intention on her part—to restrain herself from him—her legs wouldn't hold her up, and almost as soon as she stood on her own, she collapsed. He caught her easily, and held her in his arms momentarily until she again struggled against his hold.

"Do not fear," he said. "I will take you back to your sleeping robes, where you can invoke your need to be away from me if you choose."

"That would be most kind."

He picked her up in his arms and stepped toward her bed. No sooner had he started, however, when she said, "Sir, I fear there are further problems. If I do not recover my memory, there will be no option for me but to remain close to you. This would be difficult for us both, I think."

He dipped his head in agreement. "True," he said, "but if we have to do it, we will. I cannot leave you here on your own. To do so would be as to commit murder, for I do not think that you could easily forage for yourself."

She paused. "Yes, of course." She stared away from him. "But let us pray that my memory does return, the sooner the better. For the well being of us both, I think."

"*Nyah-weh.* I will pray that it will be so."

He set her down on the softness of the pine boughs and blanket, and as soon as he did so, she lay back and took several deep breaths. He watched as she gazed up at the ceiling of the cave. She was silent. He was the same.

At some length, she said, "'Tis quite a dark place that you have chosen for our shelter, is it not?"

"That is the way in which caves and other passages underground are formed, for they do not have the warmth of the sun to light them."

"Aye. I have wondered," she said. "When I first awoke, I heard water running here in the cave, but I have not been able to find the source, since my legs will not hold me. Tell me, is there water near here?"

"There is an underground stream that flows not more than a hundred or so feet from us. It is farther into the cave and so there is no light there. It would be hard to find on one's own."

"Ah, that accounts for it," she said, then she sighed as she turned her face away from him.

Watching her, he felt helpless. He realized his words might have seemed harsh to her after he had held her in his arms and kissed her, but there was little he could do about what he'd admitted to her. He had spoken the truth.

After some deliberation, however, he decided to talk of trivial things, much as she was doing, and he said, "I have brought us fresh meat. It is a deer and should provide a good source of food for days. We can make dry meat, and from the bones, we can boil a broth that should supply you with the necessary nourishment to keep your muscles from becoming painful."

"I . . . thank you, sir."

He hesitated and stared at her. "I will bring the carcass near the fire, where we will be able to skin it at our ease. Would you like to help me?"

"Yes, very much, I think." But she didn't sound as if her heart were in it.

Feeling utterly powerless, White Thunder rose up to his feet and stepped to the front of the cave. Retrieving the game, he placed it around his shoulders and brought it toward the fire, where he set it down.

"Would you like me to take you up and bring you to the fire?"

She didn't reply at once. He waited.

At last she said, "I think I would like you to prop me up so that I am in a sitting position, and can watch you from here."

He did as she suggested, being careful not to touch her overly much. "Are you comfortable?" he asked.

"Yes, I am, and thank you."

He nodded and returned to the fire, where he set to work over the deer.

To ease the undercurrents that were awash between them he continued to talk, and he asked, "Have you ever skinned a deer?"

"No, sir, I have not."

"It is not a hard task to accomplish if you know how to do it. If you will come here, I will show you the way of it." Almost sheepishly, he asked, "Will you?"

"Yes, sir, though I fear you must again help me to the fireside, for I cannot make it there on my own."

So quickly did he jump to his feet to come to her aid, he wondered if he'd startled her. Reaching down to take her in his arms, he said, "Know that if I were able, I would—"

"Please, sir," she interrupted. "There is no need to belabor the point. You are committed, and I . . . I don't remember my past. I could very well be committed, also. We are both doing the best we can in a very poor situation, so do not feel there is a need to explain."

He nodded, and placing his arms beneath her, carried her to the fireside. But it was like magic. It took no more than a mere touch to again send his body into readiness.

Were he not sworn to his obligation, were he not consumed with duty, he might like to come to know this woman better. But these ideas were useless to consider, for they could not be.

Indeed. They simply could not be. Why, he wondered, didn't that feel right?

"You make a slit here in the belly of the animal from the rump to the throat, and when you pull the skin away, it comes off whole with little trouble." He showed her how to do it.

Sarah nodded, but at the first sight of blood, she realized that this was a skill she might never use. Propped up so that she was in a sitting position, she watched him work, her attention focused on his hands.

But there was danger in letting her thoughts drift in that direction. Was it only minutes ago that those hands had held her?

To keep her attention focused on other matters, she looked away. Truth be told, Sarah was upset, but not with him. Her upset lay with . . . circumstances.

How could she have encouraged him to kiss her? Hold her? How could she have practically begged him for his embrace—only to be turned down.

It was a sobering realization.

"You are quiet," he said after a while.

"Aye," she returned, "that I am." She didn't offer further communication and he didn't seem inclined to press her.

After some moments, however, she decided to confront this tiger, stripes and all, and said, "I don't blame you for what happened."

He paused. "I am glad."

"However, I think you should have been honest with me about your wife and your feelings toward others in your life before you kissed me. Perhaps before you massaged my legs, also, for I believe that is what started this."

"I agree," he said. "I am sorry. But massaging your legs is not what started it, I fear."

"Is it not?" she asked, sparing him a glance.

"*Neh*, it is not."

"If not that, then what? When?"

He exhaled on a breath, then throwing her a sharp glance, he said, "I will tell you, but in doing so, I do not wish you to think I am trying to change the conditions between us."

She nodded briefly.

"I have been watching you and admiring you since I first found you, for you are fair of face and figure," he went on to say. "My feelings have been building up to this since I first found you, awaiting only an outlet."

She swallowed noisily, before saying, "You compliment me, sir, but I hardly think that would cause you to want to make love to me."

"Then let me say it to you this way: Had I been massaging my grandmother's legs, I would not have felt the need to kiss her and leave my imprint upon her."

"Oh, yes, of course." She paused. "In not knowing this, I did encourage you, didn't I? And you are, after all, male, and . . ." She frowned and turned her head away, rubbing her forehead. It was as though her thoughts hurt.

"Did you remember something?"

"No," she said, "but I do seem to be possessed of numerous opinions—which require no memory a'tall. 'Tis strange."

He nodded. "It is. What opinions are these that appear to worry you?"

"I fear I cannot say them."

"Why can you not?"

"Because, sir, they are hurtful opinions, and perhaps not based on fact."

"Hurtful to whom?"

"If I were to tell you that—"

"Tell me."

She breathed out on a sigh, and glanced down at her hands. "Then it would be toward you, sir."

He nodded. "I thank you for sparing me."

"You are most welcome."

"But I think," he went on to say, "that I would know the worst of it."

"I cannot say it, sir. I should never have brought it up,

for I simply cannot bring myself to use my lips to say the things that have been told to me."

Laying down his knife, and ripping open the carcass of the deer, he commented, "Someone has said that the Indian man is a beast and will rape women and children, hasn't he?"

Again, she hesitated. "I cannot recall . . ."

"And you believed it?"

"Until I met you and one other . . ." She scowled, and again she grabbed her head. Suddenly, it hurt.

"Another memory?"

"Almost, sir." Sarah cast her gaze upward. At last, she said, "After all you have done for me, I fear I now believe that the opinions I have been told are based on nothing but terrible gossip. And, sir, I have remembered something."

He glanced up at her, eyebrows raised in surprise, but he didn't push her to relate her memory. He didn't say a word. Instead, he waited.

"I recall a man, sir," she began. "An older gentleman, who was well-to-do, I believe. He had . . . some business with the Indians, I recall. It was he who told me this gossip, and it was, indeed, similar to what you said."

"I thought as much, for it is common for a man to accuse another of those things he does himself."

"Is it, now?"

"It is. Have you never observed this for yourself?"

"No, sir, I don't believe that I have."

He sighed. "I will tell you the truth, though it is probably useless to do so. But even if you do not believe it—and I fear you won't—you will at least have both sides of the story, and can make up your own mind about what is and isn't true."

"Yes. Please. Go ahead."

"*Nyah-weh*. It is a story," he said, but he didn't look at

her. His attention was taken up in preparation of the game. "Long ago, before the French, the English and the Dutch came into our country, our women and children were safe to travel on their own, even into the woods, often without accompaniment. Certainly, they were safe in their own homes. However, with the arrival of the European into our country, this and many other things changed. Disease came with the English and the French, killing many of us. But for this, we did not blame the new invader. If he brought it, it was unintentionally done. No, what we disdained, what we could not understand, were this man's unhealthy desires to seek his pleasure from our women and children."

Sarah gasped. "Surely, Mr. Thunder, you are not suggesting that—"

"It is a matter of fact. It is written in the sacred wampum—it is recorded in the memory of our elders."

Sarah sat gaping at him, unable to muster a response.

"Because of this," he continued, "to this day, when a white man whom we do not know enters our villages, we hide our women and children until we are certain of his intentions."

Sarah paused, choosing her words. "You are right, sir," she said. "I find that hard to believe."

He didn't answer. Rather, with a shrug, he went on quietly with his work.

But Sarah wouldn't let it go, couldn't let it go, and she said, "Mr. Thunder, are you telling me that good Christian men—"

"I did not say they were either good or Christian."

"But—"

"In the two years I lived with the missionaries, I came to observe that there were two different kinds of people among the English: those that take and those that give. And the two do not mix. Those that take are not good, and they are not Christian.

"They do not live by the book that they tell the Indian

and others to obey," he continued. "They lie and they cheat. So much is this true, that our wisest men warn that if such people say a thing is so, it is the opposite. These kinds of men or women are few among the English, fortunately, but they give your race a bad name. Someday all the Indian Nations might blame your people for the injustices they suffer beneath the hand of these few—which would also be untruthful."

"I'm sorry that you feel this way."

"It is not a feeling. It is an observation."

"Yes," said Sarah, "so you have said. But, sir, are you implying that your society has no stragglers, no men who serve their own ends?"

"No, all societies have such people. Perhaps the difference is in how a tribe treats a man who lies or serves his own ends. It is an Iroquois law that if a man is seen once to lie or to serve only himself or his family, the women of the tribe dismiss him from his seat on the council, or if he is not a council member, he is banished from the tribe. He is considered a thing of horror, and no child will even look upon his face. He is a disgrace.

"But this is not so among the English, who tend to believe the wagging tongue of the man who cannot and will not associate himself with anything but lies."

Sarah became silent. Indeed, she realized that what this man said was very near true.

"Until the English find a way to show this man up for what he is, until they serve him real justice, he will leave a disgrace upon the graves of the innocent Englishman, who in his heart is a good, God-fearing Christian."

Sarah stared down at her lap. In truth, she was stunned. Stunned because what this man said was too astute to be readily dismissed. She said, "I hope, sir, that your look into what the future holds for the Englishman is not an exact look."

"I, too," he said. "But I fear this will be as it is unless some force comes into the world to change it."

Again, Sarah sat silently by, watching him.

At length, he changed the subject, and said, "Would you like to try to help me take the layer of fat from the skin? I could bring you here beside me, and guide you so that you could do it again if the need ever arose."

And be that close to him?

She said, "No, sir, I believe not. I am still recovering, and I am happy watching you."

He didn't comment, though he did allow his glance to scan over her features. Silence again commenced between them.

While cutting up the meat into strips, he spoke, saying, "We will dry this meat over a smoky fire so that we can make a mixture that will nourish us on the trail."

"And where will we be going, sir?"

"Either I will return you to your people, or if you have not recovered your memory by the time we are ready to leave, I will take you to my village."

"To your village. Ah, yes, I do remember you saying as much to me." Sarah's stomach dropped. The prospect was frightening. However, if her memory didn't return, there would be little option but to follow him. She said, "But we are not ready to go yet, are we?"

"Not until you are up and able to walk on your own. And whichever path we take, whether to your village or to mine, we will need food. And since we will be traveling fast, it is best to prepare it now."

Sarah nodded. "Then I will help you do it . . . tomorrow." She grinned at him, and heaven be praised, he smiled right back.

Eight

It was only a few days later when, with the aid of the cane that White Thunder had fashioned for her, Sarah struggled up onto her feet and slowly, with one foot placed carefully after another, began to walk. Soon, within a matter of days, she was walking without aid. And though her muscles still spasmed with pain now and again, neither she nor White Thunder had dared to repeat the deep massage.

True to his word, White Thunder had concocted many meals' worth of bone broth soups. As he offered the soup to her, along with the other foods he had in store, gradually the muscle contractions in her legs lessened.

It was liberating, she discovered, to be able to amble about again, and she realized a limited truth: Lack of movement created, to a greater or lesser degree, a sort of enslavement. Certainly it made one dependent on the good-will of another.

Within days, Sarah could leave the cave on her own and though at first she was reluctant to venture too far, eventually she conquered her fear and strolled out farther and farther into the woods. As she became stronger, she realized that for all practical purposes she would be able to leave this place soon. Not yet, if only because her legs wouldn't always obey her every command. But soon.

Where would she go? she wondered. What would she do? The worry hung over her like a dark cloud, since, to date, her past life still remained a mystery to her.

One factor had changed recently, however. It had started to rain, which was causing Sarah to stay close to the cave out of necessity. Along with the downpours came a coldness that had settled over the land. Even the autumn leaves, so bright only weeks ago, now hung dismally under an often-gray and threatening sky.

It happened late one afternoon, suddenly and without warning. One moment Sarah had been safe and warm in the cave, the next she had ventured out of it only to come face to face with a bear: a big, fully grown black bear.

Sarah froze.

The bear growled, stood up onto its hind legs and pawed at the air. Sarah was dwarfed by it. It howled again, the sound terrorizing. All at once, adrenaline and fear washed through her.

She remained frozen to the spot. Though the bear made no forward movement, it was close enough that the very air around her became scented with the animal.

Suddenly something changed and the bear came down on all fours and started toward her.

Sarah screamed.

Stunned at the noise, the bear stopped, and looking right and left, it pawed at the ground. Finally, bringing its attention back to her, the bear slowly, carefully, closed the distance between them.

"Put your arms up over your head and growl!" It was White Thunder. "Do it! Now!"

She did as White Thunder ordered. Raising her hands over her head, she opened her mouth and snarled at the bear.

As before, the bear stopped, sniffed at the air, gave her a cautious look, but plodded forward.

"Keep growling! Louder! Make your voice more savage!" ordered White Thunder, who was crouched atop a high ground next to the cave. "He's tired and looking for a place to sleep. He may decide that you're too much for him. Keep growling."

Adrenaline pumped through her as, following White Thunder's orders, she mustered up her loudest voice, as well as what she hoped was her most ferocious-looking face.

Again the bear hesitated, but hearing White Thunder, the bear finally took notice of him. Sensing that he was the greater danger of the two, it came up onto his hind legs and growled at White Thunder, as though warning him away from his find.

When White Thunder did nothing but stare back at the bear and snarl at it, the bear came down again to all fours, and ignoring White Thunder for the moment, turned back to continue its path toward Sarah, as though by deed to say that she was the least likely to give him problems.

Step by step, the bear progressed dangerously close. All at once it rose again to its hind legs and roared at her, this time extending its sharp paws outward. Only one thought surfaced: She was dead. She was dinner. Never had the desire to own and have a gun in her hand been more prevalent than it was at this moment.

Suddenly White Thunder shot straight in front of her, placing himself directly between her and the bear. And if the bear was roaring and kicking up a fine noise, so, too, was White Thunder. Indeed, so loud was it that Sarah could hardly tell what was man and what was beast.

Then White Thunder did what was either the most courageous act she had ever witnessed—or the most reckless. He bent forward, sticking his face into the bear's, which was only a few feet away, and he snarled and snapped as though he were the more dangerous creature.

The animal yowled right back at White Thunder, and so shrill was it, Sarah thought her eardrums might never mend. Then suddenly, White Thunder was yelling directions at her.

"Make noise!"

Without delay, Sarah screamed and clapped her hands.

"Now we back up," he shouted at her, "so as to tell him we give him the cave. We are no threat. Slowly, we back up, all the while we make as much noise as possible."

Though White Thunder was holding his gun pointed directly at the bear, Sarah knew it wouldn't be protection enough against a head-on attack. After all, the musket had only one shot, the next shot requiring priming and reloading.

He took a step back. Sarah followed suit. Another step back, another and another.

The bear came down onto all fours again. It roared so loudly, Sarah wanted to run for cover. But it was impossible.

"If he starts toward us," yelled White Thunder, "and paws at me, you are to turn and run—do you understand? Run downhill. A bear cannot easily follow if you go downhill. You are to run as fast as you can and don't look back!"

"I won't leave you!"

"You have no choice! I give you no choice! If I say run, you are to run! If I am to fight him, I cannot worry about you!"

Another step back, another and another.

Suddenly, the bear chose to take a leap toward them.
"Run!"

Sarah turned to do exactly as told, but her legs suddenly refused to move. What was she to do? Even taking painfully slow steps was impossible. It was as if she were suddenly crippled.

That's when she spotted it. There inside the cave. Fire! Weren't all animals afraid of fire?

The bear was already attacking White Thunder. She could hear their struggle, though because of the fear gripping her, she didn't dare to look back. But her legs suddenly responded, and rushing back into the cave, she was able to pick up several of the sticks that were burning red-hot at their tips.

Without thinking of what she was about to do, she rushed out of the cave. Later in life, she would wonder where her courage and strength had come from on this day. Until this moment, she'd never been aware of being particularly brave. She could only thank the good Lord that when valor was necessary, it was lying dormant within her.

White Thunder was on the ground, the bear over him. She rushed at the bear with the fire.

"Shoo! Get out of here!" Her voice was piercing and loud. She waved the weapon at the bear and tried to get close enough to light its fur on fire.

But her attempts did almost nothing to the beast; its fur was too matted. Startled, the bear jumped back, allowing White Thunder a moment to bring up his musket and take careful aim.

BOOM!

White Thunder shot off a ball aimed straight into the eyeball of the bear.

It hit.

Still animated, the bear struggled forward. Had the shot served no purpose? White Thunder was reloading as fast as was humanly possible, and as she watched him struggle against time to prime his weapon and reload it, she wondered, was this it? Was life suddenly over? This easily?

Memories of her past instantaneously rushed through her mind. They came with no fanfare, no bells. Rather, they swamped her. Moments from her past flickered before her so quickly, she could barely take hold of them.

Indeed, so overwhelming was it, she rocked back on her feet.

Meanwhile, the battle with the bear was coming to a close. The animal took one final step forward, and fell over, dead.

Sarah watched it in horror, almost afraid to turn away from it, fearful that it might only be catching its breath. Even as she looked at it, she wondered: What damage had it done to White Thunder?

No sooner had the thought formed within her mind than she was struck with another truth. She cared for White Thunder. She honestly cared for this man.

She was breathing hard and fast, and she could hear White Thunder behind her, doing the same. At least, she thought, he was still alive.

Though out of breath, he called out to her, and said, "I told you to leave!"

"I could not do it, sir!" she cried. "You forget that my legs do not always obey me."

At last she turned toward him. He was on the ground, his shirt torn with claw marks. There were several gashes on his chest and arms where the bear's claws had found their mark. As Sarah caught her breath, she could only thank the good Lord that, because of the cool weather, White Thunder had worn a shirt this day.

But his clothing was blood-soaked, and was becoming more so by the minute.

"Look at what he's done to you," she said as she took several steps toward White Thunder, and came down on the ground beside him.

"They are scratches," he said.

Then White Thunder did the unthinkable. He opened his arms to her and she went into them willingly, both of them uncaring that he was bleeding all over her.

"You saved my life," she whispered.

"As you did mine."

"You came to my defense. You jumped in front of me and confronted the beast head-on."

"Of course I did. Did you expect me to leave you to fight a bear on your own?"

"I didn't expect anything, sir. I . . . I thank you." She paused significantly. Then a little shyly, she added, "I think also that my mistress will thank you as soon as I manage to find her again."

He pushed her back from him and stared at her.

Tears were streaming down Sarah's cheeks as she said, "It's true. I have remembered my past life and who I am. It happened suddenly. I remembered everything."

"This is good." He was smiling.

"Yes, it is very good. I will tell you more about it later. But come, you are hurt and first I must do something about that."

"I think I will need little attention. They are only scrapes," he reiterated.

Sarah drew back to look at him. "I will be the judge of that. Come."

Placing her arms about him, she helped him to his feet, taking a great deal of his weight upon her. Together they limped into the cave.

Using a piece of her torn-off petticoat that had been soaked in water, Sarah washed the blood from White Thunder's arms and chest wounds. There was something very intimate about sitting with White Thunder as he reclined on his own bedding. But she ignored the feeling.

She asked him, "Why did the bear not back down? Did he not understand that we were retreating?"

"He was threatened by me, and a bear's temper is bad even in the best of circumstances. He must have been hungry, too, for he dared much to come after you. So even though we were retreating, he could not pass up the opportunity to place his brand upon me and at the same time have a tasty dinner."

"Place his brand on you?" She paused to look up at him in open astonishment. "He was trying to kill you."

"And he might have done so had you not rushed in upon him and startled him into backing away."

"He did not back away, sir."

"No, but he was frightened enough to pause, giving me time to aim a shot."

"Yes," Sarah said as she resumed her work over him. "Thank the Lord you are a good shot."

"Do not thank the Lord. Thank my uncles and my father, who taught me to shoot."

"Aye, I shall do so. I will send them my praises, and the Lord, too, thank you very much."

He grinned at her, then winced as she dabbed at a deeper cut on his arm.

She frowned. "You will need stitches there, sir, at least on this one cut that is deeper than the rest."

He gazed down at the open wound on his arm. "Do you know how to do it?"

She shrugged. "I saw a doctor do it once. I think I might be able to sew it together, if I can find the right material to use as thread."

"Sinew from the deer can be used once my wound is cleaned, and a piece of bone might be made into a point so as to poke holes in the skin to pull the thread through. Did you spit on it?"

"I beg your pardon?"

"Did you spit on the wounds?"

"Of course not, I know better than to—"

Bending over double, he spit onto the wounds himself, leaving Sarah to watch, gaping. She said, "There are germs in your mouth, sir."

He grinned at her. "*Nyoh*, and there are other good things there, too."

Sarah shook her head, but held her tongue.

He was frowning. "I doubt that we have the right roots and herbs to put on the wound to prevent infection," he went on to say, "but there is water near here and it can be boiled and placed on the wound to speed its healing. The water is perhaps a hundred to a hundred and fifty feet from us here in the cave, but it is downhill from this place, and it is in the complete dark." He looked at her sheepishly. "I fear I may not possess the strength to take the path to the water."

"I can do it."

"Good, but bring a good fire stick with you when you go there. You will need light to find the stream."

"And what shall I collect the water in?"

"I have several bags, there by the fire." He nodded in the direction indicated. "They should do. There is also a large, hollowed-out rock that can be used to gather water, if you need it. Take more than one of the fire sticks with you when you go there, not simply one. Do not let the fire go out. If it looks as if the fire is dying, return here while there is still light by it. Once blackness falls, it is complete and there is no way to tell where you are. You could get lost. Do you understand?"

"Aye, I do."

He breathed in deeply and settled back on his own bedding of pine boughs and blanket. "I will reload the gun while you are gone."

"Yes," she said. "Please do."

He smiled at her. "Are you a good cook?"

"Yes, sir, I am—in the right circumstances."

"That is good," he said, "for I believe your skills will be needed while I recover."

"I'll do my best, sir."

He stared at her a moment. "If you have any trouble at the stream, signal me by a cry, high-pitched and loud. I will rouse myself and come and help you."

"Very well, but I think I can manage."

"Yes. We will talk when you return. After all, I would like to hear what it is that you have remembered."

"Aye," she said as she stood to her feet. "It is important, I think, although it seems to me that there are still pieces of the puzzle that I haven't recalled yet."

"Then we should discuss it. When you return here from the underground stream, I will listen while you talk."

She nodded, and rising up, she made her way to the underground stream. It was not an easy task, considering that she was carrying three bags, one heavy hollowed-out stone and three different fire sticks.

Even collecting the water proved to be almost impossible, since she dare not let the fire on the sticks go out. In the end she made several trips from their camp to the stream and back. But her problems were only beginning.

What in the good Lord's name was she going to use to boil this water? In the end, she did finally discover the smoked and toughened rawhide bags that White Thunder used to make soup. They were ingenious, actually. When she heated stones and threw them into the liquid, it was as good as boiling the water over a fire.

It was not the easiest way to go about things, but at least they would be able to eat. It could be worse, she decided. They were alive. Indeed, she thought as a shiver ran down her spine, their situation could be very much worse.

Straightening her shoulders, she set about locating the

sinew that White Thunder had mentioned. With both it and a knife—well prepared, she would be able to perform the necessary surgery to his arm.

Hopefully her hand would be steady.

Nine

"What do you mean that there is nothing to numb the pain? Are there no roots that I can dig, no plants that will deaden the nerves, even a little?"

"There is nothing."

"But if I'm to cut into you, there should be something to ease the trauma."

White Thunder's look at her was cautious, she noted, but surprised. He said, "There are herbs and plants that might do this, but there is not the time to prepare them for use. We will do without them."

Do without them? She didn't think so. She said, "Am I to presume that you intend to remain awake while I poke holes in your skin? And also while I sew up this gap in your arm?"

"*Nyoh*, that is exactly what I have in mind."

She scowled at him. "Are you one of those strange people who enjoy pain?"

He grinned at her, and again she was astonished by the

appealing effect a smile could create upon his countenance. He said, "I am not that kind of person, but I will withstand the pain."

"No, sir, I beg to differ."

He raised an eyebrow at her, but said nothing.

"You won't have to withstand it," she continued, "because I simply won't do it. There must be another way."

He didn't answer all at once. Instead, he frowned as he turned his attention inward. After a lengthy pause, he said, "Perhaps you might push the skin together and wrap it tightly enough so that when it heals, the skin will grow together. If you can do this, we may not need the stitches."

Her gaze sought out his. "Do you think that will work?"

"I have no reason to think it wouldn't. If I understand it correctly, the reason for sewing it together is to ensure that the wound heals completely and will not leave a gash on the skin. I believe that if you push the skin together and wrap it tightly, it might accomplish the same thing."

"I suppose it might work," she agreed, though her tone was noncommittal. "We could try it."

Given their circumstances, it might be the best that she was going to be able to do. She came up to her feet and turned to step to the fire. She said, "I'll boil the water."

He nodded, and leaning to the rear, flopped back against his bed.

She was beautiful. She was sweet. She was incredibly female, and despite his injuries, White Thunder was experiencing again the realization that he was nothing, if not all male.

At present, she was working over the last of his wounds, and she was so close to him that he could smell the clean, tantalizing fragrance of her femininity. It teased him. It baited him. And every now and again, one of her stray, blond curls brushed against him. Involuntarily, he shivered in response.

It wasn't her fault. He was more than aware that it wasn't her intention to become the object of his sexual fantasy. That knowledge, however, didn't change the fact that she was fast becoming exactly that.

White Thunder rocked back against the backrest of the pine branches that she had painstakingly placed between him and the wall of the cave. He shut his eyes.

In truth, he wasn't certain which was the more difficult to endure: the pain from his injuries or her soft touch upon him. At present she was washing his chest with a cloth soaked from the cave's freshwater stream.

As her fingers worked over one of the injuries to his chest—a cut that came dangerously close to his nipples— he thought he might likely sink into giddiness. How was a man supposed to endure this? Indeed, he thought, a man might very well welcome the pain instead of the unwelcome sexual stimulation.

At last, as her fingers dabbed at a cut up close to his right nipple, he caught hold of her hand. Immediately, she gazed up at him.

"Did you want something, sir?"

You. He wanted to say it. He dare not. Instead, he took a deep breath, and uttered, "A man can bear up under much, even torture, but ofttimes, a woman's touch, sweet and soft though it might be, when so close to sensitive areas of a man's body, can produce more agony for him than an enemy carving out his heart."

She stopped and stared into his eyes, her lips barely open as she gaped back at him. He wondered if she were aware of how kissable she looked. At last she said, "Have I hurt you, sir?"

He sighed yet again. "Oh, that you would."

"Sir? If I have hurt you, I apologize—"

"There is no need," he interrupted as he rubbed his

fingers over her hand, which he still held within his own. "But there is a problem."

She looked up at him inquiringly.

He didn't know how else to put his thoughts into words, except to admit the truth, and after some deliberation as to how he might say it, he blurted out, "I am a man. You are a woman. You are beautiful. And you are working on injuries on my chest."

"Oh."

At last she understood, and he nodded.

But instead of drawing away—as she should have done—she said, "Do you object, then?"

She hadn't taken her hand away from his either, nor did she back off from him, as he had thought she might, as he knew she ought.

"It is not that I object," he answered. "Rather, I am tested almost beyond my endurance. If you mean to tempt me, this is the way you might go about it."

"I'm not trying to tempt you, sir. I am simply endeavoring to clean your wounds. If you please, I have almost finished the task, the worst injury being to your arm. But 'tis wrapped now, and if you will permit me, I think I might attend to the rest of your injuries more easily."

"But those places you are cleaning are dangerously close to parts of my body that are . . . sensitive."

"I'm sorry, sir. I cannot help where the injuries lie. I am simply taking action to ensure that your other wounds are clean. If it will ease your mind, I will be finished here soon, since I need to stop and prepare us something to eat."

He swallowed hard as he stared back at her. It appeared to him that in this instance, he had few choices. Either he must silently endure the cravings that she was awakening within him, or he must take her in his arms and make ardent love to her. Here. Now.

Considering who each of them was and the barriers placed upon them by their respective societies, neither option seemed a good choice. After some deliberation, he decided to proceed with caution and changed the subject to something less personal. He said, "I have not forgotten that something today jogged your memory. You have yet to tell me what you remembered or even how it happened."

She didn't answer at once. Instead, she extricated her hand from his and pressed the cloth against another of his wounds. And though he sighed under her care, she seemed not to notice.

At length, she said, "Please excuse me for taking so long to tell you of it. It has not been my intention to hide it from you, 'tis only that I'll be done here in a moment and I had thought that we might talk about it over our supper."

He hesitated, then asked, "Are these memories bad, then, that you hesitate to tell me?"

"No, not necessarily." She frowned. "'Tis only that I little know how to relate everything to you, and since it was more important that I attend to your injuries, I thought I would first concentrate on mending those, then fix us something to eat, which would free my mind to tell you what I have remembered and what it might mean to us both."

He scowled. Something in her manner didn't seem right. Shouldn't she have been anxious to tell him about her life? Especially since she hadn't recalled anything previously?

Had she recollected something unpleasant?

That thought brought up another. Was she running away from some wrong done to her or some wrong she had done to another? Either of those scenarios would explain how she had come to be in these woods, alone. After all, such circumstances were not unheard of. In the past, the Seneca had given shelter to a few of those men his people called the black white men, those who had escaped their English masters' chains.

Staring at her, he realized it was best to put his ponderings into words, and leaning forward, he again took one of her hands in his, but this time he clasped it within both of his own. He said, "Is there something particular about your past that you feel you cannot tell me?"

"No," she replied immediately, perhaps too quickly. "It's only that—"

"Are you running away from something?"

She frowned. "I don't think so."

He nodded. "Are you married to a man who was cruel to you?"

"No, I am not married."

"No?" He made a face. "Did your husband die, leaving you alone?"

"No, sir. In truth, I have never been married."

His frown deepened as he contemplated what her confession might mean. At length, he said, "I am attempting to understand this, but I am having difficulty. Perhaps you might help me. How can a woman as pretty as you have not seen the marriage bed?"

She bit her lip and looked away, and he was afraid she wouldn't answer at all. However, after some moments, she replied, "The truth is, sir, that I am not free to marry."

Not free to? How could this be? He said, "But you remarked to me just now that you are not married."

"That is true. I am not, sir. What I am is an indentured servant."

His brows drew together in thought. He knew what a servant was, but an indentured one? He must have appeared as puzzled as he felt, for she went on to explain, "I have five more years of service to give to the man who owns my papers. Until that time, I cannot marry anyone."

"The man who owns your papers? Are you like the black white man, a slave?"

She coughed. "No, sir," she managed to say after clearing her throat. "I am a servant, which is different from a slave."

"Is it? How is it different?"

"Well," she explained, "a slave is owned by his master

for his entire life, and he must toil without compensation for himself or his family. A servant, on the other hand, works for another for compensation or in some cases, he or she toils for another in repayment of a debt. At the end of a certain amount of years, which are needed to repay the debt, he or she is free."

White Thunder thought about her words momentarily, then, "By compensation, you mean money?"

"I do."

"And repaying a debt?"

"A debt is money or services owed to another."

He scowled, not at her, but rather because of the subject matter under discussion. "Do you work for compensation or to repay a debt?"

"I work to compensate an obligation, I believe, although I'm uncertain how that obligation came to be. That part of my memory is still unclear to me."

He nodded. "Now, you say that a man owns you?"

"My services, yes."

"Tell me, how can a human being own another human being?"

She might have had a good explanation to the question, but he didn't await her response. Rather he went on to say, "Are we not all part of the Creator's plan?" He paused, and warming to his subject, he continued, "This is a fact of the Englishman's society that we of the Seneca have not understood. By what authority does one man feel he can own another?"

She shrugged. "I little know, sir, except perhaps in the matter of debt, since a man or a woman cannot produce all he or she requires in order to live. He or she must work, then, for money in order to buy the necessities of life. Sometimes a man lacks the finances needed for basic things like food, clothing and such. In that instance, he might borrow the money from another and become indebted to him.

Thus, he works for another to pay for the money loaned to him."

White Thunder's frown deepened. "Am I to understand, then, that a man exists who does not give what he has to aid another of his own kind? Without expecting labor and servitude in return?"

His confusion must have been easily witnessed on his countenance, for he noted that she immediately replied, "I can see how strange it must seem to you, for you have not been brought up by the English and are not aware of their system of culture."

"I spent three years with missionaries."

"That's not the same thing. Perhaps this explanation might help. In English society, there are those who are rich enough to be beholden to none. They are free men and women because they have the necessities of life and don't owe another their work to simply live. Then there are those who are not rich enough to obtain such things as food and shelter. These serve those who are free. It is necessary in order to simply live. I am among those who serve others."

Slowly he nodded, but in due time he had a further question, and he asked, "And who gave these men, who are free, their freedom, and the right to rule another's life to the extent of restricting another's free choice?"

She frowned. "I . . . I don't know. It has always been this way, I believe. It has to do with money, I suppose. Perhaps the king grants their favor?"

"Ah, the English father. And who gave the English father the right to rule over another's life, and take away his freedom?"

She pulled a face. "You ask me questions I have never pondered. But I believe that the church gives the king his power . . . God?"

White Thunder breathed out on sigh, then said, "If that is so, then I ask you this: According to the good book that the missionaries preached to me, does not the Creator make each of us with the same amount of love? I do not remember the missionaries saying that He smiles more favorably on one of his creatures than another."

"That is true," she replied. "In the eyes of God, we are all equal."

He dipped his head in understanding. "So it is," he said. "And now you understand the Iroquois way. A man is subject only to his Creator and to no other. It is in your good book, and it is also part of the Iroquois religion. The fact that according to the Creator, all men and women command their own lives is understood by those who serve the Iroquois government also. A man rules his own life. No other. Nor is he allowed to rule another. Such things were unheard of before the English came to this land."

"But, sir," she said, "if what you say were true, there would be nothing but confusion in a country. If all are free, how is one to pay for his necessities? How is another to secure the things he needs in order to work?"

"This is a false idea. Do you see confusion surrounding the Iroquois?" He paused. "Or do you see unity?"

"I . . . I don't know, sir. I haven't had the pleasure of being among your people."

"Then I will tell you. We of the Iroquois are united. We have laws, but our laws are those given to us by the Creator. Only these must a man obey. And I will tell you this: The Creator made no man to be another man's slave. He who would say differently seeks to enslave you for his own benefit."

She fell into silence. At some length, she said, "You seem quite ardent about this, I think."

"Should a man not be impassioned about his own soul, about his own freedom?"

"Yes, yes, of course, it is only that in my society, I have considered that I am lucky to have the position I have. I am housed well, I am clothed. I have good food. Though

I am not free, without this position, I little know how I would live."

"You would be married to a man who loves you, and who would take care of you and your children. You would be happy. Your aunts, your uncles, your parents and all others of your clan would ensure your health, also. That is how you would live." He stated it emphatically. "What of your parents? Your aunts? Your uncles? Where are they? Were they also servants to this evil man?"

She gasped, causing him to frown. And he said, "You seem startled that I am so frank, yet the practice of owning another human being is unnatural. Any man who would dare to try to own another man's soul is committing one of the most wicked acts a man can accomplish. Even your own good book says so."

"It is not that," she replied. "I, too, believe the custom of slavery is sinful. Why I reacted is not due to that, but rather because I don't remember who my parents are or what happened to them. I know nothing of aunts or uncles. And, sir, in English society, there is no clan to see to my protection."

"Have the English then done away with the family, so there is no one to protect you? Without the family, one could fall easily victim to men with deceitful intentions— as it appears you have."

"Of course the English haven't done away with the family," she said. "I gasped not because of what you were saying, but rather at the mention of my parents. Indeed, sir, simply bringing them up, I felt suddenly sad."

His gaze narrowed. Her hands were sweating. Her eyes looked fearful. What had happened to this woman that a simple remark would cause her such anxiety?

However, he didn't ask. Instead he said, "I am sorry that I have brought up a matter that brings you sadness. Perhaps in time, you will remember more."

"Perhaps. But it is maddening. At first it seemed as if

my memory returned in full, and yet I can't recall anything about my own parents, nor under what circumstances
I became indentured to this man. I even remember his
name—the man who holds my papers—John Rathburn.
But about my parents, I recollect nothing."

Sitting forward, White Thunder took both of her hands
into his, and as gently as he could put into words, he said,
"It will come back to you. It will come."

As she gazed at him, and as he stared deeply into the
deep blue of her eyes, he thought he had never witnessed
anyone quite so beautiful. Again, desire ravished him.
Again, he cautioned himself to do nothing.

Ah, if only he were free to hold her. If only. . .

Ten

Sarah sat back on her heels and loosened her hands from White Thunder's. She hadn't expected his outburst concerning a person's liberty or lack of it.

His reaction worried her, since she could not predict what his response would be to the request she must make. However, since her memory had returned, and since she had no option but to ask, she began as simply as she could. "Sir, there is a circumstance that I've remembered, and a favor I would beg of you."

He nodded, as if to say, "Please continue."

Warily, she began, "Recently, before my accident, I was engaged upon the task of accompanying a young woman who was in my charge. We were traveling through these woods on our way to New Hampshire. Obviously, I am now lost from her, sir, and if you would be so kind as to help me, I would like to find her and ensure her safety. Since I have recalled who I am and the obligations I hold, I find that I'm worried about what has become of this young woman to whom I owe my loyalty."

White Thunder hesitated before he said, "Tell me more about this woman. Is this the same person you mentioned earlier? I believe you called her your mistress. And if so, is she one of the people who thinks she owns you?"

"Oh, no," Sarah said at once, "not at all. She's a young woman who was put into my charge long ago. I've been her friend and companion for many, many years. It was her uncle who assigned me into servitude because . . ." Sarah stopped and rubbed her forehead again. "Pardon me, for I still cannot remember why I am indentured to this man; all I can recall is that I've five more years in his service. As for Marisa—"

"That's her name?"

"Yes. She is truly innocent of all her uncle's doings, and she is more like a sister to me than a mere friend. She loves me and I love her."

"Yet," he countered, "if she is related by blood to the evil one . . ."

"No, no, she's not. He's not really her uncle, he's her step-uncle, so they are not related by a true family line. Indeed, she was trying to take me beyond her uncle's influence—and that is how I came to be here . . . I think."

"You think?"

"Forgive me, but I don't recall what happened that I became separated from her, at least not now. Perhaps in time I will remember it all."

"*Nyoh*, yes. In time, I am sure that you will." Drawing in a deep breath, he reached out again for her, and taking one of her hands into his, he brought it to his lips, whereupon he kissed it. In response, Sarah's senses suddenly jerked into life, and sensation, carnal and erotic, swept along her nerve endings. Furthermore, from deep within her arose a response that was as pleasant as it was a mystery to her.

What was this? Certainly she liked the man, but this? And from a mere touch?

She did her best to ignore the perception, however, if only because he was doing nothing more than looking at her—perhaps to ascertain her response. Indeed, after a moment, he continued. "But let me tell you this so that you may know my stance about your people."

"Yes, please. Continue." She loosened her hand from his grip.

He seemed not to notice her withdrawal from him, however. He acknowledged her with a nod, then he said, "Although I told you that when you remembered who you were and who your people were, I would lead you back to them, I little realized at that time that 'your people' might include a man so degraded that he would try to own a fellow human being. Let me be clear on this: I will not take you back to this place where a man deems that he owns you. Not while there is breath within my breast would I do this to you, or to any other person. I will bring you to my home, instead, where you will be free."

Sarah wrinkled her brow. "But free to do what, sir?"

"Free to be your own person. Free to live your life as you see fit. In my village, there will be many who would admire you, many who would want to spend the rest of their life with you. You would have a full life there."

Well, she thought, this was certainly a new problem to face, and she fidgeted as she considered how best to approach it. After a moment, she said, "You are kind to suggest this, sir. But I think I would be unhappy if I failed to find and assume my obligation for the young woman who was in my charge. Besides, it would only be a matter of time before those who searched for me would discover me in your village, and then there would be trouble."

"Trouble matters little to us," he said, "for we of the Seneca are used to adversity."

She gazed back at him, and gradually her solemn look transformed into a smile. "I appreciate your kindness, sir," she said, "and I thank you for your consideration. But I am not Indian and I'm not part of your tribe, and sooner or later, I fear the past would catch up with me. Besides, I worry for the life of the young woman who was in my charge, and I don't believe I'll rest easily until I can discover her whereabouts and what has happened to her."

"I understand," he said. "It is good that you feel this way. But before I agree with what you ask, tell me: If I aid you in finding her, will she lead you back to this man who thinks he owns you?"

"Indeed not. But let me correct a false impression that you have, sir. That man doesn't own *me*. He owns my indenture papers."

"There is little difference that I see."

"But there is a difference. And please understand that Marisa would never take me back to her uncle. She had gone to great pains to secure me away from him. I believe that's why we were traveling in the woods. We were escaping him and his influence over me. But as you have been open with me, speaking your thoughts, let me also speak with clarity: Even if Marisa were to escort me back to her uncle, I would not object."

"I would."

"But don't you see, sir? Better it would be that I serve out my bond now to this man than never to return and spend the rest of my life in hiding. Surely you can understand this. At the end of my servitude, I would truly be free to be my own person, and I would then be at liberty to live my own life without having to leave my own society."

Sarah watched as he bobbed his head up and down, his attention turned inward. At last, he said, "I understand that you believe this, but I fear you will only become free in your society if this man can find no other reason to detain you.

Beware. At the end of five years, there could well be some other reason he concocts to keep you. I say this because any man who would flaunt the ways of the Creator is also a man who would lie. And such a man would do so without thought of consequences, I think."

"But, sir," she countered, "in order to keep me, he would have to tell untruths in a court of law, and I don't believe he would dare to do it. After all, a court requires a man take an oath."

"Hmph! A man such as he has already sold himself into the ways of darkness. Therefore, an oath would mean nothing to him because there is so little life left within him. What would it matter to him if he were to lose a little more of that life by telling untruths?"

"Sir, I fear I am not following your logic. That man is as alive as I am. Isn't he?"

White Thunder scrutinized her features while he took his time answering. Speaking slowly, as though choosing his words carefully, he said, "There is a wise, old sachem among us who proclaimed that a man or a woman such as this man does not truly live, because living encompasses not only caring for yourself, but caring for others."

"But—"

"Tell me," he continued, "how can a man who pleases only himself and no other be happy?"

"But aren't there many who do exactly that?

"Perhaps, for a short time. That person might even appear to be happy," he said. "But true happiness of the mind, body and spirit is not possible to such a man. The laws of the Creator forbid it."

"I . . . I don't understand. What laws?"

He frowned at her, before stating, "Let me tell it to you this way. Can a man find bliss and also ignore the child who goes hungry? Can a man be secure in his own needs when he pretends not to hear the cries of his slaves?"

She opened her mouth to answer, but he saved her the necessity, when he went on to say, "No. Such men, by the laws of God, must shut off their understanding of others. They must have ears that do not hear and eyes that do not see. Thus they understand less and less, not only about others, but about themselves and the nature of creation. Because of this, such a man cannot experience life as you and I know it. He can only eat and sleep and perhaps ruin the lives of others. He does not truly live.

"If it were different, a man would have empathy for his fellow human beings, and would not own slaves, not merely because it is wrong—which it is—but because he would understand that all men and women are alive, too. He would respect it. That is why we of the Seneca say that such men merely exist. Happiness cannot be found at the expense of others, and particularly at the expense of those who you could help, and do not."

Sarah bit down on her lip and stirred uneasily. It sounded so good, so wise, and she was struck by this man's observation of life. But she'd lived in this world a good many years, and she'd observed otherwise. And so she countered, "While you speak wisely, sir, and these things that you say could be true, I fear that I have witnessed that such men appear to be happy. Marisa's step-uncle, for instance, is this kind of man, and he certainly is able to accumulate many things that should make him happy. Plus, he surrounds himself with the finer qualities of life, and these things alone give him a life of ease."

"Ah," White Thunder replied, "but is that really living? Do we live out our lives only to gather objects and things? After all, happiness is not a thing, and it cannot be bought by the Englishman's treasure."

"True."

"Know that he who would seek to own another's soul, through debt or otherwise, is the kind of man who infects the world around him with the unhappiness of his own blackened soul. It is why when we Seneca discover that a man holding office has lied to the people, he is removed from his position and banished from the tribe. He is an object of disgust."

"Banished? Disgust?" Sarah shook her head and smiled at him. "I fear, sir," she commented, "that in my society, if we were to do as the Seneca, there might possibly be no men left."

Sarah gave him a brief smile, for she'd meant it in jest. But it appeared White Thunder didn't share her mirth, and he said, "Perhaps you speak as you do only because the Englishman is allowed to lie. Whereas our people know that he who would tell an untruth about one thing will do so again about another. And if this is so, how then is one to ever trust that man again?"

Sarah weighed his words carefully as she sat back. "You could be right. But, sir, as I mentioned before, there are legalities within the English justice system that would prevent the man, John Rathburn, from subjecting me to slavery."

"And you believe this?"

"I do. Our courts are good and are just. They will see that justice is done." Bending at the waist, she sat forward. "But I am confused about one matter, sir. You speak of slavery as if it were an evil that your people have never engaged in or ever considered. However, it is my understanding that there are slaves among the Indians, also. I've heard that when Indians conquer a people, they take captives as slaves."

"Who has told you this?"

"I . . . I don't remember their names at the moment."

"Perhaps it is the way of societies that some men see one thing, but tell another. Or perhaps they seek to blacken the reputation of another, by seeing in another those things they, themselves, do. I say this because what you have heard is not true."

"But the people who said this, and they wrote it also, had lived among the Iroquois."

"I cannot account for these people or their honesty, since I have no knowledge of them. I will tell you what is true, however, and how it really is if you would care to hear of the Seneca's version of the story?"

"Indeed, I would."

He rested back against his cushion, and once again reached out to grasp hold of her hand, causing her to follow him down. She lay by his side and, seeing her settled, he began, "When the Seneca conquers a people, it is true they often take prisoners. These people are brought back to the village, where they are either put to death to atone for the anger of one among us who has lost a loved one, or the captive is adopted into a family, where the person takes the place of a relative who was dearly loved. These prisoners are treated the same as the people they replace, and they are no more slaves than I am. They have a voice in their family, they have a say in the government of their new people and of their clan. They are certainly not owned by another. Indeed, they are a free people."

Sarah absorbed his words in silence until at last she murmured, "If this be true, then I apologize, sir. It is evident that the information I have been told is biased. This is how it is for all captives?"

"Not all," he said, "but most of the time, this is true. In all societies there are men who practice cruelty. The Seneca are no different than other peoples. To say that a man or woman is always adopted would be wrong. But on the whole, what I have told you is true."

"I see," she said as she leaned in against his side, "I believe you." Time passed as they lay silently against one another until at last she said, "Sarah. My name is Sarah."

He grinned down at her. "I am happy to know it. It is a

pretty name. Sarah. Miss Sarah. It's almost as pretty as the woman who bears the name."

"You flatter me, sir."

"No flattery. What I say is fact as I see it."

"Thank you. I am honored." She paused for a moment, then asked, "Will you do it, sir? Will you help me find the young woman who was entrusted to my care?"

"*Nyoh*, yes," he said, "I could do that. Or perhaps," he hesitated, as though he were choosing his words with great care, "you might consider staying with me."

Stay with him? What did he mean?

Sarah sat up on her elbows so that she could stare down into his countenance, trying to read his thoughts. But it was impossible. All she witnessed upon his handsome face was his own serious intent.

And so she asked, "Are you referring to marriage between us, sir?"

"*Neh*, no." He shook his head gently. "Forgive me, for I cannot."

Her stomach fell, and she looked away from him, embarrassed. Of course she'd known this had to be his answer. However, this was the second time she'd introduced the subject of marriage in his presence, only to be rejected. It wasn't as if she could marry him either, even if he asked her. Since her memory had returned, she was now aware of the many reasons this could never be.

Still, his rejection stung.

At length, she said, "If not marriage, then I suppose I don't understand what it is you are proposing."

He didn't speak, at least not straightaway. Indeed, minute after minute seemed to crawl by as he appeared to reflect inwardly. Was he searching for the right words to thwart her? The thought had her leaving his embrace, and she sat up.

He followed her up into a sitting position and at last said,

"Let me speak plainly so there is no doubt in your mind as to my meaning. In a man's life, there are many people who come and go. This is to be expected. However, now and again a person appears in his life who he would like to keep close to him. You are such a person."

"I . . . thank you," she said, looking down at her lap.

"It is my thought," he continued, "that rather than you and I going our separate ways, perhaps you might like to stay with me until I fulfill my duty to Wild Mint. And then . . ."

She didn't speak for several minutes, and when she did, all she said was, "And then?"

He didn't answer.

What could she say? On one hand, what he proposed was appealing. After all, she was more than aware that this man stirred feelings within her that were best experienced between a man and a wife. But to stay with him while he was committed to another—even if that commitment were to a person who was a mere ghost?

She couldn't do it. Always she would wonder about herself and about him.

Besides, there were their separate cultures to consider. Where would they live?

There was also her servitude that might interfere. Five more years . . .

When she didn't immediately answer, he uttered, "It is a foolish idea, for I have no right to keep you with me until I am free to make you mine."

Sarah knew she should say something, but what?

At length—perhaps because of her extended silence—he drew back from her. He said, "Perhaps you are right. Maybe we should find the one you call Miss Marisa. But we can talk more of this later, after I have had a chance to think over what we have discussed so far."

At last she blurted out, "It's not a foolish idea, sir."

She watched him as he swallowed. And she was struck by the observation that her response might indeed be important to him. It gave her the courage to ask another question—one more directly from her heart.

"Sir," she said. "I would make another inquiry of you, if I might."

He nodded, as though to encourage her to speak. But it wasn't an easy question to put to him, and she hesitated.

At length, he asked, "You have a query?"

"Aye, sir, I do." Sarah raised her chin, if only to give herself courage. Then she said, "I fear my hesitation accounts for my confusion as to how to ask this of you."

He nodded as if he understood her exactly. Then he said, "Be at ease. You can ask me most anything and I will answer and give you my opinion."

"'Tis not that sort of question, sir." She drew in her breath and looked away from him. But in the end, she knew that once begun, she needed to carry this thought to its end, and so she said, "I thank you for your offer, sir. But you must know I cannot stay with you. We were, the two of us, raised so differently, and I believe this might eventually cause dissension between us. Besides, as I've already mentioned, I fear my servitude would ultimately catch up with me. Therefore, in my mind, I have no option but to fulfill my debt. However, it's also because of my debt, and my servitude, that I would ask this of you, sir."

He nodded, and she paused while she gathered her courage together. At last she said, "'Tis my consideration that if I am to serve out my next five years before I'm allowed my freedom . . . then I . . ." She sighed. "Oh, I can't do it. I shouldn't ask," she declared. "I know I shouldn't. 'Tis silly, really." She made to raise up and get to her feet. "Forgive me. I'll go and fix us our supper if I can find . . ."

But he, too, rose up along with her, and grabbed for her wrist when she would have left, and he asked, "I thought my idea was foolish, yet I asked it. Please tell me, what is in your mind?"

She sat down again and looked askance at him as she said, "Sir, I . . . I . . . would like to know . . ."

"Is it something to do with my people? Or perhaps a thing you fear to ask about my people?" he supplied. "If so, do not hesitate. I will answer as best I can, and I am not easily insulted."

"No, sir, were it a subject easily spoken of and not personal, I wouldn't be having a hard time putting my thoughts to words."

Again he nodded.

"Sir, I . . . I would know . . . I would know . . ."

Both of them were sitting perfectly still. Both of them were staring at one another.

". . . Love."

He frowned, and she wondered if she'd said something wrong. What was he thinking?

She waited until he spoke at last, saying, "*Nyoh*, yes, many men and women would know more about this if they could."

She sighed. He didn't get it. "Yes," she said, "you are right. But, sir, I fear you still don't understand me," She gazed away from him, so embarrassed was she. Thus, as she prepared to say what was in her heart, she found herself looking at her hands, instead of at him. She continued, "If I'm to serve out my next five years—and I feel that I must—then they will be years spent without love. Therefore, it occurs to me that I'd like to come to know love . . . now, sir."

He didn't move a muscle. In fact, he looked as if he might have been struck by lightning.

"I'm sorry, sir, if I have shocked you, but—"

"You have not shocked me," he said. Then he sighed as he closed his eyes. But within seconds, he was leaning in toward her, and once again, took her hand in his.

She didn't understand. Why didn't he say something . . . anything? Was he now the one teasing her?

She tried to remove her hand from his, but he wouldn't let go of it. Instead, he gathered her into the shelter of his arms, brought her in close, and he said, "I thought you were never going to ask."

Eleven

He turned her head into his and rubbed his cheek over hers. Then as though she were a sweetened treat he'd long been denied, he buried his face deeply within the crook of her neck. At length, he whispered in her ear, "I have been waiting for these words from you for days."

"But you said nothing to me," she complained, "and not by a single action have I thought that you—"

"Of course not. Did I not promise you?" His hands were massaging her back, moving up and down her spinal column, and everywhere he touched, he sent shivers of delight over her body. Sarah melted in against him.

"Please fear not that I am trying to encourage you to marry me, sir," she whispered against his shoulder, since she felt she owed him an explanation. "Indeed, you have made yourself clearly understood on that account. And though I still believe that a man and woman should be married before they commit the act of love, it is only that . . ."

She sighed into the crook of his shoulder. "I little know how to explain it. Seeing you with the bear and realizing I could lose you . . ."

"Shhh," he murmured, putting his forefinger over her lips. "That is all behind us now. I understand."

And then he kissed her.

At first it was a soft kiss, nothing more than his lips against hers. But then it became something far different. Slowly his lips beset hers, his tongue tracing the outline of her lips before he kissed her eyes, her nose, her cheeks. His actions were prolonged and slow, as though he might memorize every contour of her countenance.

However, what was happening to her was far from slow. Sarah felt as though wave after wave of excitement had taken control over her senses. Even her stomach responded to him, creating a giddy sensation deep within her, making her feel as if she might have jumped off a precipice.

Sarah moaned, trying to fit her body in close enough to his to satisfy the fiery tide of passion that had taken possession of her. It seemed impossible. Indeed, she couldn't get close enough. She wanted, she needed, to feel his imprint against her. She wanted all of him.

He moved, bringing her down into a lying position and onto her side, where he settled in next to her. But he didn't end the kiss. Instead it became more intense.

Where his lips had adored her, his fingers now smoothed over her eyes, her cheeks, her ears. And Sarah lost track of time and place.

Indeed, his simple kiss might have been working magic over her, for it seemed to Sarah that the world around her disappeared. As his lips paid homage to her face, her neck, her shoulders, Sarah found herself squirming in against him, searching for . . . something.

When he lowered her so that she was lying down on her back, not a single thought of objection occurred to her. He came up over her, but he didn't press his weight over her. Rather, he found new places to kiss and caress.

Gradually his kiss found her lips once more, but this time, he encouraged her to open to him, and as soon as she acquiesced, his tongue invaded the hot recess of her mouth, making love to her with nothing more than tongue and gentle persuasion. She answered him back in the age-old rhythm of love.

Their tongues danced as though with feverish delight while he explored the inner sanctum of her mouth. Was this heaven? she wondered. She wanted to embrace him, to love him, to give him the essence of all she was. If only he could be hers. For if he were, she would give all that she had, all that she was, to this one man, alone.

As his kiss took possession of her, the exterior world did, indeed, vanish. There was only him, her.

And it was a thing of beauty.

Eventually even he had to break away for air and when he did so, he groaned, he growled, and when he next kissed her, it was with the passion that only a man can give a woman.

Gone was the soft, gentle possession. In its place was a sexual appetite so real, it took her breath. As his tongue again claimed ownership of her mouth, his hand trailed down over her face and neck to her shoulders.

The erotic feeling was out of proportion to what he was doing, and she rocked back and forth as the hunger for all that this man could give her took over. She'd never wanted anything more in her life. Dear Lord, was it merely her opinion, or was this man a rare breed of human being?

"It is good between us," he whispered against her lips.

His words were such an understatement that Sarah couldn't help responding by saying, "'Tis a bit of heaven, I think."

"I, too, believe this," he said. "I, too."

His hand unerringly found her breasts, and she sucked in her breath at the ultra-rich sensation. Again, she squirmed against him, setting back her shoulders, as though only in this way might she better experience the love being made between them.

"Dear sir," she said, "what you are doing is exquisite. I fear I never knew I had the capability to feel so much pleasure."

"Dear Miss Sarah," he murmured against her, "I, too, am overwhelmed with feeling. It is not always this way between two people. What is happening with us is uncommon, I think."

"Is it?"

"I believe so."

Then he shifted position again, bringing his head down to her chest, and with his lips, he made love to her breasts, even through the barrier of the linen of her corset and chemise. First he adored one breast, then the other.

For Sarah's part, she had never felt more loved. She swayed back and forth, first putting herself into one position so that he had easy access to her, then another. She was still dressed in her underclothes, but it didn't seem to curtail him in any manner. He kissed and caressed her as though she lay naked before him.

And when his hand trailed on down over her belly, massaging and caressing as he explored farther and farther down her form, her hips rose up to greet him. Her petticoats might have presented him a barrier, but thank goodness for the English style of dress. There was nothing under those petticoats but her.

His touch unerringly found that most feminine place on her body, and she again reacted as though she had taken a steep plunge off a cliff. Her stomach felt as though it was as light as a feather, and her hips rose up and down in a rhythm that was as old as time itself.

Of their own accord, her legs opened to him.

"You are wet," he murmured as he rose up on an elbow. "Do you know what this means?"

"I . . . do not, sir."

Softly, he explained, "Your body tells me it is ready for me. My only question is, are you?"

"Yes, sir. I believe that I am. Please."

Her reply seemed to send a flurry of emotion over him, for he shut his eyes momentarily, as though only in that way might he control the passion within him. He said, "It has been very long for me since I made love to a woman. I will try to hold back my seed for as long as possible, so that I might give you much pleasure before I seek my own. Know that if that doesn't happen this time, if I cannot hold myself back, I will next time."

"Mr. Thunder," she said, "you could do most anything at this moment, and I believe it would pleasure me."

At her words, he groaned, and coming up onto his elbows, he settled himself over her. "You realize," he said, "that it will hurt at first."

"I know."

"But it won't always hurt."

"Will it not?"

For a moment, his countenance mirrored his confusion over her reply, but it was quickly gone as his gaze mirrored a spark of understanding.

"Mr. Thunder," she said, "I do believe you are beautiful."

"I?" Even as he spoke, he was positioning himself over her. "It has long been my observation that a person sees in another those things that he or she is. Therefore, if you see beauty in me, it is most likely because you, yourself, are beautiful."

She smiled.

"And so you are," he observed. And then he brought their bodies together in the ancient dance of love.

The moment was charged. Sarah expected the pain of lovemaking and she braced herself for it.

This was it. She rocked under the pain . . . this part of the act she remembered. She also recalled that it got worse.

She had asked for this?

But, strangely, this time, it didn't get worse. He hadn't thrust any deeper into her. Instead he waited for her passion to rise up again as he leaned down to encourage that ardor by showering one kiss after another upon her lips, her eyes, her cheeks. And with his hand, he molded her breasts.

His patience worked. Gradually the pain subsided, as pure sensation took command over her. She moved her hips. It felt good.

When he thrust a little deeper into her, she waited for the pain to accompany the maneuver. But there was none. Indeed, instead of pain, a whole new realm of pleasure opened up to her.

He whispered against her ear, "Someone has mistreated you." It was no question. He knew. Perhaps it was because their thoughts were as one.

She didn't answer. She didn't know how to express what was a part of her very personal history.

He said, "The man who did this to you should be tortured slowly, first by fire and then by the knife, until he begs for his death."

"I think not, sir," she countered. "I would not have the miserable torment of anyone on my conscience."

He nodded slowly against her, and then he kissed her, lingeringly and gently, as though she might break if he dare heap too much passion upon her. He said, "We will talk more of it later."

"Perhaps. But, sir, if I might ask, I would beg you to continue your lovemaking as before. I will not break."

For a moment, he came up to gaze down into her eyes. At first she recognized surprise there within the depths of his dark irises, but then, ever so slowly, it changed, and he grinned down at her.

"No," he said, "I don't believe you will."

That was all it took to spur him into action. She raised her hips to his, and in response, he took possession of her, all of her.

She met him move for move, thrust for thrust, amazed at the incredible measure of emotion building within her. It was like being presented with little bit of heaven here on earth. Surely, this was pure grace happening between them, instead of . . .

She wouldn't allow herself to recall the horror of her past. She would hold that part of her back. But then her body was pushing her, driving her for more. It was as though a fire had been lit within her, and something deep and divine was begging for release.

Suddenly, and without warning, it happened. Pleasure consumed her, cascading through her body.

It was exquisite. And she wanted more of him, deeper, faster.

As though he knew just how to please her, he presented her with exactly what she craved. Like the rush of a moving stream, it was a dance like none other.

The sensation built within her, until all at once, Sarah tipped over the edge with so much rapture, she cried out. Over and over the elation swept over her body, until at last the ache within her was satiated.

It was over for the moment, but not so for their love. Coming up onto his elbows over her, White Thunder smiled down into her countenance before he took her lips in his own.

"Sir," she murmured against him, "I was unaware that the act of love could be so . . . I know of no words to adequately describe it."

"I, too, have no words to recount it, except to say that it is good between us. Always," he said, "should it be this way. But it is not over yet."

"Is it not?"

"I have not yet met my pleasure. Come, let us do it all over again."

And perhaps he might have taken her back into the realm of ecstasy once more, but it wasn't to be—at least not this time. All at once, he burst forth his seed within her. And Sarah, wrapping her arms around him securely, felt as though she had never welcomed anything more.

In the aftermath, they lay in each other's arms, he still a welcome part of her.

This was a surprise, she thought. A wonderful and welcome surprise. Indeed, the only detail she could recall from her distant past had been the feeling of revulsion and embarrassment.

There was none of that here. There was only beauty. There was only her. There was only him.

And what was between them was a thing of magnificence.

Twelve

"I have much feeling for you," he admitted after their breathing had returned to normal.

"As I have for you."

"But come, I do not wish to crush you," he whispered against her ear, and he promptly moved to her side. But he didn't leave her. He held her tightly within his arms, as though afraid that if he let go, she might disappear.

"You were not crushing me, sir."

"I am glad." He paused, but only for the beat of a moment. His next question took her by surprise. "Who is this man who has done this to you?"

Sarah bit her lip. There was no point in denying that she didn't know exactly what he was asking. Although the assault upon her person had happened long ago, it had left its scar upon her, even if that scar were only emotional. For good or for bad, this man whose arms were around her was now privy to her most intimate secrets.

As she debated what to say and what not to say, she

hesitated. In truth, so drawn out were her thoughts, time passed, and after a while, she wondered if he had perhaps focused his attention elsewhere. Turning her head ever so slightly, she was able to steal a glance at him as he lay by her side, and she was amazed to discover that his eyes were fixed intently on her, and that his look had not lost any of its fervor.

She said, "If I tell you who he is, does that mean that you will have to seek him out and kill him?"

"I will."

"But you already are hunting a man for that purpose, are you not?"

He nodded.

"I fear I have little desire to add to your burden."

"It is not a burden. It is a duty."

"Still, I wouldn't make your obligations any worse than what they already are."

He paused, but his look at her was as ardent as ever. At length, he sighed deeply and put the same question to her again, saying, "Who is this man?"

She stared away from him. "If I recall it well, it happened when I was young . . . 'Tis odd that I can remember this, while other things remain a mystery to me."

He waited. "Yes? . . . You were young?" he prompted.

"You must first promise me that you'll not go looking for him with the design and intent to kill him."

"I cannot give you my assurance on that," he said as he shifted his position so that he was lying on his back. He continued, "He deserves to be killed. What this man did to you is a crime. Know that in my society such a man would be taken before a council and sentenced to a torture so gruesome that he would beg for death. And he would beg for it for many days, because we would ensure that he was kept alive for as long as possible. All would see what befalls a man who would stoop to so low an act."

Sarah gasped, and came up to her elbows, where she leaned over him. "I . . . I can't let you do that."

He didn't answer. Instead, he gave her a quick glance, and asked once more, "Who is this man? Is it the same man who owns you, this John Rathburn?"

"You remember his name?"

His eyes narrowed a look at her. "You change the subject. Is it the same man?"

"I . . . I cannot tell you. In your culture you would be expected to seek him out and kill him. In mine, I must forgive him and get on with my life."

"It is he, is it not? The one who thinks he owns you?"

She flopped back against his arm, causing him to wince. She'd almost forgotten that this man had only recently been injured. Instantly, she sat up and said, "I'm sorry. I didn't mean to hurt you."

"It was nothing," he replied. "Is it he?"

"Please don't ask me about this any further, White Thunder. I cannot tell you because I cannot meet my Creator knowing that the death of a man is on my conscience."

"And I will not meet mine without seeking true justice. Does not your good book say an 'eye for an eye'? 'A tooth for a tooth'? In this same book, even a thief is put to death. Tell me, in view of this, what would your good book do with a rapist?"

Her look at him was frustrated. "Sir, you are putting questions to me that I can't answer," she said, "but I can say that there's another book contained in that good book—the one that you so nobly quote—and that book teaches a person to forgive."

"I will forgive this man," he stressed, "after he is dead."

Sarah inhaled deeply before saying, "Please, let us not speak of him any further. Can we not talk of us, of what we are doing and how we can go about solving our own problems? You must see, sir, that there are many problems between us."

"You will not tell me his name?"

"No, I won't."

He sighed. "You are a beautiful woman," he stated. "You are a good woman. But you are not following this to its conclusion. What will happen if you do not accuse this man and see that justice is done? Do you wish to have that on your conscience?"

"I . . . I don't understand."

"Do you think that this man has the moral fiber to withhold himself from doing the same thing again? If no one stops this, and he thinks he can abuse you with no consequence, how many more people will be harmed by him? Have you considered this?"

"I . . . No, I haven't. But I fear I'm not in a position to bring this man to justice. I'm an indentured servant. I have no legal sway over what this man does. Besides, even if I did—which I don't—if I were to go to the authorities, what court is going to believe me over a man of wealth and influence?"

"Nyah-weh."

"What does that word mean?"

"Thank you."

She frowned at him. "Thank you? What are you thanking me for?"

"I now know who this man is. I will find him."

Sarah sighed.

"Since I know who he is, tell me how it happened."

She tore herself away from the look in his eyes before she said, "I don't know if I can. I've never spoken of what happened to anyone except to my friend, Marisa, and then only in a most general way."

"Come here." He opened his arms to her and when she fell into them, he brought her body in close to his. It was an odd, yet erotic feeling. She was still clothed in chemise, corset and petticoats, but he was naked, and in her heightened state, the touch of his body next to hers was as enticing as if he were beginning his kisses all over again.

He brought her head in close, in the crook of his arm,

and said, "You should tell someone about it, and since I am here, I will be that person. Besides, what happened to you is important to me. There was pain; I saw that when we were making love. Tell me, how old were you?"

"I was fourteen. I had come to live in his household as a servant because . . . well, in truth, I still can't recall why I was there." She frowned. "I do remember that I wasn't always a servant, though. Once, like you, I was free."

"Did he force himself on you?"

"Yes, sir, he did."

"How many times?"

"Perhaps as many as ten. It did stop after a while. Within months after my arrival, another came to live under his roof. That was Marisa. Her parents had died at sea and her only living relative was John Rathburn. Because she was only four years old, he required a companion for her, which became my duty. When that happened, the assaults stopped. I don't know why. I am only glad that they ceased."

White Thunder pulled her even closer into his embrace and simply held her. He said, "Together, we will take away the pain so that in the future when you think of the act of love, you will only remember how good it is."

"Yes, I would like that. But, White Thunder, are you going to kill him?"

"I am," he said without the least hesitation.

"You mustn't."

"I must. But that time is in the future, and I must plan it well. He is white, and if he is influential, as you say, it might be difficult. The killing of a white man is not ever an easy deed to accomplish, for one's actions will often revert back against one's people. I will have to consider how to do this thing in detail. I know only that it will be done."

She shook her head, as if her slight disagreement might have him changing his mind.

She might have said something more, but he was continuing to speak, and he said, "There is one other matter between us that we must discuss."

"Oh? What is that?"

"It is this: By our actions today, as you know, we may have conceived a child."

"I doubt it," she countered. "In all those times when Mr. Rathburn forced himself into my life, I did not conceive."

"I am not Rathburn."

"Yes, thank goodness. But I'm thinking that my lack of conception might hint at the fact that it may be hard for me to become pregnant. This is sometimes the case with certain women. Perhaps I am one of them."

"Perhaps," he said, as if in agreement. But there was enough doubt in his voice that it rebutted at once any such understanding. He said, "I suspect that the fault wasn't yours. It would most likely be his, for the seed of such men, due to their own acts of violence, is often impotent."

"Hmm. That's an interesting observation. Do you suppose it's really true?"

He shrugged. "It matters little. The important reason for us to speak of this is to agree that if you are with child, you will stay with me, regardless of whether I have found Wild Mint's murderer or not."

Something in his tone had Sarah bristling and she backed away from him slightly, enough to take her body out of his arms. She said, "I am flattered, sir, by your attention to me on my behalf. I see that you are trying to protect me, and I thank you. But you must see that I cannot stay with you. It was one thing to speak of marriage, as I did, when I had no memory of my past. But now that my mind has healed, I fear there are many reasons that I know of, to keep us apart."

"And these reasons are?"

She glanced away from him before saying, "We have spoken of some already, but some are obvious. We have dissimilar values because we've been raised differently, and in two separate worlds. There is the matter of my servitude, as we have discussed, and the fact that I have pledged my word of honor to employ myself for the benefit of another for a certain amount of years. We spoke of this earlier. Surely you understand."

He turned his head to stare at her, and he said, "You will not go back to that man."

"You fail to understand. Whether I like it or not, I must go back. I have no choice."

"You always have a choice," he said. "The Creator made it so. Now, certainly, I grasp that you have been tricked into believing that you are not free to determine your own destiny and fate. But to tell me with all sincerity that another has the 'right' to tell you what you can and cannot do in your own personal life, I will never understand, nor will I ever agree that such things are binding. If there is a child created from our actions, all will have to change, and whatever is left of your servitude will have to be forgotten. Instead you will live with me in my village as my woman."

When she made to speak, he held up his hand. "There is no need to argue with me, for that is the way it will be."

His words had the effect of causing her to draw back farther from him. As she did so, she asked, "And who suddenly made you my master?"

His look at her was surprised, but he said nothing.

And she went on to say, "I beg to differ, sir."

He exhaled slowly, then responded, "Differ all you would like without consequence—as long as you are not pregnant. If that happens, we will marry."

She shook her head and frowned. "You are a contradiction, sir. You speak of freedom, yet you attempt to tell me what I can and can't do in the same breath?"

"Because you must think of the child. I cannot fathom that you would presume that taking responsibility for our child would endanger you or weigh upon your conscience."

"Sir, you now put words in my mouth that I have not spoken." Anger had her sitting up, moving even farther away from him. "You go too far, sir, with your demands. I am trying to take responsibility, not only for a child that you and I don't even know has been conceived, but for myself and my bond to others whom I have promised to serve. But there is more that weighs upon my mind: There is you, your injuries and your problems, and my desire to help you. All this in addition to the gaps in my memory. I am doing the best I can, sir, in a situation with which I am unfamiliar, so do not judge me, for there is much here to be considered, not simply one aspect of my life."

His look at her was one of thoughtful consideration, and he was nodding, faintly, as though he might be deliberating on the delicate points of contract negotiation. At length, he said, "You speak well and you speak wisely, for I had not taken all this into consideration. I forget, too, that you have been raised differently than I, and as you say, with different values, because to a Seneca, there is nothing more important than a child. And no agreement between two human beings, regardless of its legitimacy, would supplant the necessity to put all aside, and to concentrate on the rearing of a child.

"But I see what is in your mind," he went on to say, "and I respect all you have told me, and I respect you." He breathed out slowly, casting his glance up toward the stone "roof" of their shelter. "If you are pregnant, how then would you attempt to raise that child?"

"I little know, sir, for I have not had the reason to consider such a thing."

"If you were to return to the English settlement with a child, would the English put that child into servitude because you are its mother?"

"No, sir. Service to another is, indeed, a different matter than slavery in that the child I would bear would have no pledge or bond of servitude, which must be given before servitude can commence. Thus he or she would not be bound by the same oath that I am."

White Thunder appeared reflective for a moment, then said, "This would be true, even if you failed to finish the last five years of your servitude? A child of yours would not be forced to answer in your place?"

"I think not, sir," she said, although strangely, she had a bad feeling about this. Illogically and all at once, her eyes felt suddenly misty, and quite incidentally, her temples had started to pound.

"Is something wrong?" he asked after she had begun rubbing her forehead.

"No," she said, "'tis only that . . . I have a strange foreboding, as though there is some memory that I can't quite grasp." She tossed her head. "Or perhaps it's a feeling that I have done this before in some manner . . ."

"And have you?"

"I little know. Although I begin to think that perhaps, I may have . . . Do you suppose, sir, that my parents had something to do with my own servitude?"

He quirked an eyebrow at her, but at last said, "I have no method by which I can answer that. Already I find my wits challenged to understand your viewpoint, let alone that of the English slave master."

"Yes, I can see 'tis true. But 'tis also curious, don't you think, that I can now remember so much, yet nothing of my parents or how I came to be placed into the position that I hold. But I was young when it happened. I was only fourteen . . ."

"And you are twenty and nine now?"

"Yes, sir, that's right."

"It is strange."

"What is strange?"

"Fifteen summers ago, about the time when you were being forced into servitude, I lost Wild Mint."

"Indeed," she replied as she looked down and away from him, "it seems it was a bad year."

"*Nyoh.*"

Silence fell upon them then, until at last, Sarah took note that he could barely keep his eyes open. Sitting forward, she straightened the boughs and blanket around him, and said, "Rest now. I assure you that I'm fully capable of fixing our supper, and when you awaken, we shall eat."

He yawned, then smiled at her, before saying, "It's a good plan. A very good plan."

There it was again, she thought as she stared down into his eyes. His smile could be likened to a shaft of light descending down into a forest of gloom, and despite herself, Sarah found it difficult to pull her gaze away from him. She did accomplish it, however, and she said, "I thank you for all you've done for me, sir, and I pray that you will be able to rest well, and long before—"

"I would sleep better if you were here beside me." He patted the space next to him.

Sarah cast him a surprised look, then said, "Better perhaps, but not for as long, I think. No, you rest, while I cook."

"Very well," he agreed, "but when I awaken . . ."

He never finished the sentence. No sooner had the words left his lips, than he fell into an abrupt sleep.

And Sarah, watching him, smiled.

Thirteen

Her touch was as cold as a blizzard in the dead of winter. He reached out for her, but she giggled and moved out of grasp.

He followed her. "Wait for me," he called, but she had the advantage of floating over the grasses and tree trunks.

She stopped suddenly, allowing him to catch up to her. She gazed up at him and smiled, her round and pretty face mirroring her delight. Then she pointed to the plant that grew directly beneath her feet.

He recognized that plant. It was one his grandmother had often collected. Its root was used for . . .

He awoke suddenly. Where was he?

Glancing to the right and to the left, he at last realized he had never left the cave. It had been a dream, of course. Looking around further, he took note of Sarah in the foreground, working over the fire, and he sighed.

Ah, beautiful Sarah.

She was stoking the flames of the fire in an effort to cook something—and it smelled very much like a stew. The aroma of it was intoxicating and rich with the scents of bone broth and wild spices and fresh herbs, and as he inhaled deeply, his stomach growled.

Narrowing his glance toward her, he studied Sarah more closely. Her beauty was, indeed, without comparison, and remembering all she had told him earlier, he found it singularly odd that, indentured servitude or not, she had never married.

Her blond hair had escaped the knot that she'd used to tie it back, and golden-blond tendrils fell in loose ringlets around her face. Her dress was simple, a casual affair consisting of a tight-laced structure with elbow-length sleeves that made her waist look as if he might span it with his hands. Petticoats that were stiff and hooped on the side brought her a measure of dignity, though the front of her gown was dangerously low at her chest, beneath which her nipples played an enticing game of peek-a-boo with him.

He watched as a curl bounced around her face while she worked and he knew a desire to twirl its softness around his finger so he could study the differences in its color, from pale blond to tawny to daffodil. She was a delicately built woman, small and feminine, and without consciously willing it, his loins stirred to life as he watched her work.

To counter the effect she was having on him, he sat up, yawned, stretched and then said, "I believe I know how to keep you from becoming pregnant."

She clasped her hand to her chest, and sent him a surprised look. "You gave me a fright, sir. I didn't know you were awake."

"I have roused myself only recently."

"Yes, you have been asleep for some time. I'm glad you were able to rest easily and long. I have meanwhile made us a soup for our supper. There were many roots and vegetables that you collected, and I have used some of them."

"It smells like a feast," he commented, "and I am hungry."

She picked up one of the shells that he had fashioned into a bowl and using it, scooped out some soup. "Shall I bring the stew to you?"

"I can come there to you," he said, whereupon he struggled to get up to his feet. It wasn't as easy as he'd thought it would be, and he had almost collapsed before she rushed to his side to steady him.

"What are you thinking?" she scolded. "You need rest

in order to recover. One would suppose, the way you are acting, that you battle with bears daily."

He smiled. "Almost."

She helped him to sit back upon his bed, then straightened the blanket and pine boughs around him. "I'll bring you the soup."

"Good," he said, shutting his eyes momentarily. "Good."

She was gone only a moment. "Careful," she said as he made to take the shell full of broth and vegetables out of her hands. "It's hot."

He grinned at her and caressed her fingers as he accepted the shell. When she didn't pull away, he stared straight into the depths of her gentle blue eyes, as though by doing so, he might see into her soul.

He murmured, "I was watching you as you worked."

"Were you, sir?"

"Yes."

"And what did you see?"

"A beautiful woman. A woman I would like to spend the rest of my life with, if only things were different."

She gazed away from him. "But they are not different," she said, and pulled her hand away from his. "Do you like the soup, sir?"

He took a sip. It was very good. "You spoke true," he remarked. "You are a good cook."

She smiled at him, and as she did so, it was as if the sun shone upon him in this dark and dreary cave. It was good, if strange, for it made him feel as if he were seventeen again, complete with all the wild impulses of the very young. So lovely was she, he thought, he might likely die a happy man to simply look at her.

Upon that thought, he drank the rest of the soup without once dropping his gaze from hers. Indeed, with his eyes, he caressed her. At last, the stew was gone and he handed the shell back to her.

"Would you like some more?"

"*Nyoh,* yes, please." He watched as she came up to her feet and stepped toward the fire, his glance admiring the feminine sway of her hips as she moved. When she returned, he again caught her hand, only this time, he didn't let it go. "I have found a remedy for one of our problems," he said.

"Oh?"

"Yes, I have come to realize that there is a root that grows with profusion in these woods, and that, if I prepare it in the correct manner, it might well keep you from becoming pregnant. I used to watch my grandmother make medicine from these roots. Hopefully, it is not too late in the season for me to find this plant and pull it up, roots and all. I will begin a search for it as soon as I'm able."

As he stared at her, he took note of the rosy color that was flooding her countenance, even as she glanced away from him. But again, she didn't withdraw her hand from his.

In due time, he said, "In my dreams, Wild Mint showed me this root. I had forgotten it. But I was never apt at learning all that my grandmother knew, though she did try to instruct me in it."

Sarah frowned at him. "It is a shame that your grandmother wasn't able to teach you all of her skills. I'm certain she knew much more about these things than I will ever know. But, sir, I would like to note an observation."

He nodded.

"I notice that you speak of Wild Mint as if she were a living being."

"Indeed I do. That is because she does live," he said, "but no longer in the flesh."

"I see. I have said it before, so forgive my repetition. But I am sorry for your loss." She retrieved her hand from his hold, and fetched the shell from him. "Would you like more?"

He nodded, and she again arose to step toward the fire.

When she returned, she began at once to speak to him. "I must admit, sir, that your logic at times confuses me."

He slanted her a frown. "I'm sorry. What have I said now that seems to defy logic?"

"Some of the things you spoke of earlier—there are a few of your ideas that are troubling me."

"Tell me."

"One of those notions is that you spoke of marriage and told me without reservation that if I were to become pregnant, I must marry you. On the other hand, if I were not to become pregnant, then you don't wish to marry me at all."

"Yes, I did," he agreed. "But I spoke without understanding you completely. When you told me how it is with you, I changed my mind. This is why I'm happy that I've been shown this root. It might prevent the problem of pregnancy from occurring altogether."

"Yes," she said, but she sat silently before him, staring at her hands. Something was wrong.

"Is there another concern on your mind?" he asked.

"Yes, sir, there is," she replied. "By bringing up this subject of pregnancy, I am urged to think about marriage. Now 'tis not that I'm trying to marry you, sir. On the contrary, 'twould be most implausible to do so, considering who you are and who I am. But why were you suddenly demanding that I marry you, as though you were a tyrant?"

"This is a good question," he answered, "and I can see how it might confuse you. Let me explain: A child is a most valuable person to a tribe, and it is agreed upon by my people that a child must be brought into the world in the right way. This requires many sacrifices on the part of the parents, whose duty it is to bring their baby up right. He must receive training in the ways of the tribe, but mostly he must be raised with love and devotion. It is my belief that a child prospers best when he has two parents who are deeply in love with each other. It is as though the couple passes on this love to their child."

As he spoke, he watched her closely, for the subject was an important one. He saw her hesitate and frown before she said, "You speak of marriage, sir, and you speak of love. Tell me, since this is how you see it, do you love me?"

Her question took him aback for, though skilled in the powers of observation, he hadn't seen it coming. Carefully, he schooled his features into a frown, so that his countenance wouldn't mirror his surprise.

Did he love her? He certainly wanted to make love to her. But that wasn't the same thing and he knew it.

Was it possible for him to love another woman besides Wild Mint? Unfortunately for him and the problems that confronted him at this particular moment, he had no answer to that.

Therefore, to avoid giving Sarah a direct answer, he asked, "Have we not already made love?"

Her stare at him was more than a little annoyed. "Sir," she said, "you are avoiding answering my question."

He took a deep breath, then agreed, "You are right, so let me say this: There is much passion between us. It is a good foundation for two people."

"But do you love me, sir?"

Feeling a little trapped, he stared at her, and despite the fact that she was putting pressure on him, he couldn't help but admire the gentle rise and fall of her lashes. Did he love her?

At last he responded, asking, "Do you love me?"

She shook her head and bemoaned, "I asked you first, sir."

This was the sort of discussion, he thought, that a man, regardless of race, would rather avoid. However, that wasn't possible in this situation, simply because she was sitting directly in front of him, and she expected an answer.

In the end, he opted for the truth, and he said, "I little know how to answer you, so let me say this: Because of you, my world has grown brighter. Because of you, I look to each new day as a day that I might share with you, and it is good feeling. Do I love you? It is possible, and I wish I could say yes without reservation. However, I cannot. But this I do know, and this I can tell you true: Because of you, I have returned to the land of the living, and I no longer ponder upon death longingly. Moreover, when I look at you, I admire all that you are. I desire your embrace in the most elemental way a man can, and I would like to see my children growing in your belly. If that be love, then *nyoh*, I love you."

She was silent for a moment, while her gaze sought out almost anything but him. At last, she asked, "But you are also in love with Wild Mint?"

"I am," he said. Ah, he was beginning to understand where this was all leading. He added, "All that I do is because of my love for her."

"Is there a place then, truly, for me in your heart?"

"You are already in my heart. You have been there for many days now."

"But in second place."

He didn't pretend to misunderstand her. Instead, he leaned toward her and took her in his arms, bringing her in close and nestling her head against his shoulder. Spotting that lock of hair that had teased him earlier, he grabbed it and twirled it around his finger. He took a deep breath and inhaled the sweet fragrance of her before he said, "I see that we need to speak about this so that we understand each other better. Know that my intentions toward you are those of marriage. Now that we have shown each other our passion, we should follow that up by making the pledge of devotion to one other. But, even as I know this is how it should be, I cannot do it, unless there is an urgent need to do it. A pregnancy would be such a need." He hesitated briefly as he chose his next words with care. "Otherwise," he continued, "I can marry no one until my obligation to Wild Mint is brought to a conclusion."

A long pause followed, until at last, she said, "Yes, so you have told me. But I suppose what I little understand is why? I fail to grasp the problem with your marrying another or even falling in love with another, as long as it wouldn't prevent you from scouring the countryside to find Wild Mint's murderer."

He sighed deeply. "I cannot do it because . . ."

Sarah waited. "Because?"

"Because . . . she is still with me."

He felt her body start. She said, "I beg your pardon?"

"She is still with me."

"But she is dead, is she not?"

"*Nyoh*, yes."

"Then you mean she is still with you in spirit?"

"*Nyoh*, yes, and also in body . . . sometimes."

"In body? Sir, I fear I fail to understand."

"Neither did my family. It is why I left my village and ventured out on my own to find her killer. To those who loved me, I became a brooder, a loner, for I spent all my days with her, a ghost, and ignored my family. They feared my influence over others in my clan, for they thought that at her death, I had lost my wits. But I had not lost my sanity. She was truly with me.

"Often I would return home from a hunt and find a fire lit for me," he continued. "My meals were fixed as she had done when she was alive, and my living space within the longhouse was cleaned. On inquiry, I discovered that no one had been in my quarters. Over time she began to appear before me; she would share my meal and we would talk."

Sarah sat back to look into his face. That she was disturbed by his confession was evident, and she said, "How bizarre. How long did this continue?"

"To this day."

"To this day?" she repeated, her astonishment almost tangible. "And how long were you married?"

"A very short time, although we had been in love all through our youth, almost since the time we could walk. But our marriage was no more than a few seasons old—perhaps two or three seasons."

"About nine months?"

He nodded. "Sometimes she would appear before me, a misty image of how she had looked in the flesh; sometimes she would merely talk to me. We walked together. We laughed together as of old. And though her touch upon me was as cold as the ice on a winter river, still, she comforted me in my grief. She comforts me even to this day."

"You are still in love with her." It was no question. "Tell me," she said, "is she with you now?"

"Sometimes."

"At this very minute?"

"No. She is not here now."

"And so the truth, as I understand it, is that you can't marry anyone because you are still married . . . to her?"

"*Nyoh*, that is true."

His confession rocked her back on her heels, and she asked, "Is that why you said that I have brought you back from the dead? Because you were slipping more and more into her world?"

"*Nyoh*. Yes."

"You wished to be with her."

"I did."

She glanced away from him, then back. "What will happen if you find this murderer and kill him? How will that affect the two of you?"

"She will be freed from her grief, and so will I. I had once thought that when that happy moment occurs, I might join her and bring about my own death through battle. But now, I think not. Life itself holds much for me. Indeed, I find that I have changed my mind about death."

Sarah nodded, but when she remained silent, White Thunder went on to say, "You say that I saved your life, and

I see how this is so. But if I am to be honest, I would admit that you have saved mine, also."

"Truly?" she asked as she sank in against his embrace.

He tightened his arms around her. "It is true. And so I will do my duty to Wild Mint, who has been with me all these years, and to whom I gave my devotion so long ago. But when I am done with my duty, and the murderer found and justice served, I would like to have a new life, one that includes you . . . and if you will have me . . . as my woman."

Sarah, who was nestled in against him, was silent.

After a time, he asked, "Tell me, what do you think? Have I been touched by the sun?"

"No, sir," she said, "you have not. Indeed, if your sanity is to be in question, then so, too, is mine. However, your story does raise some questions with me, and I wonder, does Wild Mint know about you and me?"

"She does."

"And does she hate me? Women can be jealous of each other."

"*Neh*. She is happy that I have found you."

"Happy? Are you certain?"

"She is joyous to see that I have begun to smile again. For most of these years, I have been like a dead soul, existing but not really living, except by my desire to exact revenge. But as bad as it was for me, Wild Mint was more tormented than I."

"She was?"

He nodded. "She not only lost her life, which is most precious, but she lost her unborn child, as well as me and our marriage. This loss also came at a time when she was to be honored by her clan for her charm and her assistance to the clan mothers."

"It came at the height of her success," Sarah commented.

"*Nyoh*, yes. She is suffering still, and will continue to

be tormented until I can find this man and kill him. Only then will she be free to move on to the next world."

Sarah was quiet for so long that he was astonished when he heard her say, "I will help you."

"Help me?"

"Aye. I am not without feelings for you, sir. Twice I would be missing from this world, were it not for you—and I . . . I care for you. So, yes, I will help you . . . and Wild Mint."

"I would welcome your assistance." He drew her in closer to him and proceeded to massage her spine, his body reacting with all the renewed strength of a young man who was easily aroused.

He closed his eyes, doing nothing more than glorying in the emotional rush. He wasn't expecting it, but from out of nowhere came a feminine voice that said, *"Nyah-weh."*

White Thunder knew well who was speaking, but Sarah pulled back to gaze up into his face. She said, "Did you say something, sir?"

"Not I," he replied. "But if you listen closely, I think you will hear Wild Mint saying thank you to you. She is grateful to you, as I am."

Fourteen

Two days had come and gone. But there was something unnerving in sensing that a ghostly presence might be watching your every move. Indeed, it did much to curtail one's activities and romance.

It also caused Sarah to feel more than a little reserved toward White Thunder, and as she sat beside him, checking over his wounds and bandages, she avoided his gaze. Happily, she noted that despite the lack of stitches to his arm where the cuts were deepest, he was healing well.

"It appears that your suggestion on wrapping the wound is working," she commented as she sat forward to tightly rewrap the bandage.

He nodded, his glance intent on her, although all he said was, "Yes. It would accomplish the same thing."

Silence stretched between them until at last, he declared, "There is something bothering you." It wasn't a question.

Because Sarah was becoming accustomed to this man's unusual perception of her moods, she didn't take the pains to contradict him. Instead, she said, "I . . . I wonder how much longer you plan to stay here, and if, when we go, you will help me to discover the whereabouts of Miss Marisa."

The intensity of his glance hadn't changed, although he responded to her softly, saying, "We will remain here to make dry meat and pound roots and berries so that we may take these foods with us. In this way we won't require a fire or the necessity to go on the hunt each day in order to survive. And yes, we will attempt to find the tracks of your friend, Miss Marisa, though those prints may be gone now. It has rained considerably."

"Yes, I know, but I must try . . . so I thank you." She tied the bandage in place on his arm. "As I've said, I'm uneasy about her; it seems to me that she might be in trouble, and I don't think I'll rest easily until I find her."

"That is to be expected," he replied, "since she was in your care, and you are friends. But I fear this is not what is really bothering you. Is it?"

"No, sir, 'tis not."

He waited in silence, and Sarah found it hard to force her gaze up to meet his. Rather, she gathered up the rag that she was using to wash his wounds, and set it over the gashes on his chest.

But he caught her hand, and placing a finger beneath her chin, he raised her head up until she was looking directly into his eyes. He said nothing, but then, he didn't have to.

At last, she said, simply, "I'm afraid, sir."

"Afraid?"

"Perhaps afraid isn't the right word. Mayhap a more apt expression might be *concerned*. Since you told me about Wild Mint, I worry that she might be here looking over my shoulder. 'Tis not a good feeling to think that someone might be watching me from afar."

"There is always someone watching," he said with a shrug.

"What?"

He brought her hand to his lips, where he kissed her fingers. "This is well known to the Iroquois. Is it unknown to you?"

"Yes, sir, it is unknown to me. Of what are you speaking?"

He frowned. "Think of all the people who have come and gone before you. Some have moved along to the next world, but some have not. That's why there is always someone watching."

"As in God looking over you?"

He nodded. "But for your peace of mind, let me assure you that Wild Mint is not here, not now."

"How do you know this?"

He turned aside. "I simply know. I'm sorry this has bothered you."

"'Tis an odd situation, is it not?"

"Perhaps, but not to me. I've lived with it these past fifteen years."

Their eyes met, and she was certain a moment of empathy sprung up between them, for she realized that if she were troubled, so, too, was he. Circumstance had forced him to live amid distress all these years, as he had tried to appease a woman he had once loved, and loved still to this day.

He opened his arms wide to Sarah. "Come here," he said simply.

She didn't pretend to be coy, not when she'd been yearning for this exact moment. Rather, she fell in against him at once, as though he were a magnet and she were made of iron.

He closed his arms around her, and Sarah felt him nestle in against her. It was a delicious feeling.

He said, "I thought there might be something weighing heavily on your mind, but I had little understanding of how to unburden you. I missed you last night. I had expected you to sleep next to me."

"Yes, I know, but I couldn't. I'm doing the best I can in a difficult situation, sir. We are not married, and are not likely to ever be—"

"A condition we should remedy in the future, after we are both free."

"No, you know we cannot. We are from two different worlds. Once we are away from here, we will share nothing in common, and we will both have to return to our own people—and those people don't marry well, and—"

"Shhh." He laid a finger over her lips. "Most anything can be done if one wishes it."

"But, I—"

"Shhh." This time he placed his lips over hers. Slowly, his mouth ravished hers, and with a sigh, Sarah capitulated to his mastery, putting aside for the moment whatever it was she'd been about to protest.

His hands cupped her face as his tongue stroked hers. Meanwhile, his fingers grazed her cheeks, her eyes, her ears, her neck. It was enchantment pure and simple, and with a sigh, Sarah settled in closer to him.

He exhaled heavily, his breathing hard and fast, as he said, "Do you know what you do to me?"

"I little know unless 'tis a little like what happens to me. 'Tis soul-stirring."

As she spoke, White Thunder had begun to press kiss upon kiss against her neck and with a high-pitched groan, she succumbed to the mastery of his skill, falling in completely toward him. She arched her back, that she might partake of his ardor more fully, and he was quick on the uptake, his fingers caressing her every sensitive spot, while he worked his way down to her breasts, where he kneaded each gentle mound.

She sucked in her breath and as she did so, his brisk, musky scent filled her lungs, while the hard, yet smooth feel of his skin next to hers acted like an aphrodisiac. It was as though this man belonged to her, as though he were hers to explore. Perhaps she, too, belonged to him.

But it could never be, she reminded herself. She was not so out of touch with reality that she had lost track of what each of their societies expected of them. Nor was she unaware that what was happening between them was forbidden.

Still, being here with him, like this, was akin to ecstasy, and opening her eyes, she made a mental note of the time and place, and what was happening to her and to him, anything that she might be able to commit to memory. Never would she forget him. Never.

"Mr. Thunder," she said, "has it occurred to you that perhaps we are not meant—and have never been meant—to marry? Maybe we have been thrust together for one single purpose, which is for you to save me, and for I to help you with your burden."

He paused shortly, his attention riveted on her, though she could have sworn he was deep in thought. But it wasn't long before he shook his head, obviously disagreeing with her.

However, there was more she needed to say, and she continued, "Perhaps we are here to do nothing more than help each other and make memories—memories that will comfort us in our old age, memories that when we think of them, will bring a smile to us both."

He groaned. "I already have too many memories," he said, grimacing. "Rather, I would like a flesh-and-blood woman in my arms for the rest of my life, however long or short that is." He paused. "But if it is memories that you wish, I will make memories with you."

She was frowning. "Perhaps we could even pretend."

"Pretend?"

"Yes, as in make believe. Maybe, for just a little while we could imagine that the rest of the world doesn't exist.

That there is only you and me; no duty to bind us, no social order to pass judgment on us. Just us. For as long as we're in this cave, perhaps we could pretend that we're married."

His expression went grim. "Until?"

"Until we are forced to leave here and go back to our own worlds."

His look at her was brooding as he said, "What you suggest is to love without responsibility." His eyes narrowed at her. "What man could possibly walk away from such a proposal?"

Was he being sarcastic?

She didn't answer him, and when it was evident that she had nothing more to say on the matter, he continued speaking, saying, "I would be foolish, however, if I didn't bring to your attention that there is a danger in what you ask."

"A danger?"

"You might truly fall in love with me, as I might with you, also, and yet our marriage would be based on pretense."

"But if we did fall in love, the memories would be all the more precious."

"Memories." He snorted again. "There is a saying amongst the Seneca that goes: To love a woman without a lifelong commitment is either the action of great youth or one of stupidity." He paused. "I am not that young."

She swallowed hard. "Then, sir, your answer is no?"

"It is not. My answer is yes. Let's do it. Let's pretend. But beware: I fear you play with fire."

She was still frowning. "Your warning is well taken, sir. But still I would like to chance it."

He nodded. "When the time comes, you will remember that I warned you?"

She stared deeply into his eyes. "I will."

What had happened to her? she wondered. Indeed, it was with a great deal of shock that she realized that she had changed. She was not the same person she had been before she met White Thunder.

For one thing, his viewpoints about life and the dignity of man were having an effect upon her thought process. Not that she would let her servitude go unfulfilled. Rather, she would treasure this time with him, these moments of complete freedom from the chains of her bondage.

Bondage . . . It was fast becoming a naughty word in her vocabulary, and she wondered, was a person meant to be fettered to another by reason of debt?

Perhaps not, she thought. There was something to be said for living off the land and being beholden to none. Though there was no money to be made here and no toil to be done for another in exchange for coin, she and White Thunder yet had all they needed, provided by Nature. In many ways, the experience was proving to be more than a little uplifting.

White Thunder shifted positions so that he could rub his palms up and down her spine, and the hard feel of his muscles next to her, the pressure of his touch, the way their bodies fit together flawlessly, seemed somehow perfect.

At last, he came up over her, and smoothing one of his hands over her face, he caressed her cheeks, her lips, her nose, her eyes. He said, "Do not think because I warn you of the dangers of what you propose that I am against what you ask. I would be honored to make memories with you. Let us start now. Let us remember this moment always."

"Aye," she said. "Yes."

With a gentle touch, he trailed his fingertips over to her ears, down her throat and around to the back of her neck. Everywhere he touched, her body responded as if it had never known such joy. She shut her eyes and moaned, and as each new wave of passion consumed her, she swooned in against him.

He kissed her, his lips paying respect to her everywhere, while his tongue traced each delicate feature. And he whispered, "You possess the bluest eyes I have ever seen. But it is not only their color that holds me spellbound to you. It is the fact that when I look into your eyes, I am presented with the glimpse of a spirit that is as gentle it is true. You are an unusual woman, Miss Sarah. You are also a good woman. Every day of your life, you should be told what a treasure you are."

He lay back and brought her onto her side against him while his fingers continued to massage her back.

"I have never been able to fathom the dress of the English," he whispered against her ear, and it became evident that he was trying to untie the strings that held her stays together.

She said, "'Tis not so different from the way you dress. But, sir, what is it you intend? We have never had to remove my corset before."

He grinned at her. "What do you think, Miss Sarah? We have made love, but I have yet to see you naked."

"Naked?"

He nodded.

"What you are suggesting, sir, is unseemly."

"It is not unseemly," he argued. "It is beauty, and it is my wish to view you—all of you."

"But, Mr. Thunder, not even a married woman will allow her husband to behold her in the altogether. Dignity alone would ensure that she would at least wear her chemise, even to bed."

He shook his head. "The English are, indeed, a strange people. What man would not like to see his wife naked?"

"Perhaps there are many," she replied and smiled at him.

"I would still like to undress you completely."

"But . . . I cannot allow it."

"Not even if I beg?" he asked. "Or do this?" His hand

slipped down to caress her breasts. "Or this?" He bent to suckle on each of her breasts.

It was seduction, pure and simple, and she drew in her breath. "You cheat, sir." But even as she said it, she was already moaning and settling herself in closer to him.

"Of course I cheat, as have all men throughout history. And any man who is a man would cheat against such vulgar rules."

"They are not vulgar, sir. The opposite is true."

"Not to me. When it comes to making love to my wife, I wish to do it right."

"Right . . . but what is the right way?"

"It is the way that my wife and I decide is right."

"Hmm . . . I like the way you say that . . . your wife . . . even though it's not really true."

"But it is true," he said, casting her a seductive grin. "Are we not pretending? Miss Sarah, I am but a man, and I have dreamed of seeing you with nothing between us but the sweat of our exertions."

Again she moaned.

"Please," he said. "Show me how to remove this."

She found herself weakening, and why not? She realized that she was fighting a losing battle anyway. Even now his hands were all over her, and it felt good.

Perhaps he was right. Maybe it was natural for married couples to make love naked.

At last she said, "Very well, but we'll take off the stays and no more."

He didn't disagree, but then he didn't agree either. She sat slightly away from him, presenting her back to him. "My stays lace here and tie here. Do you see?" She guided his hands to the laces. "If you pull the string here, the entire knot comes out and they loosen."

He pulled.

"You will have to free them completely up and down before the garment can be removed."

He did so, and the corset relaxed, allowing him to pull it away from her. But there was another set of clothing beneath this, her chemise, and he seemed as perplexed to find it as she was overjoyed to be without the tight pull of her stays, even if only for a few moments.

He commented, "You have on more clothes."

"Aye, sir, I do." She grinned, and he immediately took advantage and kissed her open mouth. It was utterly erotic, completely seductive, and melting in against him, she kissed him back one for one.

He asked, "What do I take off next?"

She pretended to misunderstand, and said, "Your shirt."

Almost as quickly as she'd said it, he discarded his shirt, then he returned to her. He murmured, "And now, what of *yours* do I remove next?"

"Oh, did you mean *my* clothes, sir?"

"Exactly."

"Perhaps that would be my petticoats, then. They tie around the waist here." She took his hands and guided them to the garment's knot.

He was a quick learner and had untied her petticoats without difficulty. In barely a moment, the garment was off.

"And now what?" he asked.

"My chemise is the only item left, as you can see," she said. "But I would advise you against taking it off. I am naked enough, just like this. I feel I must stress that proper women undress no more than this, even to bathe."

"I think you are a proper woman," he said, "but this is still not naked enough for me." And so saying, he pulled the garment up slowly. Once it had been raised over her knees, he bent down to trail kisses along its path, to her joints and thighs. And as the chemise gradually rose up higher and higher over her body, he followed its progress with his lips, lingering there at the junction of her legs. He parted her legs and kissed her . . . there . . .

Sarah immediately raised her hips. Dear Lord, what was this? The feeling was extraordinary. And though embarrassment might have consumed her, it simply wasn't possible to be feel guilty and pleasured all at the same time.

But he didn't linger there, and as he pulled the garment farther upward, his kisses followed the trail of her clothes until at last he found her breasts. First he kissed one, then the other. Curiously, though he was raising himself up over her, one of his hands had never left the delicacy between her legs.

"Open for me," he said between kisses.

She spread her legs, never thinking to disobey him. Then, with his fingers taking possession of her femininity, he did love her. He watched her as a tempest took hold of her, and she rocked with the rhythm of his fingers. It was as though she were a one-woman exhibition, a show played only for him, and no matter how long he looked, he couldn't see enough.

She had never felt more adored.

In due time, with his fingers still creating their magic at the apex of her legs, he moved up over her chest until he had come up to her bosom. First he kissed one of her breasts, his tongue encircling her nipple erotically, then he shifted to the other. It was as though she were a delicate instrument and he were playing her.

The feelings he was arousing in her were so finely luxurious, Sarah began to wonder how she had lived without this all her life. But he wasn't done. Indeed, it appeared he had only begun. With one hand, he pulled her chemise up over her head, while his kisses followed the garment's path, to her neck, cheeks and on upward, to the top of her head.

And then it was done. She was fully exposed. She lay before him in nothing more than the manner in which she had come into this world. However, there between her legs, White Thunder's fingers were still loving her, even more urgently than before. Momentarily, he rose up over her so that he could gaze at her in full. Her legs were spread, his hand was upon her and still it seemed he couldn't get enough of her.

At last, he whispered, "Your beauty should be the subject of art."

Even as he said it, his touch was stroking her, encouraging her to raise up to heights that, prior to this, she had only imagined. Indeed, she couldn't lie still. She was wet, wild with desire, and she cried out, "Please make love to me. I can hardly wait another moment."

His first response was to groan. Then he said, "I would be pleasured, Miss Sarah. Deeply pleasured."

He laid himself beside her, next to her, and his fingers were creating so great a stir within her that she thought she might burst. As he watched her, his groans grew more labored.

She was more than aware that she was struggling toward that ultra-fine release, and as feeling took over thinking, such joy crescendoed within her, she could hardly hold back the pleasure. Indeed, that pleasure was coming in on her so fast and furious that when the rapture burst within her, an exquisite kind of euphoria flooded her system, literally rocking her physically. It needed outlet, and as she cried out, he echoed her with a moan of his own. She gazed up at him, finding him watching her, looking at her as though he were witnessing grace in motion.

When she at last had settled down, he whispered, "I have great feeling for you, Miss Sarah. All the days of my life, I will remember this moment. This, I promise you."

She smiled at him, and reached up to grab hold of a lock of his hair, flicking the long strand behind his shoulders. Then he brought himself up over her, and without delay, joined their bodies together.

Briefly, she remembered that the first time she had made

love with him, there had been pain, then. She expected it now.

But it didn't materialize. Not this time. At present, there was nothing but enchantment. She welcomed him, fully, completely.

They began to move as one. One thrust from him followed another, her bliss heightening as she tightened her muscles around him. When he pushed against her, she met him. When he withdrew, so, too, did she.

It was an erotic sort of dance. On and on they swayed as they drew closer and closer together. But it seemed as if it wasn't close enough . . . at least not for him.

Breaking away from her, for a moment he came up onto his knees before her. Taking hold of her legs, he placed them around his neck. At once Sarah found the position most erotic, sensuous, and utterly stimulating. In this position, she was able to gaze up into his dark, almost black eyes.

She smiled at him, and it seemed her simple action was his undoing. In response, he thrust again and again within her.

As their bodies came together in the act of love, so, too, did she meet him on a different plane. She held that look in his eyes, she wanted that look, even as the dance between them became fast, then faster.

Never, she thought, had she ever seen a man so magnificent. His groans were pure music to her ears, inspiring her, bringing her up again so that she was spiraling up to that same pinnacle she'd met earlier. Faster and faster, deeper and deeper, until finally with one last cherished thrust, he gifted her with his seed. And she met him all the way. When he burst, so, too, did she.

And not once during the entire deed, had they dropped their heated gaze from one another. It was as though she'd been presented with a glimpse into his soul. Perhaps, he, too, had glimpsed her soul. But it little mattered; for a moment, if a moment only, she knew exactly who he was.

Moreover, he was spectacular.

As he collapsed against her, she rubbed her hands up and down his spine, savoring the feel of his hard muscles against the cushion of her touch. And despite all the logical reasons why she shouldn't, she knew she would never be the same again.

She had changed. Never again would she look at the world in the same way. This man was hers.

Fifteen

Days passed. Days that were filled with lovemaking, with mounting respect for one another and with the pleasure of becoming even better acquainted.

Of course, there was always work to be done, too. White Thunder instructed Sarah in the best ways to prepare a food made especially for travel. It was a dry meat pounded into a powdery substance and spiced with fat and berries. Apparently a handful of this mixture could sustain a warrior throughout an entire day.

They made plenty of it. They made plenty of love, too. Indeed, so idyllic were their days, Sarah began to wonder if it were possible to remain here in this cave for her life through. To her, it had become home.

Meanwhile, the weather outside the cave had turned cold. But it hardly mattered. Inside their little haven, Sarah and White Thunder were scarcely aware of the change in temperature. They seldom ventured far from the cave. There simply was no need.

There was only one problem, and that was due to their activities. Sarah had become sore, and in the worst of all places. However, once she had made White Thunder aware of the difficulty she was having, he had treated her to mud and clay baths, administered lovingly by him. Amazingly, the pain went away.

Days turned into a week, then another. And though White Thunder's strength had returned—as had Sarah's—still they lingered—with good reason.

Here they were spared the wagging tongues of spiteful gossips, the damning looks from prejudiced eyes, the scornful opinions of others as were bound to occur were they to return to society. Here they were free, they were married, at least within their own eyes . . . for a time.

But as the days plodded forward, Sarah's worry about Marisa increased. What had happened to her? Would the young warrior who was so smitten with her protect her from harm? She assumed that he would do most anything to keep his love safe.

But what if Marisa needed her? What if there were problems, and she had no one to turn to?

And so Sarah came to understand that the time had at last come to leave.

She and White Thunder were cuddled up in front of the fire when White Thunder said, "Are you prepared to go?"

"I think so, but do we have to?"

"You know we do," he said. "You have mentioned on more than one occasion that you worry about your friend. And I have a duty to perform, which cannot be accomplished here."

Sarah shot him a sad smile. "Surely," she said, "there must be something else we need to do to ready us to go. Is there anything we missed?"

He smiled at her before he bent to rub the side of his face against hers. He said, "We have smoked and dried all the meat, pounded it into meal and mixed it with berries and fat. We have packed it in bags. We have no more food here to prepare. It is all stored in the bags we will carry."

"Yes, but you could hunt for more food and we could prepare that."

"I could, but it is unnecessary. We have all the food we will need."

"Oh." Her voice sounded as disappointed as she felt. "But, sir, 'tis cold. Don't we need warmer clothing?"

"What we have will be enough. We have already made two warm shirts and extra moccasins for us both from the deer kill. It will be enough."

"Then how about the root that is needed to keep me from conceiving?"

"I have dried much of it. It, too, is packed."

"Yes, that's true," she said. Then again, "Yes."

"If we linger here too long," he declared, "the snows will come and we will have much difficulty finding your friend."

Sarah frowned. "Do you think we'll encounter trouble?"

"I little know. I have seen enemy tracks in my travels to find food. War rages across this land, making traveling, even upon the lakes and rivers, dangerous. I have given it much thought, and I think we will do best to make our path through the forest. Although an enemy can hide there easily, so, too, can we."

Sarah turned to stare at him grimly. "Now that you speak of it, I remember this war. I recall that the whole world seemed afire."

"And so it has been since the English and others have come to our borders. It has been a series of one war after another. Once, many years ago, the Iroquois were at peace with themselves and with their neighbors."

"I have heard that this was so. Tell me about it."

"In the long-ago time," he replied, "hundreds of years before the white man ever arrived on this land, there was the Great Peace. It was started by two men and a woman, who took the idea of ending war from tribe to tribe. It was not easy to do, for not everyone desired harmony, and some were great, but evil magicians. However, eventually these three accomplished it, and they united six heroic nations together under one branch, and offered to bring all other Indian nations under its branches. It was what united the Iroquois. It is this that has made us strong."

"And you have a government, I believe. Is that not right?"

"We do, but it is not like the English, who are subject to a king. Our towns are ruled by the people, and he who has power, but who would govern for himself and his family, alone, is quickly warned, and if he still doesn't behave, he is removed from the council."

"Fascinating. And there is no confusion?"

"Confusion? Not about government or who we are or how we make our laws. We council together, and when all agree to a law or to a suggestion, only then is it passed by the council. But even then, if the people don't like it, they don't have to follow it. One is always left to make up his own mind."

"And this unites you? It doesn't pull you apart?"

"It unites us, yes."

Both were silent, until at last, Sarah asked, "When do we leave?"

"Tomorrow."

"'Tis quite soon."

He nodded.

"I will miss it here. I've been happy, and I've even started to think of this cave as mine."

"I, too."

"But I suppose we can't stay here forever."

"So it is. We both have duties that weigh upon us."

"Aye," she said. Then, "I've had you to myself for all these days and I have become used to thinking of you as my husband. But when we leave here, that's all behind us, is it not?"

"That was our agreement, yes," he said. "It will soon be at an end. However, we still have tonight. For a little while longer, let us pretend that we are a married couple, with no other responsibilities except to bring pleasure to one another."

She nodded. "I would like that."

He sighed and tightened his arms around her. "On this night, I would like to think of nothing but the many different ways to love you."

"Yes, Mr. Thunder, please." She smiled at him, but she feared that at present, even her smile reflected her loss. However, when she spoke, she didn't speak of sadness. Rather, she said, "Let us make beautiful memories."

He, too, seemed grim, but as he turned her around toward him and proceeded to do as she suggested, their lovemaking transformed them both. Once again, there was only him. There was only her.

The extreme darkness before dawn ushered in a new day. They had made love through the night, as though only in this way could they keep the morning from coming. But here it was already. She was tired. He was tired, also, but White Thunder had already assured her that they would rest throughout their journey.

Amazingly, she wasn't sleepy. Just tired.

They had swept away all traces of their stay in the cave—a necessary procedure, according to White Thunder, so that their time here might be invisible to the eye of anyone who should be looking for them. He had recently stepped from the cave to say his morning prayers while Sarah had stayed behind to attend to her toiletries.

She was settling her open gown over her petticoats and straightening its bodice when White Thunder came back into the cave. He stopped almost perfectly still when he saw her, and he stared at her as though he had never seen her until this moment.

"You are ready?" he asked, but he said nothing more to her.

"Almost," she replied. It was the first time she had worn her gown since before she'd awakened to find herself in a cave and in the presence of a man she didn't remember.

The gown had once been one of her best. But traveling over open ground and practically drowning in it had done irreparable damage.

Long ago, however, it had been beautiful, made of a rich, gold-colored silk brocade. Her petticoats were a quilted cream color, almost matching the gold of the dress, and as was the fashion, they were displayed in front of the gown. Somewhere in her adventures, however, she had lost her white muslin apron, although her white neck handkerchief had survived. She wore it now, covering her chest, up to her neck.

On her feet were moccasins, since her own slippers were flimsy and wouldn't provide her with the needed protection against the cold. Sarah had also managed to tie her long hair back, although she hadn't been able to contain the blond ringlets that fell forward against her face.

"You look very English," he said.

"Thank you," she replied, "I think." She smiled at him. "Was that a compliment?"

"Perhaps." It was all he said.

She looked toward their luggage, which consisted of several buckskin bags, as well as her own hand-carved cane. "What is it that I'll be carrying?"

"Our bags."

She frowned at him. "All of them?"

"No, I will carry some, but my hands and arms must remain free so that if we come upon enemies, I will be able to protect us. That this requires you to bear the brunt of carting most of our food is to be regretted, for I know this is not the English way."

"Yes, that's true," she said. "It's not the English way. But your point is well taken. Where shall we go to pick up Miss Marisa's trail?"

"I have given it some thought, and I believe that we'll start at the beginning, where I found you: by the side of the Lake-That-Turns-to-Rapids. We will backtrack to the falls, since I believe that is where your accident occurred. When I found you, you were almost drowned."

"So you have said. I do wish I could remember."

"It matters little. What I have explained is the only conclusion that makes sense. So I believe that if we begin at the falls, we may yet find some trace of your friend."

Sarah smiled at him. "I will be happy to see her."

White Thunder nodded, but otherwise remained silent. Then, he said, "Come here. I would begin our journey with an embrace, if you would humor me."

Happily she went into his arms, where he buried himself in the folds of her hair. He murmured, "There is a war raging across this country. Stay close to me. We will move fast, but not so swiftly that I cannot go back on our trail and erase our prints from the ground. Are you ready?"

She nodded, and with the both of them bidding adieu to the cave, they set off into the woods. Perhaps it was her imagination, but for a moment she thought that a certain squirrel had come out of her winter hideaway to say goodbye.

It was cold, it had rained and the ground was both hard and wet. There was a scent in the air of decaying, wet leaves, as well as the earthy smell of dirt. The trees were naked of their leaves and looked to be little more than skeletons waving their branches against the gray beginnings of the day. Sarah's toes immediately protested the chilly weather, but as long as she kept moving, her feet cooperated.

They had been gone for no longer than an hour when Sarah began to wish for the relative comfort of their cave. But she knew it was not to be. They had to move on forward; there was no turning back.

Their progress through the forest was slower than what Sarah would have imagined it would be, if only because she was weighted down with their supplies, thus their stops were frequent. And although Sarah realized that each day the burden would become less—if only because they would be consuming the food—here at the start of their journey, the bags were still cumbersome and bulky.

White Thunder never strayed too far ahead of her, even though she was certain she was holding him back. While they were on the move, his rifle was held in a ready position, always. He was well armed: Attached to his belt were tomahawk, war clubs and knives. Strapped across his shoulders were bags, a powder horn and balls. And within the folds of his leggings, there at his calf, were two more knives. He looked, she thought, like a walking arsenal.

But it made her glad. He also appeared fully capable of protecting the two of them.

She took a moment to admire his look, for it was different from what she had become accustomed to. For one thing, he was dressed for the weather with a white linen shirt worn inside a buckskin coat. On his legs were buckskin leggings and moccasins. His blanket, which also was used for warmth, was thrown over one of his shoulders and belted at his waist. Quite incidentally, his leggings didn't reach all the way up to his shirt, which left her with an alluring view of his thighs. And, indeed, she did look. Truth be told, she found her gaze lingering there more often than perhaps it should.

She knew his moccasins—and hers as well—were winter- as well as waterproof, having been carefully smoked and sewn with the fur turned inside. She knew this because she had helped to sew them.

He had insisted that her clothing also be winterized, and she wore a blanket over her shoulders in a style much like a cape. Also, there had been enough deerskin to fashion herself an outer buckskin petticoat, made and worn for warmth. She had long ago lost her hat, a shame, for it would have been a good addition to protect her against this weather.

Suddenly White Thunder came to a complete stop. She almost ran into him. Quickly, he glanced to his right and left, surveying the lay of the land. He pointed toward a stand of trees, then, gazing at her, brought up a single finger to lie across his lips.

Trouble. Her stomach suddenly churned and again, adrenaline pumped through her system.

As noiselessly, yet as quickly as they could, they fled toward the stand of the distant trees he had indicated, their feet scurrying over the wet mosses and ferns littering the forest floor. What was it? she wondered—or rather, who was it?

Her questions were all too quickly answered, however, when she witnessed a war party of perhaps twenty-five young men round a hill. At the same moment the war party came into view, both she and White Thunder had reached that stand of trees. Immediately, they ducked beneath the weight of a pine tree's branches.

He settled her up close to the trunk of the tree so that she was almost completely hidden by its long and extending boughs. Then he left. What was he doing? she wondered.

And why, in outfitting her gear for the trip, hadn't she considered a weapon? In a land torn by war, one needed some manner of self-defense.

Soon White Thunder returned and crouched down beside her in a position that afforded him a view of the enemy's approach. He held his rifle in a ready position and gazed out toward the path the warriors were making.

Perhaps they were lucky this day, or mayhap this particular group of men was overconfident because their numbers were great, or maybe they were returning from a battle, and thus were unaware of their environment. Whatever the cause, they missed seeing the tracks of the two people who had been on that path minutes before them.

Still, it seemed to take the war party forever to pass by, and when at last their rear was no more than a distant speck, White Thunder continued to wait, his body and his gun held in a position to do immediate battle.

How many minutes passed, Sarah could not estimate, but it must have been at least a half hour. At last, with his weapon still held in a primed position, he whispered, "Huron war party. We will no longer travel over known paths. They are dangerous. Our way from here on will be hard, but safer because we will travel through untouched land."

"Untouched?"

He nodded. "Land through which there are no known paths," he explained. "It will be hard for you, but it must be done, since it appears the Iroquois Trail is no longer safe for travel. Be that as it may, we will, of necessity, go where few wish to travel. Have you a weapon?"

"No. A terrible oversight on my part," she said.

"Do you at least have a knife?"

"Yes."

"Keep it ready to use. I little know what to expect. Wait here while I go back and erase our most recent tracks, but then we must leave quickly before they at last see our earlier prints and backtrack to find us."

"That could happen?"

He nodded. "Easily." Rising up, he left to erase their passage as thoroughly and quickly as possible.

Sixteen

"In the days before the European came to our country, a person could walk the Iroquois Trail from one end of it to the other and never meet with any danger . . . at least not from a human source."

"Truly?" she asked, her voice barely louder than a whisper. "And what exactly is the Iroquois Trail?"

She scooted closer to White Thunder as he took his time answering her question. They were sitting within a temporary shelter White Thunder had fashioned from tree branches, leaves and dirt. Since it was made from materials gleaned from the environment, it literally blended into its surroundings, disappearing to all but the most discerning eye.

The night was cold, they had no fire, nor did they dare to light one, since, as White Thunder had said, "The smoke from a fire travels farther and faster than a man can easily flee."

They sat close together, not only because they wished to remain close to one another, but for warmth, as well. They were huddled on one of their blankets; the other he had wrapped around her. Even still, she shivered.

"The Iroquois Trail," he explained, "is a path forged through the forest long ago that links all the villages of the Iroquois Confederation, one to the other. It stretches between the land of the Mohawks in the east to the far western tribe of the Confederation—my tribe, the Seneca. Always in the past, the trail was kept clear and free of branches or other debris so that a runner or anyone, even a child, could easily travel upon it. In the old days, no enemy dared to use it or molest anyone upon it, because the Iroquois were strong and could defend what was theirs. But all this has changed since the English and French have come here to stay. Now we see war parties of enemy tribes traveling upon our trail, where never they used to go."

"I'm sorry. It sounds as if it had once been ideal," Sarah commented. "But I still don't understand. We've talked of this before, about how the coming of the English and French changed your people. But, sir, weren't the Indians at war long before the Europeans arrived?"

Again it took him some moments to answer. "The change took place over a long period of time, a few hundreds of years. Before the English arrived, the Iroquois were a powerful nation, a peaceful nation. But it wasn't always so. In the very long ago, perhaps as long as seven hundred years ago, there were revenge killings and the people were often crying, for there seemed no end to it. But two great men, Hiawatha and the Peacemaker, brought about a better way to settle grief and to appease the spirits of the departed. They sought to end all war because at that time most wars were started due to the need to avenge one's dearly departed.

"They set up a system of government that, with certain ceremonies, would pacify the grief of their loved one, and it would ensure prosperity and peace. When this was done, a great calm fell upon the land.

"This was how it was when the European first came to this country. But we soon learned that the Europeans quarreled among themselves—not out of revenge, as we had, but due to a thirst for wealth. They had, themselves, no great peace. It wasn't long before we also realized that not only did they quarrel with themselves, but they sought to incite the Indians to their different sides in their disputes. Witlessly, Indians took sides. Thus, the great peace ended, and all with the coming of the European, for soon, there was one war after another on this land."

"But this is fantastic, sir. You must know that the English tell the story of their coming entirely differently. According to our history, it was the Indians who were treacherous, who were always at war, while our own English ancestors tried to restore peace among them."

He gazed at her askance, then said, "It has long been noted that when a man has no defense against the truth, his only option is to accuse another of those things he does himself."

She frowned at him. "This you have mentioned to me before, and it is a bit of wisdom I have never heard."

"Simple observation will show you this is true," he said, then continued. "Now, there are many of my brothers within the Iroquois Nation who have made friends with the English, though I think they are unwise to do so. They fight his wars. They take up his arms. They think they must, for they have become dependent on the things the English can give them. But not all the Iroquois have been bought by the English or the French. Not all of the Iroquois experience the greed that the trade has caused among our people."

Sarah sat silently for a moment. "Then you must very much dislike the society that is springing up all around you."

"Dislike is not the right word," he responded. "What is more correct is that I think it is unwise to become so dependent on a people who do not know you or need you. Do you think that we of the Seneca have blind eyes and have not seen how the English and French treat the white black man who escapes into our country? Do you think we have not noticed the white black man killed or enslaved when the English can get their hands on him? And what about people like you, his own kind, whom he enslaves by means of finance and rules? Do you believe we do not realize that if he could, the English, the French, too, would do the same to us? But he cannot enslave us—at least not now—because our Confederacy is too strong. We are united."

Her lips parted as though she might respond. But upon further consideration, she closed her mouth. In due time, however, she said, "I truly don't know what to say. If this is your honest viewpoint of my people, it is not a complimentary one."

"So it is not."

She shivered.

He drew her into his arms and said, "Too much talk and not enough lovemaking."

Sarah smiled. "Surely, sir, you're not thinking of making love here? Here beneath a ceiling of tree branches and leaves?"

"I am," he said. "It will keep us warm, if you are willing."

"'Tis not a point I can argue . . . sir." She smiled.

He grinned back. "What?" he questioned. "You do not disagree?"

"Am I that bad, sir?"

"Bad? You are good. Very good." As he took her in his arms, he brought her into a position up and over him in a straddle-like pose, and he repeated, "You are very good, indeed."

They traveled through thickets and brambles with stickers that stuck to her dress and petticoats. They stepped through streams that froze her moccasins to her feet, requiring the two of them to stop while White Thunder rubbed them back to life. And always it was cold.

"Why do you not warm your own feet?" Sarah had asked once, after observing that White Thunder never attended to his own needs. Indeed, were it not for her, he might not have stopped at all, but would have continued on their path, acting as though nothing untoward had happened.

"My body does not require attention," he had explained. "I have bathed in cold and icy water all my life. Even in the dead of winter, the wintry swim is a necessary part of life."

Sarah shivered. "I can't imagine anything worse."

"It is not bad," he said. "Over time, the body craves it."

She shook her head at him. "If you say so."

Soon they were back on the trail, even though it had begun to rain and drizzle. In the distance, the roar of a waterfall was becoming more distinct, for this, according to White Thunder, was where he'd found her.

At last they reached the area of the falls. Though Sarah witnessed them only from afar, their roar drowned out all other sound.

I had fallen down those? She shivered as she watched the utter power of this natural wonder.

But it wasn't White Thunder's intention to stop and admire the marvel of the falls. He was plodding on ahead, and was so far distant from her, it required her to run to catch up with him. Perhaps she was making too much noise in her mad dash toward him. Whatever the cause, at last White Thunder turned and stopped, waiting for her to draw even with him.

"Is there a reason you usually travel so far ahead of me?" she asked as she came to stand beside him.

"There is," he answered without looking at her. He pointed forward. "The danger is in front of us, not behind us. I must stay well in advance should there be peril, either from man or animal. In this way, you might escape while I fight the menace."

"Oh," she murmured in acknowledgment. "It is interesting because it is much different in my society. Men in English society are considered mannerly only when they follow the woman."

"I know," he said. "But I would not be doing my duty were I to lag behind you. It could cause you to meet the danger head-on, while I am in safety at the rear."

"I see. Thank you."

He nodded.

The rain had started in earnest now, and in her haste, she slipped over the wet leaves and fell to her knees. Immediately White Thunder was at her side, helping her up.

"Mr. Thunder," she said, coming up to her feet. "Is it really possible that I fell down those falls and survived?"

His arms spanned her waist as he set her back on her feet. "It is my belief that this is so."

Sarah shook her head. "'Tis a shock I wasn't killed."

He placed his arms around her and brought her into his embrace. "Almost, you were," he said. "Almost."

As the rain fell in torrents around them, they stood in the middle of the forest, clinging to one another. He said, "We will begin our search for your friend and her husband here. If they survived the falls, they would have stayed here to mend themselves and their equipment, since no warrior of any merit would dare the forest without an adequate defense. And if they stopped here, there will be a shelter somewhere in this vicinity. That is what we'll be looking for."

"I see," she replied, raising her face to his, a perfect invitation for a kiss. Happily he accommodated her.

There was something erotic and magical about kissing your lover in the middle of a rainstorm, if only because the downpour itself seemed to magnify the fire inside. It was another moment of pure heaven, and Sarah cherished it, committing this, too, to memory.

But wonderful though it was, they couldn't long stand in the middle of a forest, in the midst of a rainstorm. Soon, they were heading out again on the trail.

Somewhere along the way, Sarah asked, "Aren't you afraid that the rain might freeze our tracks to the ground so that anyone could follow us?"

"I might be concerned if it stopped raining," he answered, "but because it continues, there is little danger of that happening."

"Oh."

Onward they traveled, slowly now, searching for clues. One day turned to the next, and still they found nothing definite.

For Sarah, these days of constant wandering had begun to blur. In truth, because their path required her to traverse a muddy, cold, gray and wet land, the days were beginning to take on the color of pure misery. It wasn't that she didn't appreciate the landscape, or what White Thunder was doing. More to the point, it simply was not the sort of journey that a woman might enjoy. Indeed, the land they traveled over was the kind of terrain that even a rabbit wouldn't have dared navigate at this time of year.

Always, the ground seemed to be moist and littered with the sight and scent of decaying leaves, bushes and undergrowth. The trees were brittle, and hosted so many branches that they often scratched Sarah as she passed them by, and her clothes were torn by thorns and stickers. Her hair had long since escaped its knot to hang in curls down her back, which, due to the drizzle, had taken to springing into waves and ringlets.

But if the days were wretched, the nights were enchanting, perhaps making up for her daily travail. Each night White Thunder fashioned a temporary shelter, one that was built from whatever was to hand. Each night, after making

love, they slept in one another's arms. In the morning they
bathed, she in the relative comfort of their refuge, and he
in some nearby stream. Always the feel and scent of nature
was all around her, the dirt, the leaves and the freshest air
she'd ever breathed.

It happened on a beautiful, sunny day. They came upon
the body of a man, months decayed. He had certainly been
a huge man, Sarah thought as she turned away from the
sight.

Carefully, White Thunder bent to examine the ground
around the body.

"There was a struggle here," he said, "but most of the
prints that would tell the complete story of what happened
are long gone."

"Is the man a Mohawk, sir?"

"No, Ottawa."

Sarah breathed out in a sigh of relief. "Thank the dear
Lord. I was afraid it might have been the young man who
was so besotted with Miss Marisa. You are certain he is
Ottawa?"

He nodded. "Ottawa."

"How can you tell he is Ottawa? Without a doubt?"

White Thunder pointed toward the man's feet. "Do you
see the cut of his moccasins?"

"No. I . . . I don't want to look."

"The pattern of beadwork, the cut. His style of breechcloth, clothes, weapons. He was Ottawa. He was struck
several times, also; the blow to the head was the fatal blow.
The man who did this was protecting something."

"How do you know that?"

"It was unnecessary to beat this dead man so many
times. Whoever it was that fought him was ensuring the
Ottawa's death. One has to ask why?"

Sarah shook her head.

"Loved ones or a loved one was near, perhaps endan-
gered. Only then does a man become so savage."

"Oh, I see," said Sarah.

"Besides, clamped in the Ottawa's hand is some red hair. Was your friend's hair red?"

"Yes."

He nodded. "It is possible they camped close to here."

"They?"

"By these clues, I think we have found the trail of your friend and her Mohawk protector." Reaching into one of the bags that he carried around his shoulder, White Thunder withdrew what looked to Sarah to be a dried herb.

Carefully, he crumbled the herb in his hand, then sprinkled it around the body of the dead Ottawa. After some moments, he said some words in his own language over the body before he at last came up onto his feet.

Turning toward Sarah, he gestured. "Come, let us search for the place where they built their shelter. If I am right, I believe we will find it close to here."

In the end, it took White Thunder several more days of hunting and inspecting the forest around him to locate the shelter, which was nestled in a deeply wooded valley. Constructed as it was, alongside a fallen tree, it first looked to be nothing more than the loose branches of an old, dead tree. But as he pulled one branch after another aside, the inside of the structure was revealed.

Whoever built this, thought White Thunder, was a good man. Smart.

"This is where they stayed," he told Sarah. "Come, let's see what clues they left us."

"Then she's alive?"

"I cannot say how she is now, but when this was built, she was alive—do you see over there?" He pointed into the shelter.

"No, what?"

"Look closely."

"I see nothing, sir, but branches and grass."

He bent and picked up a small piece of white lace. He said, "Unless our Mohawk warrior has taken to wearing a lady's decoration, I think we can assume that your friend stayed here."

"Let me see that."

White Thunder handed her the material.

"Yes," said Sarah. "I recognize the design of this. 'Tis Marisa's." She brought her gaze up to meet White Thunder's, and White Thunder found himself yearning to take this woman in his arms and make love to her here, now, under the broad light of day.

He might have done it, too, were it not a dangerous thing for a man to attempt, given where they were and the circumstances of war that surrounded them. He had always been attracted to Sarah, thus he'd felt no qualms in agreeing to their pretense at being man and wife.

But since they had started out on the trail, each day brought a new facet of her personality to the fore, and he was finding himself becoming more and more besotted with her. Her gentle ways, her kind encouragement to him, her courage in the face of so much adversity, was acting as a balm to his heart.

Plus, her beauty continued to enchant him. He knew the harshness of their travels was not a woman's favorite abode. While on the move, she couldn't treat herself to the niceties that women tended to favor: she couldn't always manage the condition of her hair, her body or her clothes. Yet, oddly, he couldn't remember ever desiring a woman's companionship more . . . not even Wild Mint's. Certainly, he had loved Wild Mint. He loved her still.

But he nursed a fascination for Sarah that was new to him. Indeed, he didn't quite understand it. For one thing, he never grew tired of looking at her, and he couldn't ever seem to get close enough to her. Always he found himself inventing little reasons to touch her.

"What do we do now?" Sarah asked him, bringing him back to the present moment.

"We will stay here tonight," he answered. "This shelter can be easily rebuilt and made comfortable. The structure is Iroquois built and made."

"Is it?"

"Yes," he said. "Do you see how the builder uses the bark against the frame of the structure? The way the poles are positioned? This structure is Iroquois built—Mohawk, specifically. Your friend's sweetheart was taking no chances with her being accidently found. I can only imagine that the Ottawa somehow discovered your friend and was taking her away when she was rescued by her Mohawk husband."

"I still don't understand, Mr. Thunder. How do you know these things?"

"I don't. Not completely. But it's what I believe happened. We saw the remains of a man who was killed viciously. His attacker was protecting something. Only then is a man so vicious. And whatever he was protecting must have been close by for the attack to be so gruesome. Therefore, one must assume that the Ottawa found your friend and that she was rescued by her Mohawk husband."

"Oh. It seems simple when you say it, but I didn't see it."

"Only because you don't know what to look for and are not trained to look."

"Perhaps."

"They probably left here immediately, thinking that the shelter was no longer invisible to an enemy eye. Where they would go from here, I can only speculate."

"But what is it that you think? You must have some idea of where they might have gone."

While she was speaking, White Thunder had begun to reconstruct the shelter, filling in its gaps with bark and logs. It took him several moments before he answered. "You know your friend. Tell me, would she have taken her Mohawk husband back to her village?"

"You mean Albany?"

"If that is her village, yes."

Sarah looked away from him and frowned. "I don't think so. Her uncle was against the two of them even talking to each other, let alone marrying. Right from the start there was trouble, because of Marisa's position as John Rathburn's niece. She was expected to marry a man of Rathburn's choosing. This she knew; this she expected to do. But she rebelled at the last minute, although I do believe she meant her rebellion to be small, a one-night affair only. And so she escaped one evening to make love with this young man. She never expected to marry him. Rather, I recall her saying to me that she wished to make some memories to last her all her life."

"As you have said to me," he observed.

"'Tis true."

"So this evil one, this Rathburn, not only forced himself on you, but he felt himself so superior to others that he could dictate to your friend how she should live her own life? That he, and he alone, should pick her husband?"

"'Tis the way of the English aristocracy."

"It is their way?"

"Yes, sir, 'tis so. Is it different with the Seneca?"

"*Nyoh*, yes," he said. "A Seneca maiden picks her own husband, not the other way around."

"That is often the way of the English, too, for someone who is not of the aristocracy."

As White Thunder set the last of the branches onto their shelter, he said, "The more I learn of the English, the more I like the Seneca way."

She smiled at him, and staring down into her lovely face, he melted a little. He reached out to run a hand over her hair, bent down to kiss the top of her head and said, "Stay here. Prepare the shelter as we have done every night while I backtrack to erase our trail. I should return soon."

"Yes, sir. I will."

He smiled at her and it came to him that he was a lucky man. Very lucky, indeed.

Seventeen

Across the Lake-That-Turns-to-Rapids, a party of five men slid their canoe silently to shore. Three of the men in the party were Ottawa, the other two were French. Though they were en route to the French fort at Niagara, the Indians had a stop to make here: They had left a man, Dirty Hands, at this place almost two months earlier. Because Dirty Hands had not been in his right mind at the time, no one had desired to accompany him as he went about a self-appointed mission to find his son's killers.

But Dirty Hands had not returned to the Ottawa village, and his wife and relatives were asking about him. These few men had promised to discover his fate, and possibly to send him home if he were still alive.

Because they were a party of five well-trained men, they were not long in locating Dirty Hands' remains. It took them little time to discover that Dirty Hands had been brutally killed. Quickly, they assessed that the murder had been committed several months ago.

But what was this? Here were fresh tracks, perhaps only a few days old. Here also were the remains of dried sage, which had been crumpled and scattered over the body.

Was it his murderer returned to this place to propitiate the spirit of the departed?

They scoured the area further, looking for more footprints. Those they found were Seneca made, two different prints—that of a man and a woman.

Carefully, the five men took up the trail, if only to solve the mystery of what had happened to Dirty Hands. Moving single file they made a path and like silent shadows, they slid into the forest.

At last, she and White Thunder had found Marisa's trail.

Sarah smiled as she set to work within the shelter, unpacking their bags and setting out a meal of pemmican and water for herself and White Thunder. It was comforting knowing that this was the shelter Marisa and Black Eagle had used, and that they had somehow survived the falls.

As Sarah settled in to begin her work, quite unexpectedly, the memory of that fateful day slid into view. Again, like once before when her recall had suddenly returned, it came instantly, easily and without having to strain.

It had been a day much like this, sunny and bright, when the Ottawa and the French had attacked herself, Marisa and Black Eagle. The three of them had escaped in a canoe. But what they hadn't been able to avoid were the falls of the Lake-That-Turns-to-Rapids. At least, she hadn't.

There was another aspect about that day. Thompson, who was supposed to have been their guide, was a traitor. All those months ago on the trail, there had been accident after accident. It hadn't been completely apparent who was creating those series of mishaps, or indeed, if they were even accidents. Not until Thompson had floundered into the canoe that day and had tried to kill Marisa had he finally showed himself for what he was.

But why had he done it?

Why would Thompson . . . all at once Sarah understood. It was John Rathburn. Rathburn had hired Thompson. For some reason that Sarah couldn't fathom, Rathburn had wanted his niece dead. It had to be. But why?

Sarah strained to remember . . . There was something there that was important—something just out of reach— something that made this all make sense, if she could but remember.

But as often happened when she was straining to remember, her head began to ache, and soon Sarah realized it was useless to try to recollect it. Her mind was determined to remain blank. But at least there was one detail that was now apparent. She had to find Marisa and warn her not to go home. Until her doubts about John Rathburn were put to rest, Albany was not safe. But what if she had already returned home? Sarah's stomach churned at the idea, and urgency rose up to fill her mind.

As might be expected, Sarah could barely contain her need to leave here and find Marisa. But she couldn't go. Not yet. Not until White Thunder indicated it was safe.

In the end, Sarah busied herself with straightening their bags and placing the blankets on the ground in preparation for the evening. She was careful to be quiet. White Thunder had warned her to make no noise and no jerky movements. War parties, he had said, were out in force upon the trail.

It seemed a small thing. It shouldn't have produced the reaction from her that it did. But she thought she'd been alone in the shelter.

However, what she had missed, and White Thunder, also, was that a skunk had found this place long before they

had. Its home apparently was within one of the hollowed-
out logs that created one of the "walls" of the shelter.

Alas, one moment she was by herself, the next she was
confronting the skunk eye to eye. She should have done
nothing. She should have controlled herself and frozen all
movement.

But she was female, plus she was untrained in the ways
of the woods. Her first reaction was involuntary, and she let
out a shriek. The skunk left in haste, but Sarah was overwhelmed at what she'd done.

Immediately, she clasped a hand over her mouth and
shut her eyes.

If a war party were anywhere near, she had very nicely
given away her location. Hopefully her mistake would go
unnoticed.

Crunch!

Her eyes flew open. It was a footfall outside the shelter.
She recognized the sound at once. Worse, it was close-by.

Silently, she chided herself for her foolishness.

There were cracks in the branches that held the shelter
together. Staring out through them, she could see the fig-
ures of two men coming toward her cautiously. They were
French.

Were Indian scouts with them?

She swallowed the lump in her throat. Dear Lord, where
was White Thunder?

Presently, three Indians joined those French, and Sarah
watched as the party approached her shelter, watched also
as a red, white and black–painted face stared into the cracks
of the structure. All it would take was one of them to pull
back a few of those branches and they would discover her.

Sarah's heartbeat began to pump blood furiously
through her body, while her mind was swamped with
thoughts of regret. It was her own fault. Why hadn't she
controlled her reaction?

One of the Frenchmen took up his rifle and fired a shot into the shelter. It missed her, the ball whizzing by her harmlessly, landing in the dead log behind her with a *thunk*. But it didn't matter. She screamed.

They were upon her in an instant. They dragged her from the shelter. But Sarah was not going to go willingly. She screamed until her voice was ragged. She kicked out at them.

One of the Indians placed a hand over her mouth, while another picked her up and threw her over his shoulder.

This was it, then. Was her death to be as easily accomplished as this? The two Indians were chattering away in their own language, when suddenly a single shot split though the air. One of the Indians who had been accompanying the French fell back, hitting the ground, dead.

Sarah heard the yelp of a war cry. At once she recognized the voice: White Thunder. But, dear Lord, there was only one of him. The odds were against him. All the same, Sarah listened helplessly as White Thunder must have plunged himself into the midst of the French soldiers. What followed next must have been hand-to-hand combat. Sarah could hear the deadly clang of their weapons. Then came the cry of yet another man as she listened to him fall to the ground.

Was it White Thunder? She tried to look. She couldn't.

But it had sounded like him. Sarah hung her head as tears spilled down over her face. She began to pummel the back of her captor, cursing at him. He, in reaction, threw her to the ground, which she hit with an *oomph* that knocked the breath out of her. He bent over her and quickly tied her hands together.

Not bothering to throw her again over his shoulder, the one Indian, along with his friend, shot away from the scene of action, pulling her along with them. Sarah had no choice but to follow at a sprint and to try to keep up with their maddening pace. It was either that or be dragged. As she ran, she dared to cast a look back over her shoulder. White Thunder was still on his feet, still fighting.

He was alive. He was still alive.

But then Sarah lost her footing. She was hauled a good distance before she was finally able to struggle to her feet. There came yet another manly cry. And then she was lost to the sound and sight of the fight.

Onward they raced, into the forest, going ever farther and farther away from White Thunder. Uselessly Sarah wished herself away from here; she wanted to be back there, with White Thunder, and she cried out at her vulnerability. Was he still alive?

Dear Lord, she prayed. Let him still be alive. Please let him be alive.

Evening came at a much faster pace than Sarah would have liked. At present, she and her two captors had stopped and set up camp. Sarah was sitting upright against a tree, tied to it with a rope around her waist; also there was one tied around her hands, which had been positioned in front of her. The rope around her hands chafed and cut into her skin, and she could see blood oozing from the sores. The rope around her waist, though restrictive, was merely uncomfortable. Looking down, she despaired at the state of her skirts and her bodice, which were both torn and frayed, and her petticoats, which had been soiled beyond repair. Plus, to her shame, these men hadn't granted her the courtesy to allow her to relieve herself along the trail. Somewhere in their trek this day, nature had had its way.

She'd never felt so wretched, nor so dirty.

The two Indians were busying themselves with a fire, and it was a big one. They said nothing to her—not that she would have been able to understand them had they tried.

But human decency would have thought they would have at least ventured to attempt it.   ·

What were they planning for her? The question was one that was likely to drive her mad if she didn't gain an answer to it, and soon. If her death were fated this night, knowing it seemed more preferable than being caught unaware.

Of course, she'd never been more frightened. Nor had she ever felt more alone. Death awaited. She knew it. It was there in the way those men looked at her, and in the way they treated her.

But how were they going to go about it? Was it going to be painful?

There was every indication that it would be so. Even now, she watched them as they sharpened their knives and their tomahawks. They were even priming their weapons.

Where was White Thunder?

Many hours had passed since her capture. Hours that had been spent fleeing along an obvious trail, her feet flying over ground covered with moss, slime and dead leaves. At times she'd been dragged when she'd fallen and couldn't keep up with the pace. During those times, it had always been a struggle to get back to her feet. Sometimes she'd managed it, sometimes they had simply dragged her.

Surely they had left tracks that White Thunder could follow . . . if he were still alive.

Presently, one of the Indians rose to his feet and stepped toward her. Watching him, realizing that his intention toward her was hardly social, she gathered her courage. Without warning, he flew at her and grabbed a handful of her hair. He pulled, practically plucking it out by its roots. Then he spit upon it. Then her.

He said, "Your . . . husband . . . dead. No sign . . . him."

Sarah looked away from him, but the warrior forced her face back toward him.

"Our brother . . . killed. English kill . . . my father. You . . . pay. Will die in fire."

Though the Indian held her face so she couldn't glance away, Sarah refused to look at him, her gaze centered downward. Tears slipped over her cheeks.

"You cry now . . . cry more . . . later. Torture first . . . before fire. You feel . . . much pain."

He untied her from the tree.

"You . . . stand . . ."

He put some effort into making her rise, but Sarah refused to obey. If she were to be tortured, then die by the fire, why make it easy for him by cooperating? If the only defiance she had left in her was to sit while he wanted her to stand, then that was exactly what she would do.

He pulled her roughly to her feet, but she immediately sank to the ground. The warrior repeated the same procedure twice.

Had it not been so serious, Sarah thought the situation might have appeared humorous. It was, however, anything but amusing.

Eventually, because the warrior couldn't force her to stand, he let her sit. He came down onto his haunches before her and stuck his face in hers, smiling. His image was a horrible thing to behold, for his face was painted black, and the stark contrast to the white of his teeth made him resemble a walking skeleton.

All at once, he sliced away the bodice of her gown, as well as the sleeves of her chemise, leaving a large, red cut across her chest and exposing her entire upper body to the cold night air. Involuntarily, her cry shot through the night.

He tried to tear away her skirt, also, but she wore so many petticoats, her outer one being buckskin, that it became impossible. Eventually he gave up and said, "No matter. Soon you . . . feel manhood." And he ripped away his breechcloth, exposing a man partially aroused.

Sarah was sickened by the sight of him, by his smell and

by the idea of what he intended to do to her. Indeed, what food she had left in her stomach, she lost.

But there was no mercy to be found in this Ottawa warrior's manner. He laughed and squatted in front of her again.

Sarah gasped as he took out his knife and once more brandished it in front of her. He brought it toward her, slowly, slowly, watching for her reaction like a wolf cornering a rabbit. He sliced off a portion of her hair, grinning at her all the while. "We do this . . . all over . . . body."

Exposed, vulnerable, Sarah began to wonder if part of the torture were pure fright. If so, he was being very successful.

Again, he waved that knife in front of her as he once more cut off a portion of her hair. But this time, instead of her stomach losing its dinner, she lost what was left in her small intestines at the other end of her.

It was degrading, and perhaps that's what decided her. If this were her fate, then so be it. The least she could do was to stop cowering in fear. Since that was exactly what he wanted, then she'd be damned if she would give it to him.

Thus, when next he came close, she took action, doing the first thing she could think of to do. After all, what did it matter? They were going to kill her in the most feminine, and probably the most horrible way possible.

She spit in his face.

Immediately he slapped her. But though the hit stung, it felt good. It was all she had . . . defiance . . . and so long as she was sane, she would resist him to the end.

She hadn't counted on what happened next, however. He picked her up by her hair, brought a knife to her scalp and began to cut.

She screamed. And he laughed, the wickedness of his smile the last thing she beheld before she fell forward into a dead faint.

* * *

White Thunder heard Sarah's screams as if from outside himself. He knew at once what it meant.

Silently he cursed himself for his stupidity. He'd made two mistakes. Big mistakes.

The first was that he'd gone off the trail to look for roots. He'd seen the plants on his trek through the woods, and he'd thought there was plenty of time to dig them and get back to the shelter before any possible trouble might befall them. But his second and major error was being unaware of the environment around him. He'd been so engrossed in hunting for the roots, he hadn't felt the presence of some-one else in these woods.

It could prove to be a deadly blunder. Could he cor-rect it?

With all his strength, he shot forward, sprinting back toward the shelter. As he ran, he checked his gun for readi-ness. He felt for his other weapons, which were on his belt, awaiting only his hand to use them. Satisfied, he practically flew over the forest floor.

As he came within sight of the valley where the shelter lay, he sighted five of them. Three Ottawa, two French. He watched as two of the Ottawa pulled Sarah out of the shel-ter, one of them slung her over his shoulder, and the two marched off.

Instinct made him long to cry out and attack at once, but he held himself back. Not yet. They were five and they were ready for a fight, their guns held primed. He wasn't going to be of any use to Sarah if he himself was killed immediately.

Let him first take them down with him.

Was there anything he could use to his advantage? He could think of only one circumstance that might be in his favor, and that was the element of surprise. But even that might not be helpful, for these warriors were wise enough to know that a white woman wouldn't be in the woods alone.

Watching them, devising a plan, he crept from place to place in the environment surrounding the shelter. He waited until he had a good shot. He delayed, checking his front sight; he fired. A man dropped; it was the remaining Indian.

That was it—his only advantage—surprise. Because the musket had only the one shot, White Thunder threw it to the ground and leapt down into the enemy's midst, his hatchet and war club drawn and ready. The Frenchman saw him coming and aimed a swing at him, but White Thunder ducked, and with a back hand, sent a fatal blow into the man's middle section.

He was down.

There was one man left, but this one was ready for him, and had his rifle pointed straight at White Thunder. He fired. White Thunder ducked.

The shot flew by, and White Thunder instantly sprang up and met him with his hatchet, but the man dodged and White Thunder had to spin around in a split second to avoid a fatal backhand. He aimed his tomahawk straight at the Frenchman's head, but again the man parried, the steel of their weapons clanged.

Thinking fast, White Thunder knew he had to do damage quickly, before the Frenchman did irreparable harm to him. Slamming his hatchet straight at the Frenchman's shooting arm, White Thunder plunged his weapon unswervingly into the man's elbow. It cracked; the arm hung useless.

That did it. The Frenchman knew he was hurt beyond repair, but he was big and predatory and he aimed a fatal blow at White Thunder with his left arm. But it lacked strength. White Thunder easily ducked, then with another pitch of his hatchet, struck the mortal blow. All three men were down.

But there were two more Ottawa and they had Sarah. And they were long since gone.

Picking up the Frenchmen's guns and ammunition, White Thunder rushed back to pluck up his own gun, then darted forward to hit upon the Ottawas' trail. There it was, right in front of him.

As he sped over the ground, following their footprints, White Thunder only hoped he wouldn't be too late.

Eighteen

The Ottawa were moving fast, but they were also covering their tracks. The warriors were smart. They'd known White Thunder would come after them if he survived the fight with their three cohorts.

Their trail was difficult. Several times White Thunder had been led off on a false trail, and had been forced to go back and start afresh. It was slow work; slow at a time when speed was crucial.

But there was one thing he knew that the Ottawa didn't: He had survived. If he lingered here on their trail, if he pretended he'd been taken down by the French, and that no one was following them—perhaps waiting until the last minute to attack, White Thunder might gain an advantage.

Finally, after grueling hours spent tracking, he found them. Luckily for him, his ploy had worked, and they must have assumed he'd been killed, because no one was standing guard, a very unwise move.

White Thunder smiled.

He spotted Sarah, and what he saw made his blood boil. Tied to a tree, she was bare-chested and exposed. Plus, there was a gash over her breasts. Even now, she was bleeding. Had he been a younger man, he might have rushed in upon them now, spoiling whatever edge he might have.

Older and wiser, he positioned himself into a good shooting posture. That's when he saw Sarah spit in one of the Ottawas' eye, and he smiled again. Not only did she possess a gentle nature—one that he had witnessed on more than one occasion—if pressed, she could be as dangerous as a she-cat.

But the Ottawa went too far. He slapped her. Older he might be, but even still, White Thunder could barely contain himself from taking immediate action. He knew, however, that he must control his anger. One single, sure shot was better than taking a chance at wrestling—and losing.

White Thunder watched as the Ottawa pulled her up by the hair, watched also as he brought a knife to her scalp. She fainted, but the Ottawa was having none of that, and he shook her awake.

White Thunder couldn't remember a time he had felt more enraged. He took very careful aim, for the Ottawa was too close to Sarah, and he dare not miss.

He had the Ottawa in his front sight; it would be a fatal shot to the head. White Thunder pulled the trigger. Sarah screamed, and the Ottawa jerked sideways from the strength of the blast. He didn't move.

But his friend, the other Ottawa, sprung to his feet, and crouching low, peered off in every direction. There was one other fine point these two hadn't realized.

White Thunder possessed another rifle, taken from the Frenchmen. He leveled a clear shot, aiming for the Ottawa's head. He pulled the trigger, heard Sarah scream yet again, then watched to see the result. The last Ottawa crumpled over, dead.

White Thunder waited only a moment to determine if either of the two Indians would get up. Carefully, slowly, he himself rose onto his feet and rushed forward to inspect the men before he turned his attention to Sarah.

What he saw wrenched at his heart. Her face was wet with tears, she was naked from her shoulders down to her waist and her skirts were ripped into rags.

"Mr. Thunder," she sobbed, falling forward onto her knees. "I thought you were dead."

He rushed to her, knelt in front of her and reached down to cut the bonds holding her hands. "Not yet," he said gently. "Not yet."

Once she was free, she fell into his arms, where she cried until he thought his heart might likely break.

"It's all my fault," she said. "If I hadn't cried out, they—"

"Shhh." He massaged her head, glorying in the feel of her silky locks beneath his fingers, thankful that she was alive and in his arms again. "I share the fault, if there is any to be found," he said. "Had I been more aware of my surroundings, I would have been able to avoid this. Come, let's leave here and fast, before more Ottawa come to find their friends."

"Yes," she said. "Yes."

Taking off his shirt, he slipped it over her head, and helping her to her feet, he grasped her hand in his and they fled into the forest.

They shot through the woods as if demons were after them. Perhaps they were. Still, it was a different speed of travel than that of their earlier wanderings. Whereas before, they two had traversed slowly, taking one delayed step at a time—which had allowed White Thunder the opportunity to examine every piece of ground—now they sprinted over what was clearly a trail. They dashed up forest-covered hills, down into lush valleys and skirted every bend. They splashed through icy-cold streams, not paying any attention to their depths, and sometimes they had to swim. Always they pressed forward, and at a maddening pace.

Luckily, there was a full moon this night. It lit their path, but it didn't allow Sarah to see the changes in the elevations of their path ahead of time, and she found herself stumbling more often than not. There was nothing for it, however, but to pick herself up and match her pace as well as she was able to with White Thunder's. She couldn't see as well as she ought in the dim, silvery light cast here and there by the moon, and the stark tree branches caught at the sleeves of the shirt that White Thunder had loaned her. Sarah's own petticoats snagged on the stickers, further tearing her underclothes.

Above her the sky was black, with contrasting light from the full moon and stars, but so fast was their haste, Sarah didn't dare spare more than a quick glance upward. Instead she concentrated on placing one foot in front of the other, and keeping herself upright and on the tail of White Thunder.

The atmosphere of the forest was oxygen filled at this time of night, she noticed; its fragrance was uplifting to her spirits. It was as though the forest itself were lending the two of them a helping hand. Even the wind conspired to aid in their escape, for it was at their back.

But what circumstance were they escaping? Or who? And why were they hurrying? Weren't the Ottawa dead?

The question, though an urgent one in her opinion, went unasked, simply for lack of the opportunity of posing it.

Sarah was out of breath when White Thunder at last broke his pace and settled into a trot. Simply because she couldn't run as fast as he, Sarah had drawn a ways back from him. With his slowdown, at last she had an opportunity to catch up with him.

As soon as she came into view of him, however, they pressed forward yet again. And though the trot was more to her liking, she still lagged far behind.

At last, they came to an open meadow, and White Thunder stopped at the edge. He was gazing out at it, looking as though he had been frozen in his tracks.

Sarah was breathing hard and fast as she drew level with him, and now that she had come to a standstill, she observed her breath was mirrored on the air. Interestingly, the cold air, usually intolerable to her, felt good this night.

As soon as she caught her breath, she asked, "Why are we running?"

He brought a finger to his lips.

Immediately she ceased not only all talk, but all movement, too. But she couldn't help wondering what was wrong. Were there other enemies about? She hadn't seen any.

But then, she might not be aware of them. For good or for bad, Sarah was more than sadly aware that her experience in the woods left much room for improvement.

And then, without saying a word to her, White Thunder indicated that she was to follow him. They crept low, skirting the woods on the edge of the meadow. They stopped at each moonlit shadow and darkened silhouette.

But at last, he seemed satisfied, and he signaled to her that she was to follow, and do as he did. That he then came down onto his belly and forearms was almost asking too much of her, she thought. However, he was already crawling across the meadow. She was supposed to do the same? In petticoats?

Sighing deeply, Sarah realized that she had no option. Not if she wished to keep up with White Thunder. Coming down onto all fours, she fell onto her belly, her elbows taking the brunt of the weight of her body.

The fresh scent of grass, dirt and the nightly dew that covered everything felt lightweight on her lungs as she inhaled several deep breaths. Though they were long since ruined, Sarah realized that her petticoats would be forever grass-stained.

It was slow going, but at long last, they had crossed the meadow. Once they reached the other side, and were again within the shadowy midst of the forest, White Thunder came up to his feet, and struck out, again at a maddening pace. Sarah followed. Tired though she was, her legs still kept sending her forward. Somehow she made them obey her desire to hurry.

It was practically dawn by the time they stopped. Exhausted, Sarah fell to the ground and probably would have slept right where she had dropped had White Thunder been of a mind to let her.

Indeed, at first it seemed that he might. He let her rest while he constructed another one of his temporary shelters, made from logs, branches and leaves that were strewn on the forest floor. Sarah watched him with tired eyes as he landscaped around the shelter, fixing a log here, a branch there, so that to the untrained eye, their abode would be unseen. Then coming back for her, he bent to pick her up, straightening her hair back from her face as he brought her into his arms.

He said naught as he lay her down on their bed within the shelter. It was a bed that he had fashioned from nothing more than fresh pine boughs and the grasses of the forest, with a blanket thrown atop it. But to Sarah, the bed felt as if she'd sunk into the most comfortable featherbed she'd ever known.

He kissed her; she smiled and then, no sooner had she rested her head against the blanket than she fell to sleep.

Amazingly, her rest was dream free. And if not for the warm arms that held her securely all the morning through, she might have thought she was back in Albany, alone in her bed, and that none of this had ever happened.

* * *

They slept from morning 'til dusk that first day. Then, after a snack of dried meat, water and a few shared kisses, they again slept through the night and on into the next day. Indeed, when Sarah at last awoke, the sun was in the western sky and was showing off its artistry over the land in pinks, blues and oranges. Scents of moss, pine, twigs and dead wood assured her that she was still on the run, not back in Albany in her lonely, yet safe bed.

She awoke with a start, immediately anxious. If not in Albany, where was she? Had she and White Thunder escaped into safety? Were there still enemies hunting them? Looking up, she stared straight into "rafters" of twigs, and branches of maple, oak and birch. Nothing unusual there. These were the common "ceilings" of the temporary shelters.

Why this sense of turbulence? Was it because of Miss Marisa? Sarah hadn't forgotten she couldn't rest until she found Marisa and if possible warned her of the danger awaiting her in Albany.

Or was it? . . . Her stomach dropped. The memory of an Ottawa warrior, with black-painted face, white teeth and an evil smile, threatening to murder her in the worst possible way, stirred in front of her, as though he were here now haunting her. She almost screamed, but she curbed the instinct. Never again would she cry out without knowing who or what was around her.

She lay perfectly still, afraid to move. Eventually, however, when nothing untoward happened, she chanced to stretch. That's when it became very apparent to her that something else was very wrong: She was completely naked beneath this covering.

She didn't remember having gone to bed in the nude. Tired, she most definitely had been, but she was certain she would have remembered removing all of her clothes.

Where was White Thunder?

Most likely, he was the one responsible for her state of undress. But why? Sitting up as quietly as possible—for there wasn't the room to stand—she brought the blanket up with her, wrapped it around her and sat forward to peer out through the cracks in their shelter. Was it safe to leave?

While she sat debating the pros and cons of "stay" or "go," she caught sight of White Thunder, who was climbing up from a ridge below. Were they camped on a hill or mountaintop? Now that she thought of it, she had noticed as they had fled over hill and dale last night that the terrain had sloped gradually upward.

He was shirtless, and despite her anxiety, she took several moments to admire this very handsome man. His chest was broad and muscular, as though he were used to the hard work of carrying game for miles on his shoulders. His chest was also wet, Indeed, he was wet all over, and she wondered where the stream was that he had used for bathing. Sniffing the air around her, she was well aware that she needed to visit that stream, also.

Beneath the pale rays of the setting sun, his figure took on the appearance of being engulfed in a mystical kind of haze, and she spent several moments watching him, her spirit full of silent admiration. He wore skin-tight leggings, she noted, which accentuated the muscular beauty of his legs. Those leggings were also thigh-high, exposing the upper part of his thigh and the outline of his buttocks to the fancy of her feminine eye. And she did look.

Those leggings were tied at the knee with strips of red-fringed cloth, and they fell down and covered a good portion of his moccasins. A breechcloth of navy-and-red cloth fell down in front of him and in back, and it served two purposes that she could see: support and masculine modesty.

His figure exuded male beauty, despite the fact that his chest and arms displayed several red, blue and black tattoos in designs of circles and straight lines. His stomach was flat, and tied around his waist was his belt where hung his tomahawk, ax, war club and several knives. In his hand was his ever-present rifle and strung around his shoulders crisscross over his chest were belts and bags for his powder horn and ammunition. His arms were muscular, and except for two bands that spanned his forearms, they were bare.

His hair was clipped close to his head, with a longer strip of hair that ran down the center of his head, much like the men's mohawk style, except that he wasn't bald and this man's hair was exceptionally long in back.

He looked incredibly dear, sexy and handsome, and something very warm stirred within her. This was the man who had saved her life three times now; the same and only man to whom she had ever given her complete devotion. And she wouldn't have been quite human had she not wished to give him everything that was in her to give. But what?

He demanded so little of her.

At present, he appeared to be at his ease, which prompted her to think that perhaps they were in a safe place. On the chance that this might be so, she poked her head out through the entry flap and said, "Hello, sir."

He looked up at her and smiled. "Hello," he responded warmly as he climbed the rest of the way to the summit where he had set up their camp.

She said, "Mr. Thunder, do you know what has happened to my clothes?"

"I washed them," he replied. "They are drying."

"*You* washed them?"

"*Nyoh*, that is so."

Sarah was taken aback. Having spent most of her life

as a maid attending to others' needs, she tried to recall if anyone had ever washed her clothes for her. If it were so, she couldn't remember it.

"I also mended your blouse."

This last had the effect of startling her. What sort of a man was this, who not only rescued a maid from certain death, but then mended the clothing that had been torn in the process?

She said, "Thank you, sir, that was kind of you. But unnecessary. I could have taken care of it myself."

"True," he replied, "but you were sleeping and I didn't wish to disturb you. Your clothing, however, needed attention."

Remembering the fact that her captors hadn't allowed her the decency to relieve herself privately, she was well aware of this fact. For a moment, embarrassment consumed her, realizing that he was probably understating his case.

But she had a question, and she asked, "How did you accomplish mending my bodice? Did you bring needle and thread with you?"

"*Neh*. However, I always carry sinew and a sharpened tooth for poking holes. It is a necessity, since one often needs to repair or make new moccasins when traveling."

An emotion, similar to gratitude, but all mixed up with respect and love, gripped her and was threatening to engulf her completely. For a moment, she felt overwhelmed. Indeed, tears filled her eyes, and a knot seemed to have developed in her throat. Immediately she was gripped by the realization of how kind this man was. Yes, he was a toughened man, he was a warrior and he had shown his ability against great odds. But she thought that this one trait outshone them all. He was kind.

"Come here," he said as he squatted in front of their entrance and pushed back the pine boughs that they were using as an entry flap. "I have something to show you."

"Is it safe, sir?"

"It is."

"But I think I should stay here. You see, I have no clothes on."

He grinned. "Is that an invitation?"

She looked down, then up and smiled back at him. "Perhaps, but only after I have bathed."

"Come," he said, holding out his hand to her. "If you need a bath, I will take you where you may have one."

She hesitated only a moment longer before she reached forward and placed her hand in his. He helped her to crawl out of their temporary refuge, for she had hold of her only covering, this blanket.

He asked, "Are you still wearing your moccasins?"

She glanced down. It felt like she was, but . . . "Yes," she said, "I believe I am." She grinned. "During our travels, they have begun to feel as if they are a part of my feet. Will I need them?"

"You will. The way is paved with sharp rocks. Come."

He led her down the steep, rocky bluff he had recently climbed, lending her his support when she slipped, which was often. Trees, deciduous and pine alike, had taken root on this otherwise slippery sloop, their branches and roots creating footfalls and handholds. In the distance, she could hear the babble of a fast moving stream. Interestingly, the sound was soothing.

At last he brought her down to a ledge that looked out over a narrow valley that sat between two peaks. In the middle and at the bottom of these peaks ran the crystal-clear stream she'd been hearing, and on each side of it were lush areas of grasses, now brown, and trees, bushes and shrubs. Here were willow trees, birch, maple and oak trees, as well as berry bushes and red sumac guarding the water. The colors of brown and gold dominated the landscape, and though the trees were barren at this time of year, this stretch of land looked cared for, as though it were a park. Off in the distance, branches from the willow trees dipped in and out of the water lazily, as though they moved in time to the music of a cool wind.

Above them, the sky was a deep blue, she noted, with white, fluffy clouds spotting the heavens. There was a hummingbird that seemed interested in their goings-on, and it flitted in and around them in its quest to find a sweet treat. Sarah sighed. It would appear that they were safe here.

She said, "'Tis beautiful. Where are we?"

"We are deep in the Adirondack Mountains."

"Deep in the Adirondack Mountains. The Adirondacks. Tell me, I had heard that these mountains are named for an Indian tribe. Is that true?"

"It is," he said, "and the word itself is from our language and means 'eaters of bark.' This is what we called these people when the Seneca first came to this country. Our elders tell us that they flavored their food with bark, thus their name."

"When your people first came here? Then your people are not originally from this place?"

"*Neh*, no," he replied. "The old stories tell us that long ago, perhaps as long as a thousand or more years in our past, we lived in the west, near what the people say was a big river. But my people left that place and came east."

"I didn't know that. I had assumed you had always been here."

"Perhaps all people come from somewhere. Did you know that it is because of the Adirondacks that we of the Iroquois value freedom as much as we do?"

"No."

"Would you like to hear how that came about?"

"Indeed."

He nodded, and placing his arm around her, he continued, "The story goes like this: The Adirondack people were very different from us, and we fought many battles with them. They were good warriors and they defeated us in battle after battle, and a dark period hung over our people. We were forced to pay the Adirondacks a tribute of skins and meat, as well as much of our crops. But my people remembered how it was to be free, and they longed to be unfettered again—as free as the eagle. And so they planned to escape. They schemed for years. When at last the people had a good store of food and were prepared, they stole away, sending out their canoes upon the river that the English call the St. Lawrence."

"Were they successful?"

"Not at first, for the Adirondacks had much to lose if my people escaped, and so they came after them. My people were heavily burdened with women and children, and the Adirondack men were not. A great battle commenced and the Iroquois were almost wiped out. But the Creator heard the people's cries, and took pity on them, for He believes that all His children should be free.

"He sent a storm so forceful that day that the Adirondacks were almost wiped out. After that, they returned to their villages, never to bother us again. And so it is that we owe ourselves, our crops, our meat and food to no one. We will always be free."

"Yes," she said, "may it always be so. If there is one idea that you have impressed upon me, it is that a people should be free."

"*Nyoh*, yes," he said simply. "Now come, there is much privacy here. The creek is but a short distance from our camp and we are alone, I believe. You can bathe in the stream if you wish and wash your wounds, for this is a special place. I'll help you to the water and, if you will allow me, I'll assist you to bathe."

"*You* would help me bathe?"

He grinned at her, his look more than a little seductive. "I would. Your wounds need to be tended, and it's best if I do that. And besides, I think you might like the manner in which I clean you."

Sarah shook her head, but she smiled back at him all the same. For a moment, if a moment only, the nightmare faded. If only it would go away for good.

Nineteen

"Why is it warm here, when it's been so cold else-where?" she asked. "Aren't we higher in the moun-tains? Should it not be cold?"

White Thunder grinned as he helped her to negotiate, one slow step at a time, the grassy slope to the stream's shoreline. He said, "I think the English call it 'Indian summer.'"

"Oh, yes, of course," she said, and he watched as she cast him a tender look. "I'm glad that it's warm today," she continued. "I have great need of a bath, but unlike you, my body does not crave an icy swim."

"Careful," he said as she negotiated a steep passage. "Now, do not be deceived. The water is cold, but the air is warm. Here." He stooped down to pick some goldenrod growing close to hand, and offered it to her. "This makes a good soap for hair and body."

"It does? Just the plant all by itself? I don't have to do anything with it?"

"You have never used this?"

She shook her head.

"Then it truly is best that I wash you."

Delicate color came quickly to her countenance and spread out slowly over her cheeks. Watching her, White Thunder found himself much fascinated. It wasn't that he was intentionally trying to cause her embarrassment; these little details about her simply endeared her to him.

He said, "We have been intimate for many weeks now. And still I embarrass you?"

"Yes." She gazed away from him. "Don't you see? There's a difference, sir. I have always been fully dressed when we make love . . . except a few times recently, perhaps . . . But to undress, here in the light of day, fully upright and in complete view of you . . ."

"You will come to love it, and I will, also," he said quite honestly, "because I won't give you a chance to be embarrassed. Besides, soon the evening will be spreading its dim shadows around us, and it will give you some protection from my leering."

Again, she smiled, but still she hesitated. "I don't know . . ."

He bent and kissed her long and hard, his lips and tongue seeking out the sweet recess of hers. While it wasn't his intention to make love to her here and now, the caress caused such an instantaneous response from her that his body reacted in a way that promised much pleasure, were he to follow up on it.

But he was not in such a mind. She needed time to recover. After her ordeal, she required peace, and he would see that she had it.

But that didn't mean he couldn't tease her.

As they kissed, he rocked the lower part of his body against hers and reached down to her buttocks to pull her in close. He even fought her for hold over the blanket. But she won, clutching it firmly to her bosom.

Breaking off the kiss, she asked, "Why did we have to run so hard for so long last night?"

"Bad spirits there," he answered her. "Not a place to linger. It was also in Abenaki Territory, enemy of the Iroquois. In rescuing you, we made much noise, and the Abenaki will investigate it. When they do, they will see that a Seneca was there, and they will try to find me. But this place where we are now has long been a symbol of peace for all tribes. It is on the border of Abenaki Territory, but they do not control it. All tribes come here because here one can more easily talk to the Creator. This is His safe haven. But to arrive here safely, we had to hurry."

"Ah, now I understand," she said. "And that meadow—why did we have to crawl across it?"

"Abenaki were in those woods last night. Did you not see their signs?"

"I little know what to look for, sir."

He nodded. "Their prints were on the trail and they were fresh, meaning that they were crawling in those woods. If we had crossed that place upright, we would have been easily seen, especially because there was a full moon."

"Oh." She looked down, then up, her gaze settling on something over his shoulder. "Look there on those tree branches," she said, pointing. "There are my clothes drying. Do you think they're ready for me to wear yet?"

"*Neh*, I have only just washed them. But come," he said, "I still see fear in your eyes from your experience, and there is a sadness that I sense in your spirit. Let us bathe you in the fresh water here, and see if it might help to cleanse the body . . . and perhaps even more." Bending to kiss her again, he loosened her grip on the blanket then let it fall to the ground. He stepped back to admire her breasts, her rounded buttocks and the splattering of hair between her legs. But it was obvious that she was uncomfortable under his scrutiny, and not wishing to stir up awkward emotions, he picked her up in his arms and stepped to the water.

The shoreline was rocky, and long grasses grew up close to the bubbling water, which swirled over the rocks in its path. But there was nothing unusual in this; it was all as it should be, and he strode through the grass and waded out into the fast-moving stream.

To him, the water was refreshing, but he feared that she would find it too cold. Luckily this rivulet wasn't deep, and it would be possible to gradually acquaint her with its temperature. At this part of the stream, the water came only to mid-calf level, which allowed him to kneel, come down on his haunches, then position her over his lap.

To say that he was not sexually excited by her and by holding her naked form in his arms would have been a terrible lie. Given a chance, he would have liked nothing better than to lock their bodies in the dance of love. It was simply that he knew that what she needed most at present was comfort.

"Place your arms around my neck," he said, "so that if you slip, you won't be subjected to a cold dunking."

She did as he asked, and bending over her, he removed each of her moccasins, throwing them to shore. He washed her feet, massaging them in the process. She sighed and melted against him as though she might likely go to sleep.

However, the feel of her skin, silky and smooth against his fingertips, was having an effect on him that was purely carnal. Indeed, touching her was as potent an aphrodisiac as if she had asked for his lovemaking, and despite the cold water, he found his body more than ready for her.

But he reminded himself that it was not his intention to make love to her now. She was fearful. She was hurting. He could see it in her demeanor, could feel it in the slight jerks and shivers of her body.

His arms tightened around her. If he could, he would keep her with him always.

To keep her with him always. It was a potent thought, and as he hid his face in the silky tresses of her hair, he realized that it was time to come face to face with a truth: He loved her.

He'd denied it to himself, telling himself that what he felt for her was nothing more than an intense admiration. Certainly, he had offered her marriage, especially when it seemed likely that they might have created a child. But love?

It had come at a time when he hadn't wanted to love anyone again, had even promised himself it would never happen. Love could hurt.

But it could also be healing, he amended. Hadn't she proved that to him? Wasn't he a living result?

Because his thoughts were profound, he swallowed hard, and kissed the side of her face and her cheeks. Then he rubbed his face against hers. In time, he said, "After we wash your body of its nightmare experience, I have something to give you that I think will help to heal your fear and grief."

"Oh? What is it?"

He reached into one of the bags that were draped over his shoulders, and pulled out a string of white-and-purple-beaded wampum.

"Wampum?" she asked, and sat up, crossing her arms over her chest. She looked surprised, and amazingly, she seemed suddenly upset.

He said, "*Nyoh*, yes, it is wampum."

"I don't understand, sir. After all we've been through, I . . ."

This was not the response he had expected, and he asked, "Is something wrong?"

"Sir, what is it you are saying to me? Is this meant to be an insult?"

He frowned at her. "*Neh*, the opposite is true. I am showing you great respect."

"Then why have you suddenly decided to give me Indian money? Perhaps it's not like this in your society, but in mine when a man gives a woman money after they've made love . . ."

At last he understood her meaning, and he said, "Wampum is not money. Is that what you think it is?"

"I do, sir."

He shook his head in disgust. "I fear some trader has stuck you with a great misunderstanding. Wampum is not used as money. It never has been. The English, with his gold and silver coins, has assigned a value to wampum that is in error."

"But I have heard that people will trade fortunes for it. So if not money, then what is it?"

"Its use," he replied, "is to cure the mind of the madness of grief, to open the throat so that a person may speak openly and at free will, and it is given to take away the heartache of losing someone close to you. Come here." He sat forward to gather her into his arms and bring her back in close to him. "It is my desire to help ease the fear and grief that your experience has brought you. This is the correct use of wampum."

She sat silently for the space of a moment. "I understand, I think," she said at last. "You were trying to help me, and I misunderstood. I deeply apologize, and I thank you for your consideration."

He nodded.

"But now you have excited my curiosity. What exactly is wampum?"

"That will take some explaining," he said. "If you will settle back here in my arms, I'll finish washing you, and I'll tell you about it."

She did as he asked, and he began rubbing her legs with water and the sand from the bottom of the stream. He said, "There are three words that are used to banish what we of the Iroquois call the insanity of grief. Long ago, the two men who founded the Iroquois Confederacy sought to console a person who was consumed with grief."

While he was speaking, his touch had explored higher and higher up on her thigh.

"Hmm . . . that feels good," she said. "But tell me more. What are the three words?" Meanwhile, she shifted position so that his hand was captured between her legs, there at their junction.

He swallowed. "They are called the Three Bare Words, and they are the first few words that the Peacemaker spoke to Hiawatha in founding our Confederation. It is our Condolence Ceremony, which is performed with the intent of wiping away the insanity caused by grief, a madness that brings about endless fighting and war."

While he was speaking, she had parted her legs slightly, and he was not slow on the uptake. He placed his hand on her where he knew she ached to be rubbed, and he gave her what she appeared to need. In response, she moved her hips against the pressure he was exerting, and with the magic of his fingers he began to love her.

"We can talk about this later," he said.

As she moved her body against his hand, she murmured, "Yes."

He sighed, and keeping his voice low and his fingers intent at their task, he said, "It has not been my intention to make love to you while you are still recovering from your fear. But if you want it . . ."

She didn't answer all at one time, though her legs had parted wider and she moved in time with the rhythm of his fingers. She was laid out before him like a feast, and not only did he partake, looking his fill at her, but by his touch alone, he was bringing her to a release.

"Don't you believe, sir, that making love is part of the healing process?" And though they were speaking all around it, the truth was that he was becoming very excited. Apparently she was, also.

He answered, "I believe it might be . . . if one is willing."

Her hips were moving faster now against his fingers, and when she moaned, then whispered, "I'm willing," he thought he might likely be the luckiest man alive. He groaned.

Her lips were still parted, and the invitation she provided would have required a saint to resist; he was hardly that. Slowly his head descended toward hers, and when his lips took possession of hers, she moaned while she squirmed hard against him.

It was a long, slow kiss, during which he repositioned her, settling her in front of him, with her legs wrapped around his waist. Then he came up onto his knees and holding her up by her buttocks, he settled her over his shaft. Slowly he entered her.

She was hot, she was wet; and so aroused was she, he sensed she was already close to her peak. It was an erotic position, and they made love as if their lives depended on it.

As he thrust into her, he said, "I think I died a thousand deaths when that Ottawa warrior slapped you."

"I have never been so frightened."

"Shhh. I know."

They were working themselves up into a frenzy of sexual tension, and his thrusts had become fast, jerky and driven. He knew she was close to her pinnacle. And when she rose up to fully experience that pleasure, he met her with his own need, spilling his seed into her.

On and on the pleasure lengthened, extending way beyond the physical deed. And as he drifted back to earth, he came to realize that his life from this point forward would be different. He was not the same man he had been before he had met her. She was now as much a part of him as was his own identity. With her, he was whole.

As they continued to move against each other in the

aftermath of love, he sat back on his heels, bringing her with him. He whispered, "I would do most anything for you."

With her arms swung around his neck and her body intimately connected to his, she said, "I, too."

Twenty

The love they created between them was pure, was good and was a little like magic. Perhaps, as she'd said, it was what was needed to help her to heal. He hoped it was so, for it was not within him to purposely bring her more heartache.

At present, she was wrapped around him. And he had little desire to unsettle her. And so with himself still firmly encased within her warmth, he began to finish the job of washing her body, starting with her legs and thighs.

In time, his manhood returned to its more usual state and when it did, he lifted her up above him slightly so as to wash her there, too. Then he rinsed the dirt from her arms, her breasts and her back. But when he came to her chest, he hesitated.

Setting her slightly away from him, he traced the slash that had been made by the Ottawa warrior and asked, "Does this hurt?"

"A bit," she said, nodding.

He let off touching it to splash fresh water on the wound, then sneaked in a few massages of her breasts before he reached down into the water, his hand seeking the mud in the river's bed. Grabbing a handful of it, he dabbed it onto the cut.

She jerked a little, then settled back into his arms, her own arms hugging him firmly around his neck.

Interestingly, she didn't object to the movement of the cold water over her body or to the mud that he had spread over her chest. Rather, it seemed as if she'd fallen asleep. But he wasn't done yet.

He would wash away her fear and her grief. Somehow, he would banish it from her mind. He only wished it were as easy as cleaning the body.

He said, his voice no louder than a whisper, "Are you ready for me to wash your hair?"

Her answer was a sigh. "Will it be cold?"

"I fear it will be, for I'll have to submerge it into the stream."

"Must we?" She gritted her teeth. "Truly, sir, you needn't continue to wash me. I'm a big girl now and I can do the job myself."

"You would deny me the fantasy of my dream come true?"

She laughed, and the sound of it was as pretty as she was.

"Besides," he continued, "if I hold you crossways over my lap, it might not be too cold."

She sighed. "I think, sir, that I am putty in your hands for the moment. Do with me as you will."

He growled. And when an answering moan escaped her lips, he almost lost his resolve. But then, with trusting eyes, she stared up at him innocently, and said, "Sir, I think I should tell you something."

He raised an eyebrow in response, an encouragement for her to continue.

"It may or may not matter to you. But . . ." She hesitated. "I . . . I've fallen in love with you."

Every nerve ending within his body suddenly screamed at him to do something, anything. He pulled her hard and fast against him, practically crushing her.

So lost was he for words, he swallowed several times before he was at last able to utter simply, "I, too."

She backed up slightly from him, and said, "Did I hear that right, sir? Did you say that—"

"You did. I love you." He said it simply.

She shifted until she was so close to him that he could feel the imprint of her breasts against his chest, then she said, "But what about Wild Mint and your promise—"

"I love you," he said again, this time more firmly. "I have for many days, perhaps weeks, but until I saw you with those Ottawa warriors and realized I could lose you, I hadn't had the courage to admit it, even to myself."

Sarah sat up only inches away, presenting him with the glorious picture of a nude woman. Ah, what a fortunate man he was.

"And Wild Mint?"

"She will always have a place in my heart, and my duty remains as it has been for years," he said honestly. "But it's been fifteen years and . . . I have changed. No longer do I wish to join her in death. Indeed, I have come to know life, and it is a life I would like to share with you."

"I, too, feel this way," she said, hugging him tightly. "But we must face the fact that we are from two different worlds, sir. You know this. When we're here, separated from the rest of society, it seems that it would be a matter of simplicity to create our lives with each other. But other people's will sometimes gets in the way. And I am still an indentured servant, with five years left to serve. Surely, sir, you understand, for we have discussed this at length. After five years, I will be free, and without the worry of being found if I tried to escape, and then forced into service for the rest of my life."

"Shhh." He pulled her face in toward his until her head fit into the crook of his neck. "I know, but we have come here to wash away your grief, not add to it. Someday, we will have to face this, together. But for now, we are still married, if only because we have not yet had to part. And if we never part . . ."

He felt her smile, heard her slight chuckle there against his shoulder.

"We cannot fight all the battles that lie before us on this one day. It's true that the moment may yet come when it appears we will have to part, but that it is not here now. We have time to prepare. Meanwhile, let us have this one evening without worry."

She nodded.

"Now, it was not in my thoughts," he said, "to make love to you here, now, in this stream. I think the shore would be a more comfortable place. But first we should wash your hair."

"I am honored, sir, that you are thinking of my comfort," she said as she changed her position yet again, so that instead of straddling him, she was merely sitting in his lap. "You have my best interests at heart, and I thank you. But, Mr. White Thunder," she said, "if I am to wash my hair, then I should swim, and so should you. And, sir, forgive me, but I believe you have on too many clothes."

He closed his eyes and smiled. What had he done to deserve such pleasure? He said, "That is easily remedied."

He accommodated her at once, shifting position so that he could come up to his feet. He still held her firmly in his arms, but since he was now ambulant, he waded to the shoreline.

Once there, he let her down so that she was standing on her own, and as quickly as he could, he removed his leggings and the belts and straps that he wore over his chest and shoulders. But he left on his breechcloth, as well as several of his weapons.

"Mr. Thunder, you are not naked, as I am."

"I am as naked as I can get," he explained. "Until I am within the safety of a Seneca village, I cannot relax and leave my weapons behind me. This may be the Creator's own valley, but there are those who do not respect even the Creator of all things. Therefore my tomahawk, my knives and my war club will remain with me."

"If that be the case," she said, "then I shall swim as I usually do—in my chemise."

He nodded. "Though I fear it is not much protection," he said, "for it is so flimsy that I can see beyond its threads to the treasure beneath. But if you desire it, I'll get it for you."

"That would be most kind of you."

The tree where he had laid out her clothes to dry was not far, and he was back in an instant. He held the chemise out at arm's length. "Is this what you need?"

"It is." She reached for it.

But he withdrew it before she could take hold of it.

She gave him a puzzled glance.

His response was a smile. "Come and get it."

"Sir?"

With his hand, he urged her to come forward. Again, he held the garment out toward her.

She took a step toward him, another, then she lunged at him, grabbing for the chemise.

But he sidestepped her easily, and caught her so she didn't fall. He tickled her a little, too, and quite expectedly, she giggled.

"You have to learn to be quicker. Would you like to have another try at it?"

She gave him a wild leer. "I little know if I wish to play this game with you. sir. I seem to be the loser of it."

"Loser?" He shook his head and smiled at her. "I think you are the winner of all my attention."

That caused her to laugh again. It was a delight to hear.

"Mr. Thunder, I would like my chemise now."

"And so you shall have it." Again he held it out to her. "Miss Sarah, you simply need to be a little faster."

She shook her head, and he knew she was suppressing a smile. He held the chemise out to her.

"You have to hold it still," she demanded, "and you can't jerk it back when I reach for it."

He extended it from his body. "Do you see, I am holding it still."

"Yes, you are now. But you have to continue to hold it still, sir. Those are the rules."

He grinned at her. "And so I am holding it still for you."

She made to reach for it, but again he quickly moved it out of range.

"Sir, I said you had to hold it still."

"I was. I am," he said. "It was the fault of the wind, which moved my arm."

She sighed. "I fear the chemise is not to be seen on my body while I swim with you, is it?"

"I have no say over that, Miss Sarah. You have only to reach for it . . . and beat me."

She laughed. "It doesn't appear that this is going to happen, and I think I should take that swim while my body is still used to the temperature of the water, and while we still have light to see by. Already the sun is disappearing in the western sky."

"Then come," he said. "Let's swim before you get too cold, and while I can still look at you to my fill." He rushed toward her and took hold of her hand with his own—the hand that was holding the chemise. Quickly she grabbed it from him and slipped it over her head, letting it fall to its full length, which came to mid-calf on her.

She said, "Thank you, sir."

"You are welcome. But come, let's take that swim."

As he'd promised, he washed her hair with the goldenrod flowers, which he'd rubbed in his hands with water until they made a paste that could be spread through the hair.

"It's best to dry the plant first and then make the soap from that. But this will work," he'd said.

They'd washed each other's hair, and Sarah had curiously asked about the common Indian hairstyle of the Iroquois, the one known to most as the mohawk.

He'd run his hand over the top of his head, then said, "This is called the scalp lock, and it is a dare to the enemy. Most tribes take scalps to prove the accuracy of their war deeds. They are like the Englishman's metals, and they are honored in the same way."

"However," she commented, "one is bloody, and the other is not."

"Yet, they are obtained in the same manner, Miss Sarah, and for the same reason—war," he'd countered. "And war is not without blood. Perhaps the Indian way is better, because it is a reminder that the token is taken by sacrificing the life of another."

Sarah didn't have an instant reply to that, and so they'd fallen back into their animated romp in the water, mostly playing tag and splashing one another, for the water was only deep in particular places, which didn't allow for actual swimming. But it didn't matter. It was a perfect end to a memorable evening.

Indeed, she'd had so much fun, she'd almost forgotten about the torture. Almost.

The evening shadows finally chased the two of them from the water—that and the cold wind that arrived with the night air. By the time they were ready to leave, Sarah had discovered that her clothes were dry and she hurriedly slipped them on before White Thunder had the opportunity to get at them before her and tease her. At last she was fully dressed. It felt good.

"I'm hungry," she said as they began climbing up the slope that led to the summit, where they had set up camp. "What's for supper?"

"I fear we are still eating a diet of dried meat and berries. Perhaps tomorrow I might hunt and we will fix some fresh meat."

"I think dried meat and berries sound delicious." She followed him up the slope, placing her feet in the same footholds he'd made.

Before they reached the top, however, he turned to her and signaled her to silence and to remain where she was. Oh, no. Now what? Were they never to escape the enemy?

Her heartbeat picked up enough speed that she could hear its beating in her ears. Her stomach twisted as she watched White Thunder crawl up the remaining incline of the slope, watched as he quietly, carefully took out his tomahawk and took aim.

He let the projectile go and she heard a dull thump and the cry of whatever life he'd hit.

White Thunder turned back toward her, and signaled her to follow him on up the slope. Perhaps it wasn't as bad as she'd thought. She did as requested, dreading what she might find but knowing it had to be done.

White Thunder was grinning at her as she caught up to him, and he held out his hand to her. He said, "The Creator must have heard us speaking of our dull supper. Do you see what He put here, awaiting us?"

It was a deer, a buck.

"We will have fresh meat tonight."

To Sarah, whose duties had never included kitchen activities, the idea of skinning and preparing the meat was neither appealing nor even appetizing. Even that first time when he'd brought a deer to the cave, she hadn't helped him then. She had watched. But that was past, and she'd be darned now if she'd let him know that the task was hardly pleasant.

She grinned at him as though he might have presented her with a jeweled ring. "It's wonderful," she said. "We can make more dry meat."

"We can, but first there are parts of the animal that have to be eaten fresh after it is killed. The liver is one of those. We'll eat that tonight and make dry meat tomorrow."

"Yes, yes," said Sarah, who hoped she was feigning the same sort of enthusiasm for the task as White Thunder.

They set to work over the deer, and to Sarah's amazement, she discovered it wasn't as gruesome as she had thought. Indeed, with White Thunder at her side, she enjoyed the evening very much.

Twenty-one

The black-painted face of the Ottawa hung in mid-air in front of her. It had arms that reached out to grab her and sharp teeth to bite her. Inch by slow inch it cut her skin, taking part of it off, as though the Indian were skinning a deer.

It said, "I will make this into a robe for John Rathburn, who will enjoy it because it is made from your skin. He will like it because he owns you, body and soul."

"You shall not do this." Now it was Miss Marisa speaking, who had suddenly appeared in the middle of the Ottawa camp. "Miss Sarah's parents are guarding her and they will not let you do this to her," continued Marisa. "Come this way, Mr. and Mrs. Strong."

And then, there they were, Sarah's parents, staring at her with such loving expressions, they might have been alive. But they weren't alive. They'd been dead since . . .

Suddenly they were gone. They disappeared, and in their place came the Ottawa warrior once more, knife in hand. Closer and closer he came, and always he smiled. He brandished his weapon in front of her face. Then he reached for her, he cut off part of her hair, then plunged the knife into—

Sarah screamed and screamed and kept on screaming. White Thunder, now awake, sat up and pulled her into his embrace. He said nothing. He simply held her closely, pushing back her hair to caress her.

"It was so real," she cried. "It was as though he were here again, as though he had come for me."

White Thunder didn't reply. Nor did he ask who "he" was; perhaps he knew.

Gradually, he began to rock back and forth with her still in his arms. At length, he said, "It is possible that your body is not in harmony with itself, and that it might need some food and water to bring back its accord. Come, we have food here and water. Eat. Drink. Then let us sleep again— only I think you should remain within my arms for the rest of the night."

She nodded.

Because all their needs were close to hand, her requirements were met quickly. But Sarah was far from ready to go back to sleep. She was too frightened. Still, she settled back down, hoping against hope that because White Thunder's arms were around her, she would simply drift off to sleep again.

However, it wasn't to be.

White Thunder must have realized this also, because in due time, he spoke to her, saying, "Do you want to tell me about it?"

"I . . . yes. It was the Ottawa, but it was only his head and his arms that threatened me. However, this time he didn't stop at simply cutting my hair. This time . . ."

White Thunder's arms increased their pressure around her. He said, "That time is not now. Though it is possible his spirit might haunt you, the danger from him doing you physical harm is gone."

"Aye," she said. "Yes. Because of you, I am still here to speak of this. Again, Mr. Thunder, I thank you."

He nodded. "Does the Ottawa's spirit haunt you?"

"Perhaps," she said. "I'm uncertain how to judge that. But something else happened. I dreamed of my parents, and when I did, something good occurred. My memory of them returned, and . . ." She fell silent.

"And?" he prompted.

"My full recall has returned to me, sir. I remembered how my parents died, how I came to be an indentured servant and what those two separate experiences have to do with one another. I recalled that Miss Marisa and I were fleeing from Albany, and I remembered why."

With his arms wrapped securely around her, he nodded, and said, "Go on."

"It is complex, I fear. My parents were Dutch. They'd owned a farm, a house and had much to live for. They were happy, successful. My father was investing in raising tobacco as a crop, and had borrowed the needed finance for this from John Rathburn. All seemed good until they were raided by 'Indians,' who set the farm, the house, the barn and the fields afire. My parents died in those fires. In the end, there was nothing left with which to pay the debt to John Rathburn. No crops, no house, no barn. So Mr. Rathburn took my family's farm, he took their land and he took me into servitude for twenty years."

"He is an evil man."

"Yes, sir, I think you're right. But the terrible part is that through Marisa, I came to learn that it was most likely not Indians who started the fires that night, but Mr. Rathburn, himself, or people he had hired to do the deed for him. In other words, it was never his intention to help my father. Mr. Rathburn financed my father simply to bankrupt him and take from him what he had."

"If this be true, then your services to him were obtained through lies."

"That they were. Unfortunately, it changes nothing in the eyes of the law. I'm still duty-bound to honor my bond, sir, no matter how ill-gotten it was obtained."

"How can this be if he gained what he did through dishonesty?"

Sarah tossed her head. "Because it is hard for poor people to fight rich people in court."

"Then it is a bad system."

"Perhaps."

"How is it, then," he asked, "that you came to be in the woods, so far from your home?"

"That's another story altogether. Through a series of incidents, Miss Marisa found out what Mr. Rathburn had done, and when she did, she arranged to get me out of John Rathburn's reach—she was taking me to some friends who live far away from Albany. I think it was her intention that I should serve out the rest of my debt there."

"And now she, too, is gone from you." It was not a question.

"Yes."

He sat silently, as though lost in thought. After a few moments, he said, "All those years ago, when your house was set afire, did you try to stop your mother from going to the aid of your father?"

"That I did. How did you know?"

"Because when you were delirious with fever, you called out to your mother. And I knew there was something that haunted you. Now I understand that it is their deaths that possess you even to this day."

"Aye, sir, that is true. It is a thing from which I have never recovered."

He dipped his head in agreement. "Perhaps," he said, "it is time that I speak the Three Bare Words to console you in your grief, no matter how long ago that sorrow occurred. If I do this, it has the power to relieve the dead, who might surround you, so that they, too, may go on their journey. Would you like that?"

"Very much, I think."

"Good. Come and sit up. Though it is dark, we can climb down to the nearby stream, where I will speak these Three Words to you."

She nodded. "Very well."

He added, "I only ask that you forgive me if I make any

mistakes, for I have long been gone from my village, and my memory of the ceremonies may be at fault."

"I would forgive you most anything, sir. Know, however, that you don't have to do this. I've managed to make my way in life so far, and I dare say, I'll continue."

"But why should it be difficult for you? *Neh*, you are important to me. So come, it's late, but though night has taken over the evening sky, let us set a path to the water, where I can conduct the Condolence Ceremony as best I am able."

Grasping hold of his bags, his weapons and his rifle, he threw the straps over his shoulders, situated all his weapons on his person, then crawled out through the entry flap. Turning, he held it open for her.

As she crawled out through the flap, she froze. Not from fear, rather because it was an unusually beautiful night; it was dark, cool and still. The air was crisp, cold and scented with pure oxygen, as well as the fragrance of pine. Without the warmth of the sun, the cold bit right through her skin, and she was thankful that White Thunder had taken the time to fix her dress.

Above her, the moon was full, though at present it was half hidden behind a cloud. A million or more stars glimmered above her, some twinkling more brilliantly than others, and the Milky Way stood distinct and clear in a sky that seemed broader than eternity.

Space, she thought. Had she ever seen so many stars?

There was something about the atmosphere this high up that gave her a feeling of gaining room, and as she gazed around the moonlit summit, her thoughts seemed to spread out, away from her. Interestingly, it brought her a feeling of relief.

But there was little time to spend in admiration of the surroundings, for White Thunder was quickly pacing toward the edge of the slope. She hurried to catch up with him, and once again, she followed him down the steep incline, clinging to him more often than not when she lost her footing.

At last they traversed the level ground that led to the shoreline of the stream. She watched as White Thunder looked around their surroundings, took note as he indicated a large maple tree and followed him toward it.

There, after spreading out his blanket over the ground, he indicated that they would sit. She followed his lead, taking her position opposite him.

"Please forgive me if I err in the performance," he repeated.

"Of course," she replied. "But, sir, I wouldn't know if you made an error."

"Although that is true," he responded, "it's still important that I do it right. We will begin," he said, and he pulled out eight different strings of wampum from his bag. Holding them in his hand, he began. "Tears, Throat, Heart. These are the words that were first spoken by the Peacemaker to Chief Hiawatha, to comfort Hiawatha in his grief."

White Thunder took a string of wampum, and leaned forward to wipe it over Sarah's face and eyes. "With this string," he said, "I brush away the tears from your eyes so that henceforth, you may see more clearly, and not be blinded by the madness that true grief can bring." Then White Thunder handed her the string of white-and-purple wampum.

Sarah accepted the gift and sat before him silently. As the moon cast down its misty beams to the earth below, the light caught White Thunder in its glow. Under its silvery effect, his profile looked more like an artist's depiction of male beauty than that of a flesh-and-blood man. Though she had always found White Thunder to be handsome, to describe him as merely attractive wouldn't have done him justice. He looked warm, approachable, magnificent.

White Thunder took hold of another string of wampum

and brushed it over her throat, saying, "With this string of wampum, I take away any hindrance that would keep you from speaking freely." Again, he handed her the string of wampum.

Slowly and with great deliberation, he repeated the ceremony with the other strings of wampum. With these, he wiped away the blood that had been spilled due to her parents' death; he covered her parents' grave, that they would bring her no grief; he collected up all the bones of all her relatives and buried them deep so that not even they could cause her grief; he made the sky beautiful again and he expelled the insanity of grief. With each step, he handed her another string of wampum.

When White Thunder had only one string left in his hand, he said, "With this last string of wampum, I banish the weighty thoughts that encircle you. From this moment forward, light and sunshine shall again be a part of your life." As before, he handed her the string.

Then he came up to his feet, held out his hand to her and said, "Come."

She followed his lead, standing up to her full stature and taking hold of his hand. He then led her to the fast-moving creek, where he squatted and gathered water from a pool that had collected there.

"Today," he said, "as we were playing, I saw that this part of the stream, because of all the waterfalls that drain into it, is the clearest and cleanest."

She nodded.

"Now I'll pour this water, which is the cleanest water I can find, into your body so as to clear your mind of any distress."

He guided the water to her lips, and when she had drunk it, he said, "And now you must return the wampum to me, strand by strand, as I did to you, and give me your reply."

She understood what he meant without having to query him, and one by one, she gave each string back to White

Thunder, replying to him in the same manner by which he'd given them to her. When she stumbled on the words, he encouraged her, until the last string of wampum was returned, and with it she said, "I thank you for banishing the dark thoughts that were troubling me. I can now behold the beauty of the world around me."

He inclined his head. "And now it is finished," he said.

She smiled up at him. Soft, shimmering moonlight held him in its trance and cast the planes of his face with silvery light. She was already standing so close to him, she could feel his breath upon her. It was beautiful. He was beautiful.

Her voice was no more than a mere whisper when she said, "I do see more clearly, and it does seem as if my heart is purer. Thank you, White Thunder. I am trying to remember if anyone has ever performed such a kindness for me. Outside of Miss Marisa, I think there is no one. Please know that I am honored and deeply touched."

He bent down and kissed her gently. Then taking her in his arms, he said, "Grief for a loved one can be a terrible thing. It can cause vengeful war to commence. It can bring about paralysis, nightmares. It is like a poison to the system. This ceremony was established long ago by the Peacemaker to wipe away the grief of the people, and by doing so, to do away with war. It is my pleasure to do this for you. Just as it was their hope all those hundreds of years ago that by wiping clean a person's grief, they could do away with war forever, so it is my desire to wipe away your fear and anxiety so that you may look upon the world again, not as a place of despair, but as a world of beauty."

She reached up to run her hands through his hair. "Mr. Thunder, I am again deeply touched. Indeed, I bless the day you came into my life. I know little what the future holds for us, but this I do know: I love you." She sighed against his shoulder. "I simply love you."

He backed up, but only minutely. Placing his hands on

the sides of her face, he reached down to bestow one soft kiss after another against her lips. Meanwhile, his hands massaged her face, her neck, her cheeks, her hair, her scalp.

He whispered, "This is not part of the ceremony—it should never be part of the ceremony—but I want to make love to you."

"Oh, yes," she said. "Please."

Twenty-two

Soft moonlit shadows flickered over the delicate features of her face, her pert nose, her full lips, the dainty bone structure of her cheeks, the creamy-blond tendrils of her hair. Even her complexion appeared flawless beneath the flattering rays of the misty moonbeams, though he knew personally that her skin bore scratches from their journey and her encounter with the Ottawa.

As her clear blue eyes glanced up at him adoringly, and as he beheld the look of gentleness and trust in her gaze, he knew true happiness.

Oh, to keep her with him. But how? After the many conversations concerning their future together, it always reduced down to the same objections: He had his duty and she had hers.

In truth, even if there were no obstacles between them, there was still society's considerations that would make their life together difficult—both her society and his, but

mostly hers. Besides, didn't he know from experience what
the judgmental wagging of tongues could do to a person?

Hadn't half-truths and lies driven him away from his
own tribe?

True, he and Sarah had come together under unusual
circumstances, and it was an indisputable truth that their
love itself was an uncommon sight. However, it didn't necessarily follow that their love, once realized, shouldn't be
sanctioned. Now that the deed was done and love blos-
somed between them, there was no going back. Regardless
of others' opinions, they were in love. They would always
be in love.

Perhaps that's why they were lingering here so long.
Because once they had recovered sufficiently—both physically and mentally—he would be obligated, due to his
own pledge to her, to take her where she wished to go.
And apparently that was back to her own society, back to
servitude.

And regardless of their discussions concerning the
crime of slavery, she seemed to be of a mind that she still
owed her service.

He was no sachem, and he couldn't see into the future,
but if there were one detail that was under his control, it
was this: He could give her a love neither would ever forget. Forever, they would share this between them.

Bending down to her, he pressed a kiss against her lips,
then another and another. Over and over they caressed, as
though there were no such thing as quenching their thirst
of one another. When she swooned in toward him, and as
he caught her and inhaled her fragile scent, it was a stimu-
lant, more potent than a swig of rum. Ah, had he ever loved
anyone more? He whispered, "Open your lips to me."

She did, and without pause his tongue invaded her
mouth. She tasted of pure femininity, both sweet and salty,
and he explored her mouth as though he meant to make

love to her utilizing nothing more than his tongue against hers.

His hands explored the contours of her back as she pressed in against him, and he discovered that there were certain advantages to having mended her gown earlier this day. Now that he understood how the garment was sewn together, it took no great effort to unfasten the few hooks and pins that held it up. Within minutes he had her dress falling down around her ankles.

And still they kissed. The feel of her curvy figure, now clothed in only petticoats, corset and chemise sparked his heartbeat to race like liquid fire.

Her petticoats, corset and chemise came off without incident. And then there she was . . . enchantingly beautiful and naked . . . and encircled within his arms.

Although they might have made love in the late afternoon, that was then, this was now. As the balmy fragrance of her femininity teased him, and as the silvery beams of the moon emphasized every bend and arch of her figure, he realized that he had never craved the consummation of his passion more than he did at this moment. It was almost his undoing. But he kept himself under control. Slowly, he told himself, one step at a time. In the end, he would give all that he had of himself to her, and fully.

"Sir," she whispered against his lips, "again, I fear that you wear too many clothes. You have an advantage over me. Thus far, I have never seen you naked. Is it safe enough, do you think that I might look upon you, too?"

He groaned. What a thing for a woman to ask a man. Did she know the impact that her words, though soft, had over him? If not, she was very soon to become aware of their effect.

"Come," he muttered, and he led her back to the blanket he had placed beneath the maple tree. But there wasn't enough privacy there. Casting a quick glance around their surroundings, he said, "I think we will move this over by the trunk of the willow tree, where we will be hidden from any casual view. And there, I promise I'll take off my weapons, my breechcloth and my leggings. Even my moccasins. I give you my word of honor that we will lie together naked."

Still holding her hand, and more than aware of the feminine beauty that was within his grasp, he reached down to pick up the blanket.

Quickly, they stepped away from the maple tree and fled into the protection of the weeping willow. White Thunder spread the blanket close to the tree's trunk so as to give them maximum privacy, even if it were only privacy from the night itself. Once there, he turned toward her, let go of her hand and placed his rifle on the blanket, though she noted that he set it with care and within easy reach. Next off came his tomahawk, his war ax, war club and several of his knives, many of them hidden in the material that tied at his knees and waist.

She observed, "You are not only well-built with masculine brawn, sir, but you are well armed, also."

"Is it different in English society?"

"No," she said. "Oftentimes a man is judged by the condition of his pistols alone."

He nodded. "A man's duty is protection," he explained, "and this can only be done by having a good arsenal of weapons close to hand. All he values is at risk if this is omitted."

Next, he removed his leggings, which tied to his belt, and from across his chest, the straps of his bags, powder horn and ammunition. Then came his belt, his shirt, his moccasins and finally his breechcloth.

As he let the breechcloth fall, he was well aware that he was ready for her, and there was no hiding the obvious influence that she had on him. But if the amorous state of his body alarmed her, she didn't show it. Indeed, she took the necessary few steps to bring herself up next to him, throw her arms around his neck and say, "Mr. Thunder, you are as handsome as any Greek god."

The sensation of his sex nestled in against her stomach was exhilarating. But then, as though she were layering on one sensation after another upon him, she twisted against him. Once again he almost lost himself to her, right then and there.

He moaned and pressed his own hips against her, cautioning himself again to move slowly, inch by inch. Since it was his intention to love her and give her a love that she would never forget, he realized that he had best proceed in a manner that would allow him constant stimulation, but without him reaching the apex of their love too soon.

Perhaps, if he were very lucky, she would never again consider living her life without him. Truthfully, he held out little hope for that.

He brought her to her knees and followed her down, kneeling in front of her, where they swayed against each other as if they danced to a music of their own making. As if in collaboration, the south wind blew gently against the cool night air, the willowy branches of the tree their accompaniment.

She was ready; she was wet, and he realized there was much to be admired about his sex resting against the hot core of hers. For a moment—but a moment only—he joined himself with her. It was not his intention, however, to bring their lovemaking to a peak so soon. He only wished to arouse her passion to a fervent level.

However, he soon found that there was danger here: He had to keep himself well checked. Indeed, he was much too ready to realize the full extent of their lovemaking.

He pulled away from her and laid her into a position on her back, where he leaned over her from the side. From here, he showered her with kisses. All these were works in progress. But there was also a method to his endeavors. He was winding his way down to her breasts.

First he nibbled at one softened mound, while his fingers massaged the other, then over to her other breast. And here he lingered.

He nestled his head between her breasts, as though he were a small child needing comfort. For a moment, he wished he could stay in this position a little longer. But he was completely aware that there were other treasures that awaited him.

Gradually he slipped farther down her body, his kisses extending slowly downward, over her stomach, down farther and farther, until he had at last arrived at the center of her femininity.

With a slight nudge, he pushed her legs apart. But she was uncooperative, and as she brought her legs together, she came up onto her elbows, where she gazed down at him.

"Sir?" she queried. "What is it you intend doing?"

"To love you, my wife."

"There?"

He nodded. "There. But do not concern yourself. You will enjoy it."

He was aware that she frowned at him. "Perhaps I might wash first."

"There is no need," he said. "You are perfect as you are."

He heard her sigh, but at last, she relaxed back, and when he again parted her legs, she acquiesced.

Then he made love to her, showering her with the full extent of his admiration. At first she lay stiffly beneath him, but as his lips and tongue worked its exquisite magic over her, she settled down. After some moments, as if compelled, she began to move in synchronization with the rhythm of his tongue.

He heard her breathing catch, then quicken. He felt her

muscles contract around him. He watched as she spread her legs, as though she offered herself to him.

And he accepted her gifts, while his tongue, his mouth, his lips, gave her as much erotic pleasure as he was able. He felt the fire building, felt the fiery pressure of her hips against him, knew she was close to release. She was breathing hard now and her embarrassment seemed to have been a temporary affair. She moved, twisted and strained against him until suddenly, magnificently, she tripped over the edge of release.

It was a certain aphrodisiac for him. He might have eased off his lure over her, but instead of withdrawing from her, he gave her as much of himself as he could, even using his fingers to bring her to the ultimate pinnacle of pleasure.

She exploded with satisfaction, and he reveled in the sounds of her release. At last, as her breathing settled down into a more normal pace, he came up to his knees over her from whence he gazed down at her with all the admiration that was in his heart. And it was plenty.

"White Thunder," she whispered. "I believe that when you said I would simply enjoy it, you belittled your case."

He laughed. "You liked it?"

"I think, sir, that you speak in understatement. If there is a heaven on earth, I judge that you have given it to me, if only for a moment."

"You flatter me," he said, "but your joy brings me delight, for it is my intention to make memories—as you asked me to do—that you will never forget."

As he settled himself between her thighs, she reached up to bring him in close to her, and she said, "I think you have accomplished your purpose, Mr. Thunder. But, sir, I have yet to see that you have met your pleasure."

He sighed. Oh, the complete thrill of her. He said, "Then you are ready for me?"

"Aye, sir, that I am."

At long last he joined himself with her in passionate embrace. The warmth of her femininity surrounded him, and it occurred to him that this was home. Here, with this woman, was home.

Slowly he began his dance with her. One thrust led to another, her hips meeting and encouraging his euphoria. He shifted position, because although they were sexually embraced, he wished for more. Coming up onto his knees before her, and reaching down for her legs, he settled them around his neck. It was a position that offered him a look into the essence of who she was, for there, within the depths of her eyes, was mirrored her spirit.

He caught her glance as he bore against her. He held that glance. He watched with something akin to awe as she once again rose up to the heights of lovemaking. He stared at her as her movements became more and more intense, watched as she stretched again toward that pinnacle. He smiled at her. She smiled back. They met, man to woman, spirit to spirit, and looking at her, his love for her exploded until it consumed him.

Their struggle had become frantic. They strained against each other, they gave to each other. And when he at last felt her muscles contract around him, he gave to her every bit of him.

As she toppled over the precipice of her passion, he met her with his own need, flooding her body with his seed. And as their pleasure met its pinnacle, he felt himself become as one with her. As he did so, he was aware that he understood all that she was.

She was pure beauty; she was grace. And whatever the future might hold, he would love her. Always.

As he collapsed against her, Sarah wrapped her arms around his body. Tears stung at the back of her eyes. She loved him. They were bound together and it didn't matter if they were to be together physically for the rest of their lives or not. Always, she would love him.

Why did the two of them have to be from different worlds? She wanted all those things that women the world over want from the man they love: to stay here with him, to be his woman, to have his children and create her life with him.

But who in English society would understand? Her friend, Marisa? Yes. But that was only one against many.

As she ran her hands through White Thunder's dark, thick hair, she knew pleasure, yet loss. They had pretended to be married, and as he had warned her, she had fallen in love with him.

She'd wanted memories. She had them. But at this moment, all she desired was to be with him for the rest of her life, and even that seemed that it might not be enough.

But at least she had him with her now. And she would savor every minute of their time together. Always.

Twenty-three

They were moving fast and they were traveling by
night. Sarah had long ago learned to keep her stride
even with White Thunder. Although he sometimes sur-
passed her by a large margin, he was never so far ahead
of her that she couldn't catch sight of him. And though she
was aware that he adjusted his pace to accommodate her,
he still outdistanced her more times than not.

They weren't using the regular pathways through the
woods. "Too many war parties on the move," White Thunder had said.

So once again, branches, brambles and burrs caught at
her dress. But White Thunder had warned her to ensure that
nothing snagged and was left behind as evidence that they
had passed this way. It slowed her down, but she checked
and rechecked those areas of the trail where her dress had
caught.

They were en route to the Mohawk village of Andagoran, which sat squarely on the Mohawk River. It was where

Black Eagle resided. Interestingly, White Thunder knew of Black Eagle, and was aware of what village he was from. Perhaps this was because they were both part of the Six Nations. Mayhap somewhere in their past, they or their fathers might have counseled together.

Whatever the reason for his knowledge, Sarah was simply glad that they wouldn't be required to search from village to village in order to find Marisa and Black Eagle.

Sarah had at first disagreed with White Thunder on journeying to the Mohawk village, if only because her main concern was to warn Marisa against returning to Albany. In her mind, anxiety alone would have sent Marisa to Albany.

But White Thunder was certain that if Black Eagle intended to marry the girl—and it appeared that he did— he would have taken her to his home. After several conversations on the topic, Sarah had recognized the logic of White Thunder's thoughts, and she had capitulated.

They were already two days on the move. Back in the Adirondack Mountains, however, they had spent another two days wrapped in each other's arms. Now and again they had exerted themselves and had applied their talents to the task of drying meat for their journey. But all their work had only been done halfheartedly. It seemed that they were both more engrossed with each other than they were with food.

But at last it was done, and with the chore behind them, there had been no further reason to stay, even though the spot could be compared to a cathedral in the wilderness. Even they had come to realize that eventually they would have to rejoin society.

They had left the next day. At present, although their quickened pace didn't allow Sarah to study or appreciate the woods in detail, she did note that straight ahead of them, there appeared to be a clearing in the trees. Was this it, then? Had they finally arrived at the village of Andagoran?

All at once, the clearing was upon them, and like two deer suddenly frightened, they burst out of the forest at a speed that was as fast as it was brisk. And no sooner had they cleared the trees and undergrowth than they were surrounded by large fields. Because it was late autumn, the fields lay barren. Here and there a few black tree stumps dotted the fields, and occasionally they passed an empty sentry post, which was a lean-to that had been raised up high on poles. But outside of the remnants of these lean-tos, the fields were deserted.

Looking at them, Sarah pointed to one of the outposts and asked, "What is that for?"

White Thunder glanced in its direction and answered, "When the fields are ripening and the crops are growing, the women and children come to those posts to watch for crows and other birds. All must be scared away lest the animals eat all the food. These outposts can also be used to watch for the approach of an enemy. That's why they're built high."

"Oh, I see. And where's the village? All I can bear witness to here are fields."

White Thunder pointed toward a cliff set high and slightly back from the river.

"Ah," said Sarah. "I see it now."

Their pace had slowed but little, and though they no longer traveled at a run, their walking stride was almost as fast as their sprinting had been.

"Guards have spotted us. Come," he said, "we must sit and await their sentries."

"Truly? Why is that?"

"Because it is considered uncivil to enter a village without invitation. Even then, as soon as we are taken into a village, we'll be escorted to the Stranger's House, where we'll remain while the people are told that we are there. In this way, the people will have the opportunity to prepare food for us to eat and bring us skins to sit on in order to see to our comfort. Only once we are well fed and relaxed will we commence conversation. It is at that time that we'll be able to ask them about Black Eagle and your friend."

"It sounds very hospitable. Indeed, after all of our adventures in the woods, I will be happy to accept their goodwill."

"I think you will find it pleasant."

In due time, two old men approached them. "Brother," one of the men addressed White Thunder. "I see by your clothes and by the tattoo on your arm that you are my Seneca brother. I see also by the state of your clothing that you have traveled a distance to visit us and have perhaps encountered much hardship."

"This is so."

"Then, Brother, come let me escort you into our village, where I will take you to the Stranger's House, while I alert the people that we have a guest." He nodded toward Sarah. "Is the woman a captive?"

"She is not."

The old man nodded once again. "Come, I will show you to the Stranger's House."

The view was spectacular. The village was positioned on a cliff overlooking Mohawk fields and the Mohawk River, which flowed and gurgled over rocks and boulders in an ever continuing cascade of white waves. In the distance, mountains and hills rose up both east and west of them. Set against a blue sky, the site for Andagoran was surrounded by breathtaking beauty.

The entrance to the town was unusual, as well, consisting of overlapping logs instead of a gate. At this entrance, she noted, was yet another outpost. Big, dangerous-looking men stood guard at the entry point. That each of them stared at her, not in greeting, but as though she were an enemy, was intimidating.

Sarah looked away, swallowing hard. She must have lagged behind, because as soon as she glanced forward, she noted that White Thunder was well in the lead. She hurried toward him, following on his heels. As she and White Thunder, along with the two older gentlemen, rounded the corner of the overlapping logs, the village at last came into view.

Like a scene gradually opening up before her, her first impression of the village was that of colors: the greens and browns of dried grasses; the browns of the trees and long-houses; the oranges, yellows and golds of produce set upon the ground; the multicolored prints of the people's cloth-ing, although there were only a few people in sight. The village, she decided, was not without beauty.

She heard male voices singing and a drumming noise in the background, but the sound was muffled, as though it were coming from within a building. The scent of smoke hung heavy in the air, as well as the fragrances of farm-rich beans, squash and husks. And somewhere, someone—or perhaps many someones—was cooking food.

The flavors in the air were so numerous and delicious smelling that Sarah was reminded that her recent diet of dried meat and berries was not the only food to be had.

She and White Thunder were led to a longhouse, one that was called the Stranger's House.

"Soon," said one of the two elderly men, "one of us or another will return with food and clothing, as well as furs to sit on. Eat, be at your ease and make yourselves comfort-able. After you are refreshed, we will smoke, and then we can begin conversation."

The door to the longhouse remained open, and this was good, for the shelter smelled of dirt, bark and the charred remains of a fire. It was also dark in the interior of the structure, if only because there were no windows. The only light, it seemed, came from smoke holes in the ceiling, and from the open door.

A long corridor led from one end of the longhouse to the other; in the center were two hearths, evenly spaced apart. Glancing around, Sarah thought that the longhouse might have been forty feet long, twenty to thirty feet wide, and perhaps twenty feet high. On each side of the structure were compartments, where she supposed a guest might berth if he or she were staying the night. Attached to several posts hung corn cobs to dry, as well as gourds and other articles needed for cooking.

Both she and White Thunder had been seated only a few minutes when a woman entered, bearing a tray of food. As Sarah looked on, she saw corn cobs heaped upon several plates, corn cakes, ribs and a dish she learned was called succotash—a mixture of corn, beans and squash. To drink there were bowls of water and a sweetener that might have been maple or corn syrup. To a person from any culture— Indian, English or other—it looked like a feast.

Behind the woman followed another maid, who looked to be a younger version of the elder, and she was bearing furs to sit on, as well as a handful of clothes. Sarah saw that there were shirts, a belt, moccasins, a navy-colored breech-cloth and leggings for White Thunder. There was also a simple, trade-cloth dress in a light blue color. It was intricately embroidered with designs of pink, white and blue flowers. The sleeves were puffed at the shoulder and fell down to just below elbow length. Accompanying the dress were leggings of the same color and embroidery work, as well as moccasins.

Hesitantly, the young girl placed the clothes beside Sarah. Sarah smiled at the girl, and said, "Thank you," but the maid was shy, and outside of a brief nod, did no more than look away.

The two women left and White Thunder and Sarah were left alone with their meal.

"Are these clothes meant for us?" asked Sarah.

"They are."

"But they're beautiful. Are we to wear them only while we're here?"

"No, they are ours now."

"Ours? That's incredible. Do they expect them to be returned at some future date?"

"*Neh*, no. It is all part of being hospitable. All strangers are given food, furs to sleep on if they are tired and in our case, clothes, because ours are obviously torn and in disrepair."

"But there must be something required in exchange for this. Money, perhaps? Although I think it obvious that we are not a man and woman of wealth."

"Nothing is expected in return," he said, "except perhaps that you will remember that they treated you with kindness and respect when you were in need. It is the hope of the Six Nations and our belief that all people should honor each other in this manner. If it were so, wars would be less, I think."

"Yes," said Sarah. "I believe you are right."

Silently, Sarah and White Thunder applied themselves to the food, and once their appetite was satiated, they dressed themselves in their new clothing. What was amazing to Sarah's mind was how well the dress fit her. Even the moccasins were neither too big nor too little.

They were now well dressed, well fed and comfortable, and soon the two old men and an elderly woman entered. A pipe was offered to White Thunder, which he accepted, and while smoking, the conversation began.

"We see that you are from the Turtle Clan of the Seneca," said one of the elderly men in English. "Is this from whence you came?"

"Indeed, it is not," said White Thunder, whereupon he relayed who he was, where they had come from and the circumstances surrounding Sarah's rescue.

The conversation continued, and when asked why he had come to their village, he answered with the truth and with the information that they were seeking Black Eagle and his bride, Marisa, who was a friend of Sarah's.

The old man nodded, and leaning over toward the elderly woman, he addressed her in their own language. The woman rose to her feet and left the house, while the old man turned back to White Thunder. He said, again in English, and probably for Sarah's benefit, "We know of Black Eagle and his bride, whom we call *Ahweyoh*, Water Lily. Neither are here in the village at present, but I have sent for Black Eagle's mother and *Ahweyoh*'s sister, that they can inform you where you might find them."

"*Nyah-wah*, thank you," replied White Thunder. "Do you know how long ago they were here?"

"It was only a moon ago and a day that *Ahweyoh* was captured—"

"Captured?" Sarah sat up and bent forward, but White Thunder placed a hand over hers, as if to caution her not to interrupt the speaker.

"*Nyoh*, yes, she was captured by her own people, the English," said the old man. "She did not wish to go and there was some trouble, for the English assaulted *Ahweyoh*'s sister, that they might steal *Ahweyoh*. Her husband, Black Eagle, was away on the hunt, but he has since returned and has gone to save her. But where that place is that he has gone, I know not. However, his mother might have knowledge of this, or if not, *Ahweyoh*'s sister might know, thus I have asked for them both to come here."

Soon the two women arrived. However, neither of them spoke English and Sarah had to wait to learn through White Thunder's translation that both women believed the English had taken Miss Marisa to Albany. Although they couldn't be certain, Black Eagle had said this was where he would go to find her.

As soon as Sarah understood what had been said, she

murmured to White Thunder, "It is as I feared. She went to Albany. We must go there at once."

White Thunder nodded. He thanked them all for their hospitality, for their kindness and for their information. But, he told them, both he and Sarah would need to leave as quickly as possible, since they possessed urgent information for Black Eagle and his bride.

"And where be your destination?" asked the older gentleman.

"Albany," replied White Thunder. "We go to Albany at once."

Twenty-four

They left the Mohawk village of Andagoran in haste. Evening shadows were already falling upon the forest when Sarah and White Thunder quit the relative safety of the Mohawk village to again travel through the woods.

Their pace was that of a light run; it was fast, lively and quick, which kept Sarah warm, though the air temperature was cold and turning ever colder as evening crept in around them. Again, White Thunder took the lead and for now, perhaps because they were still close to the Mohawk village, they traveled on the well-worn Iroquois Trail.

Because the trail was kept clean and clear of debris, Sarah's trek through the woods was easier, if only because she didn't have to worry about catching her dress on the brambles and burrs of the trees and bushes.

"Aren't you concerned about war parties?" Sarah had asked White Thunder as they had slowed their pace to a fast walk.

"Indeed, I am," he returned, "but not this close to the Mohawk village, which is still patrolled by the warriors and sentries. Tomorrow, we will have to resume our more usual trek through the unkempt places in the woods, those paths where no one travels. But I think we are safe here for now."

"How long will it take us to arrive at Albany?"

"A day and a bit," he answered. "Perhaps more, depending on the state of the lesser-used paths."

"Have you ever considered utilizing the river instead of the trails through the woods? Couldn't we simply paddle a canoe to Albany? It would be faster."

"It would be faster if this land were not at war and we were not in danger of being exposed to all eyes on the water, friend or foe. *Neh*, no, better it is that we travel in the woods, concealed."

"Yes, I see. Of course."

They pushed onward through the evening and late into the night, not stopping until dawn was a dim light on the horizon. Only then did White Thunder quit and begin to set up camp.

"Will we arrive in Albany tomorrow?" Sarah asked as she and White Thunder sat beside one another in their temporary shelter, enjoying a meal of dried meat, corn cakes and berries.

"We will."

"I suppose we'll first need to visit the Rathburn estate to determine if Marisa is there and safe. But if not, I assume we'll have to discover where she might have gone and why she left."

White Thunder nodded. "It is a good plan. You forgot one important detail, though. We will go there only in the evening, when there are shadows that might hide us."

Sarah frowned. "Must we? I understand your concern

and need for stealth, Mr. Thunder. I, too, am anxious about
Marisa's safety. But to have to wait until the evening . . .
I lived there for fifteen years, and it seems to me that I
might go there and make inquiries without having to sneak
about."

"There is every reason to conceal ourselves and wait
until evening," White Thunder rebutted. "If we go there
and confront Rathburn, and he sees you, he will keep you
there as his servant."

"Yes, he could. He has that right by law."

"He does not have that right," protested White Thunder.
"Not by any law. No man has the 'right' to own and control
another human being for his own profit. And if, as you say,
there is a 'law' that states he does, then that 'law' is against
the tenets of the Creator, thereby making it no law at all,
but rather a crime."

Sarah sighed. "'Tis so logical sounding when you say
it to me. However, that is not how the courts look upon it.
And I am subject to those courts."

"You are subject to no one."

"You are if you're a woman."

"Because you are a woman? What does your gender
have to do with being subject to someone?"

"Because," she answered, "a woman is always subordi-
nate to her husband or to her father or to some other male
relative."

"This is English law?"

"It is."

"It is a bad law. Is a woman a life form different
from man that she should do nothing but serve him? Does
she not hold the welfare of the tribe and its prosperity in
her hand? Without woman, man is nothing but a pitiful
creature. Therefore, she deserves a place of honor, not a
position of servitude. You come live with me with the Iroquois," he went on to say. "The women in our tribe hold

the balance of power of the tribe and they are no man's subject."

"Truly? 'Tis much about your society that we could learn, I think. But whether we agree or not, 'tis not the manner in which English law is conducted."

"Law or no law, subject or no subject, do you forget that this is the same man whom you suspect killed your parents?"

"Yes, I have not forgotten, and perhaps if I had the finances necessary, I could fight him in the courts and win my freedom, although I still think those courts will favor a man of influence."

"Or you could stay here. Instead of putting yourself in a bad situation, I will go and learn what I can of your friend and then return to you here. Once we discover what has happened to her, or if she requires our help, we can either assist her, follow her or go into the west, where we will still find freedom and a people who will not judge our marriage because of who we are."

"It sounds so good, sir. But do you forget your duty to Wild Mint?"

"I do not," he said.

"Then what is your plan as regards her?"

"I might have to return to Mohawk Territory from time to time to search for her killer, but I will no longer make this the reason that I live. There is another now who is important to me . . . you. I would live in truth. I would be alive. And if I can, I would live with you."

Sarah glanced away from him. Oh, yes, it sounded so perfect. Except for one thing. She said, "I fear, sir, that it wouldn't work. Eventually, you would begin to dislike me because I influenced you to turn your back on a pledge you made to another. And as for me, I would always be looking behind my back to see if someone were coming for me to take me back into servitude. Better it is that we confront our obligations here and now, rather than drag them with us elsewhere."

He sighed, and was silent for so long that Sarah began to wonder if he had drifted off to sleep. At last, he said, "You are right. You are wise. We will both go to Albany, but, as I said before, we will use stealth, and we will go in the evening, when the staring eyes of the English villagers will have a difficult time seeing us together. And if you are to go back there, you must first visit these 'courts' that you talk of and tell them the truth of John Rathburn. Only then might I feel that you will be safe. Only then will I take you."

Sarah nodded. "Yes. You're right, and I will. You have been seeking to help me and I appreciate your concern. Please bear with me, however, for first I must see about Marisa and discover if she is safe or not. Then, with my mind at ease, I'll do as you say and visit the constable in Albany, where I will tell him what I suspect of John Rathburn."

"Can you not visit this constable first?"

"Aye, I could," she said. "Is this what you wish?"

"It is."

She sighed. "Then so be it."

They had camped in the wooden grove of trees on the north side the Rathburn estate. White Thunder had discovered a tree that would make a good base while they were in Albany. It was a tree that looked much like the one that Marisa had once described, Perhaps it was the same, for it was a solid oak that looked as though it had been hollowed out by a lightning strike. Here, in the hollowed-out section of the tree, they left their food, extra moccasins and a few other bags. And though Sarah would rather not have to sneak into a village where she had lived for so many years, she could readily understand White Thunder's hesitation. Besides, there would be no harm in visiting the constable before she had, of necessity, to confront John Rathburn.

With this explicit purpose in mind, she and White Thunder had visited the offices of Constable Phelps, only to discover that he was gone. They had even traveled to his home, but when that still produced no result, Sarah had insisted it was now time to find Marisa.

At present, both she and White Thunder were safely hidden by the bushes and trees of the woods that surrounded the Rathburn estate. Their plan was simple: Sarah would try to solicit the cook's help. If anyone would know what had happened to Marisa, it might likely be Mrs. Stanton, the cook. Not only was her heart good, she had always held sympathy for the girl that Marisa had once been and the young lady she had become.

White Thunder seemed unusually alert, as though his attention were not only here but scattered over the entirety of the estate, watching for trouble. At last, he indicated that they should approach the kitchen door.

They crept up to it. Sarah knocked. White Thunder stepped to the side, out of the light.

No one answered. Sarah knocked again.

This time, they were in luck. A kitchen maid answered.

Immediately Sarah asked, "May I see Mrs. Stanton, please?"

The maid gave Sarah a confused, searching glance, most likely trying to discern exactly who Sarah was.

To ease the kitchen maid's unspoken questions, Sarah said, "Cook knows me, for I used to work here, too. My name is Sarah. Please, would you find Mrs. Stanton and tell her that Miss Sarah Strong is here to see her?"

The maid nodded, closed the door and turned away. Sarah waited, trying to frame in her mind what she would say.

Without delay, Mrs. Stanton stepped to the door. Sarah

watched as the cook opened the door a crack, and peeped out, saying, "Miss Sarah? Be it true that ye are here?"

"'Tis I, Mrs. Stanton. And I have had quite the adventure getting here."

"Why, Miss Sarah, it is ye. Enter, please." She opened the door wide.

"I have someone with me, Mrs. Stanton—an Indian. May we both come in?"

"Aye, child. I could've gathered from yer dress that ye've been rescued by the Indians. Miss Marisa was the same."

"Miss Marisa? Is she here, then?"

"Nay, Miss Sarah, she is not." Cook's glance skipped off of her to stare at something at Sarah's back, and Sarah assumed that White Thunder had stepped out of the shadows to stand behind her. "But," Cook continued, "she was here fer a time. Locked in her room, she was, while that evil man tried ta marry her off to an ugly old good-fer-nothin'. Now get ye in here. Would ye like some stew? I've only jest made it."

"We would be delighted. But what happened?" asked Sarah. "Did Marisa marry the man her uncle had selected for her and then leave?"

"I daresay not. She escaped, and in doin' so, she forced that evil man John Rathburn to write out his own confession. He did it, too, had little option."

"He had little option? Why? What happened?"

"He tried to kill her."

Sarah gasped and almost swooned. For a moment, she could hardly speak. "Miss Marisa?"

Cook nodded.

Eyes wide, Sarah asked, "But he didn't accomplish it?"

"Indeed not."

Sarah let out her breath. Gingerly, she laid a hand on Mrs. Stanton's arm, then asked, "How did it happen?"

"Him and that giant Thompson tried to kill her—happened in his study, it did. That Indian lad of hers saved her—kilt Thompson dead."

"Thompson is dead? Can't say that I'm sorry. But, Mrs. Stanton, what did Mr. Rathburn confess to?"

"I wouldn't be knowing that exactly, but rumor has it that he had business with a Dutch settlement, and he destroyed it and the murdered of all those people, and—"

Sarah had sat down all at once, looking for all the world as if she might faint.

"Miss Sarah, are ye all right?"

"Aye, I am fine. I think. But please, don't stop. Please continue with your story, Mrs. Stanton."

"Are ye certain?"

Sarah nodded.

"Though it happened long ago, long before ye came to live here, Miss Sarah, Miss Marisa forced John Rathburn's hand at a confession of that Dutch settlement."

"Then he truly was responsible for my parents' . . ." Sarah placed her hand over her heart.

"What was that, Miss Sarah?"

"It was nothing, Mrs. Stanton. Please do continue."

"I be thinkin' that if he done it once, he done it many times. But I guess all we'll ever know about is that poor Dutch colony."

"Aye, you could be right."

"He has been under house arrest since he made that confession, and I daresay he'll remain that way until his trial, and 'tis Albany's own constable who be here with him tonight."

"The constable is here?"

"Aye, that he is."

"But Miss Marisa is not?"

"No. She left with that Indian gent who saved her."

"Is she truly well? She is not harmed?"

"The last time I saw the girl, she was well . . . and happy."

"And Thompson? You say that Black Eagle killed him?"

"Aye, lass. He was kilt dead, right here in this very house. He tried to kill Miss Marisa. But her Indian lad took care of Mr. Thompson, and like ye, I say, good riddance."

Sarah nodded. "He did deserve it, Mrs. Stanton. He tried to kill Miss Marisa while we were en route to New Hampshire. Had it not been for that same Indian gentleman, she might not have survived. Me neither."

Mrs. Stanton nodded. "'Tis true, what ye say. But come now, ye look like ye've been through the gates of hell and back. Ye and yer friend are welcome here in me kitchen for as long as ye wish to stay. Sit. Eat."

Sarah did as ordered. Indeed, she didn't think she could have stood to her feet at the moment had she tried. It was as though she had been delivered one shock after another.

True, she had suspected that Rathburn was responsible for the deaths of her parents. But it was one thing to suspect it, another to be confronted with the reality of it.

Still, good manners came to the fore, and with all the well-said thank-yous, Sarah picked up a spoon and forced herself to eat.

In due time, however, noticing that Mrs. Stanton was hovering near her, Sarah asked, "Did Miss Marisa say where she was going?"

"Nay, lass, she dinna."

"I suppose I'll have to see Mr. Rathburn so as to obtain his approval to go and find her, since she is still in my charge."

"Lass, dinna ye hear?"

"Hear what?"

"When Miss Marisa made that evil man write a confession sayin' how he'd destroyed that Dutch colony, she also forced him to confess that he had no right to keep you in servitude. Before she left, she not only told me so, she showed me the confession."

"She did what?" Sarah came up out of her chair.

"Yer free, lass. Yer free of him."

With a clatter, Sarah dropped her spoon onto the floor. She stood dumbfounded. She was free? As easy as that? There would be no court of law to pronounce her a fugitive from justice? No master to appease? It was over?

Turning her glance onto Mrs. Stanton, she asked, "You're certain, Mrs. Stanton?"

"I be certain. But don't ye take me own word fer it. Constable Phelps is here. Go and ask him yerself."

"I will, Mrs. Stanton. I will. But not tonight. For now, I need to sit and try to assimilate all that you've told me. For much has changed since I was last here."

"That it has, lass. That it has."

Since Marisa wasn't in residence at the Rathburn estate at present, and Sarah was apparently her own free person now, there seemed to be no reason for her and White Thunder to stay. Eventually they bid Mrs. Stanton farewell, and stepped back into the darkness of the night.

Sarah barely knew what to do with herself. For fifteen years, she had lived under the yoke of servitude. It had become a way of life for her. Now what was she to do?

She must have asked the question aloud, for White Thunder suggested, "Stay with me. Become my wife."

"Yes," she said, although her attention seemed scattered. She simply didn't know how to take it all in.

"Then you will become my wife? Stay with me? Live with me?"

"Yes," said Sarah, this time with more passion. "I would like that very much."

White Thunder smiled at her before he turned away to take the lead. Happily, they made their way back into the woods.

Twenty-five

"*He is here.*"

It was Wild Mint. She stood before them in physical form, blocking their path, although Sarah had to admit that Wild Mint's body substance was weak and filmy, as though one could easily put their hand through her . . . if they dared.

"*The man who killed me as well as our child, is here.*"

"Who is he?" asked White Thunder, looking and acting as if seeing Wild Mint in this way were most common and ordinary.

"*John Rathburn. I would recognize him anywhere. It is he, the one you have been searching for all these years. I thank you, Miss Sarah, for bringing my husband here, and I thank you for all you have done to help him. But now justice must be done.*"

No, it couldn't be. How could this happen when everything seemed so right only moments ago?

Sarah despaired. There for a while, her world had been a happy, wonderful place. But no more.

"I will kill him," said White Thunder, and no sooner had he said it than he turned to retrace his steps to the Rathburn residence.

However, coming out of her temporary distraughtness, Sarah caught up with him. She said, "And if you do that, you will be hanged, Mr. Thunder. I realize 'tis not an easy thing to give up, seeing that you have searched for this man for fifteen years. But if you kill him now—tonight, and in cold blood—the townspeople will hang you."

"Interfere no longer," said Wild Mint.

"You do not rule my life," said Sarah, "and you do not rule White Thunder's either."

"He is my husband."

"No more," said Sarah. "You are no longer alive."

But their argument was for naught. White Thunder was already striding back toward the residence, and Cook's door.

He didn't even knock. He simply let himself in easily enough, for Cook hadn't locked the door. Sarah followed, running to catch up with him.

As soon as she could, she stopped him by plopping herself down in front of his path. Arms held akimbo, she said, "Please, White Thunder, be reasonable. If you kill Rathburn now and in cold blood, you will hang. But if you let justice have its way, he will hang at the end of a rope instead of you, and you will live to have the pleasure of seeing him dead without having to risk your own life."

He stopped perfectly still in front of her. He asked, "You would have me be a coward?"

"I would have you be alive, sir."

From out of nowhere Mrs. Stanton came hurrying toward them, adding to the confusion and shouting, "Be there something wrong?"

"Aye, Mrs. Stanton, there is." Sarah turned to welcome the woman. "Apparently Mr. Rathburn killed another woman, long ago—fifteen years ago. This man, White Thunder, has sworn to kill the man who destroyed that woman, who was his wife."

"Oh, no."

What neither Sarah nor Cook had realized, however, was that while they'd been carrying on their conversation, White Thunder had darted away. He was now almost out of sight. Quickly, they caught up to him.

As soon as they reached him, White Thunder turned toward Mrs. Stanton and asked, "Which room is Rathburn in?"

Mrs. Stanton didn't answer. Indeed, Sarah watched as Mrs. Stanton cowered back, away from White Thunder. When it became evident that no answer would be forthcoming, White Thunder addressed Sarah.

"Do you know which room he is in?"

"I . . . I don't."

"It is his study," said Wild Mint, her voice floating above them. *"This way."*

Sarah took note that Mrs. Stanton didn't even bother to ask who had spoken. Perhaps Mrs. Stanton couldn't hear her. It made sense, because when White Thunder paced forward to follow Wild Mint, with Sarah running after him, Mrs. Stanton still noticed nothing out of the ordinary.

At last all three reached the study. But they halted when White Thunder indicated that they should stop and remain perfectly quiet. Tiptoeing forward, Sarah listened at the door,

"I tell ye, she forced me to write the confession at gunpoint."

"She is but a woman, John. Are you telling me you couldn't overpower a woman?"

"Ye saw the Indian with her. He would have kilt me,

too, if I hadn't written it. As it was, ye saw that he kilt Thompson."

"It was self-defense." This was Constable Phelps speaking. "The first moment you stepped into my office, you said this was so yourself. And it's in the confession."

There was a heavy pause. Somewhere in the room, a log from a fire crackled. "I'll give ye ten thousand pounds if ye'll look the other way."

"Are you trying to bribe me, John?"

"Nay, never a bribe. Jest an exchange 'tween businessmen."

Silence. Sarah couldn't hear Mr. Phelps reply. But it mattered not at all. White Thunder had learned enough.

Breaking through the door, he burst into the room. In an overpowering voice, he said, "You, John Rathburn, I accuse you of being the cause of the death of my wife, Wild Mint."

Whatever Constable Phelps had been about to say came at once to a close.

"Who is this Indian and what is he doing in my home? Guards!" Slowly, Rathburn backed up toward his desk.

But Rathburn had made a mistake. He'd forgotten that he was under house arrest. There were no guards to come to his defense.

White Thunder stepped closer to Rathburn and said, "Many seasons ago, you dressed yourself as a Huron Indian and invaded a Mohawk village of Onnontogen, where my wife was visiting relatives. There you raped her, cut her child from her belly and then you killed her. For all these seasons I have searched for you. I have dedicated my life to finding you to kill you. Now you will die."

"Ye are insane!"

But White Thunder held his position and commanded, "Why did you do it?"

"I don't have to answer any questions from a species so low as an Indian."

Both Sarah and Mrs. Stanton gasped.

White Thunder, however, had planted his feet firmly, and he demanded, "Is that why you did it? You think Indians aren't human?"

"I know they are not human. What does it matter who lives and who dies? Indians feel nothing. Besides, they were on me own land."

"The Indians who lived there had been on that land for hundreds of years."

"'Tis mine, I tell ye. I wanted it. 'Twas mine. A man must do whatever needs being done to make others fear him and drive the squatters off his land, now, doesn't he? Guards!"

Again Rathburn seemed to have forgotten the circumstances of his arrest, and sadly the only guards available were the constable and White Thunder himself.

"Please, White Thunder, no! Can't you see he's insane?" It was Sarah speaking.

"I am not insane!"

But Sarah ignored him. "Don't you see, White Thunder? You must let the constable deal with John Rathburn and treat him for the murderer he is. You must understand that if you kill Rathburn now, there are too many witnesses. You will hang. But if you leave it for Mr. Phelps to do, Rathburn will be the one to hang and you will live."

"Hush, girl!" shouted Rathburn. "It's not your place to talk."

Sarah, however, continued to ignore him. She said, "Please, White Thunder . . ."

It seemed, however, that all she had accomplished with her entreaty was to give White Thunder time to take aim. But Rathburn was nothing if not clever, and he suddenly burst across the room and grabbed hold of Sarah, pulling her in front of him. Worse, he held a pistol in his hand, pointed at her.

Rathburn said, "Go ahead and shoot, Indian! Yer shot will go through her to me. Do it if you dare."

Sarah struggled in Rathburn's hold. She bit his arm, gaining a yelp from him; she stomped down hard on Rathburn's foot, but she was wearing only moccasins and she did little damage beyond making him wince.

Taking aim at her head, he said, "Be still, girl."

But Sarah was no coward. If what Rathburn wanted was for her to be still, that was the last thing she would do. Wiggling again, she bit down on his hand and stomped once again on his foot. But still he held her firm, with the gun pointed directly at her.

Meanwhile, White Thunder had lowered his weapon.

"If ye don't be still, girl, I promise ye, I'll kill ye along with the Indian."

But even as he said it, Rathburn had suddenly changed his aim and pointed his pistol at White Thunder.

BOOM!

Rathburn's aim was quick and sure. Plus, it was a small room and they were standing at close range. However, if he'd been intending to put a ball through White Thunder's head, he missed. The shot caught White Thunder in the shoulder instead.

For an instant only, Rathburn settled Sarah to one side of him so that he could check the accuracy of his shot.

Without warning, White Thunder jumped to the right flank of the room, his motion so swift it looked as if he were in two places at once. *BOOM!* The second shot seemed to come from mid-air.

There was an instant explosion and smoke was everywhere. John Rathburn's hold on her tightened, then unexpectedly, he let go. He fell to the floor. White Thunder rushed toward her. Pushing Rathburn out of the way, he took her in his arms.

Slowly, Constable Phelps paced toward Rathburn's body, where he nudged it with the toe of his boot.

"Are you all right?" White Thunder asked.

Was she all right? Looking down at herself, Sarah saw that she was covered in blood. Plus, the love of her life had just shot a man and would probably hang for it, even though it was in self-defense. And he asked if she was all right?

Sarah didn't answer. She simply shut her eyes and moaned.

"Miss Sarah. Miss Sarah." It was Mrs. Stanton, who had come up behind her. "Did ye catch part of the shot also?"

"No, Mrs. Stanton, I'm fine."

"Forgive me, Miss Sarah." It was Constable Phelps speaking. "I was aiming for Rathburn only, and it took me a great bit of courage to pull that trigger when he was holding you. But if I shot you, too, I'll never forgive myself . . ."

Sarah pushed herself out and away from White Thunder's embrace. Addressing the constable, she said, "You? You shot him?"

Constable Phelps nodded. "I'm afraid I did."

"Then White Thunder didn't?"

"Check his rifle, Miss Sarah. I think you'll find 'tis cold."

She did. But the musket was far from cold. In fact, it burned her hand, confirming that White Thunder had, indeed, been the one to pull the trigger.

She glanced up at White Thunder, who was shaking his head. Then she looked at the constable, who winked at her. Amazingly, Mr. Phelps said, "I'm sorry you had to witness my shooting your employer, Miss Sarah, but there seemed no other way. I couldn't very well let him kill you, could I? So sorry."

Sarah hardly knew what to say. However, at last, she managed to speak, and although her voice shook, she said, "There is no need to apologize. I . . . I thank you, Constable Phelps."

Constable Phelps bobbed his head once. "Now, if you don't mind me giving advice, I'd say that the two of you should leave here at once."

Sarah stepped completely out of White Thunder's embrace, then, and coming up to Constable Phelps, she placed a kiss on his cheek.

"We will do that, Mr. Phelps. As soon as I see to Mr. Thunder's wounds. Come," she addressed White Thunder. "Let's go to the kitchen, where I'm certain we'll find plenty of bandages."

White Thunder didn't object in the least.

It was a pleasure to leave that room. It would be an even greater pleasure, indeed, thought Sarah, to leave the house entirely.

And so it was that a reign of malevolence had come to an end.

Perhaps it is true that one cannot victimize one's fellows in this life without becoming himself the victim. Perhaps karma will win out after all.

One circumstance was apparent, however. In all the days and weeks to come, no one mourned the passing of John Rathburn. Alas, the opposite was true. Perhaps he had, after all, lied to and cheated too many people.

Twenty-six

White Thunder and Sarah finally caught up with Black Eagle and Marisa in the Seneca town of Geneseo. Geneseo was another Iroquois village that had been built so that the people could live in beauty. Indeed, the entire town had been recently relocated in an area that the Iroquois called Neahga.

The two women could hardly believe their luck at finding one another again. They hugged and hugged one another until they almost had to be pried apart.

The two men, however, though obviously watching their women in open appreciation, knew that their finding one another was no accident. White Thunder had sent inquiries to all the Iroquois tribes, and runners had told him exactly where the couple was to be found.

In truth, White Thunder had discovered that Black Eagle had delayed going farther west only so that the two women could be reunited.

"We looked for you, Sarah," said Marisa. "I think I died a little when you let go of my hand that day."

"I, too," said Sarah. "But it turned out well, has it not? I was found, and by White Thunder."

"He is quite handsome, and he seems devoted to you, Sarah. I'm happy for you."

"And I'm happy for you."

The two couples had left the village to walk through the deserted corn, bean and squash fields. There, privately, the two women could reacquaint themselves with one another, the two men accompanying them to act as protection.

There was some danger, because the French had set up a fort close by. But on this day, it was doubtful that the French would attack the town of Geneseo. Apparently they were being engaged elsewhere.

"What are you planning to do?" asked Marisa. "You know that Black Eagle and I would like for you to come west with us. There, I think we'll find comfort in the fact that no one will look with disfavor upon each of our unions. Won't you come with us?"

"I would like nothing better," said Sarah.

"Oh, I'm so happy."

"But—"

"But?"

"A certain friend of mine ensured that all the rights of her parents' property was transferred to her. In truth, Marisa, White Thunder and I have thought that we might like to settle there. It's away from all the other farms—at least it is for now. But we'd like a chance to work the land."

"Yes," said Marisa, "of course. But you know, there may come a time when there are too many settlements that surround you, too many prying eyes, too many wagging tongues. If that ever happens, come see us. There will always be a place for you with us."

Tears stung at the back of Sarah's eyes, and apparently

Marisa felt much the same, for her eyes were shining and blinking.

"I will miss you, my friend," said Marisa.

"And I will miss you. But I do have something for you."

"You do?"

"Aye, I do." Reaching into her bag, Sarah pulled out a letter, which had been given to her by Constable Phelps.

"For me?"

"Aye."

"What is it?" Marisa asked as she broke the seal to read the letter. "Oh, my," she said. "Did you know this?"

"I fear I did."

"And you didn't tell me?"

"I wanted you to read it for yourself. No one came forward to claim the estate. Therefore, Constable Phelps has ruled that John Rathburn's estate shall become yours."

Marisa wiped a hand over her forehead. "But I don't want it. Albany is not a place where Black Eagle and I will thrive. I'm sure you understand why that is."

"That I do."

"But I think I know someone who would do the property good."

"You do?"

"That I do. Mrs. Stanton, our old cook. Did you know that despite John Rathburn, she helped me?"

"She helped me also."

"Yes. I think I will convey the property to her . . . or at least I will try to. Sarah, if I write a note to Constable Phelps, would it be too out of the way for you to deliver it to him?"

"No trouble at all."

Marisa grinned and hand in hand, Sarah smiled back at her.

"I think," said Sarah, "that always we'll be friends. John Rathburn might have been insane, as well as a scoundrel

and all sorts of other bad things, but he did one good deed
in his life: He brought us together."

They hugged. And this time it wasn't a simple matter of
the sting of tears that threatened at the back of their eyes.
This time, the tears flowed openly and with joy down both
of their cheeks.

"Are you certain that you'll be happy settling on our farm
in Pennsylvania?"

"Wherever you are, my wife, I will be delighted and
pleased to be there with you," said White Thunder. "Besides,
if we decide we like it very little, we can always pick up our
roots and join your friend."

White Thunder and Sarah had packed their belong-
ings that very morning, and had left the Seneca town of
Geneseo, heading back east. Meanwhile, Black Eagle and
Marisa had begun their journey onward into the west. Part-
ing had been difficult for the two women, but at last their
men had pulled them apart, and saying their goodbyes,
each couple had set off on their own separate path.

"Yes, if we don't like it, we can always go farther west.
But if we could stay for a while on the land my parents
originally purchased, I think it would honor them."

"And so it will be," said White Thunder. "Always will
we love. And so long as I live, I give you all of me that there
is to give."

"I love you," Sarah said.

"Always will it be," whispered a voice on the air. It was
Wild Mint. *"Thank you, White Thunder. Thank you, Miss Sarah. Always will you two love. Always will I remember your
kindness to me. And now I leave you to go on my way.* Dah-
neh hah. *It is finished."*

Historical Note

I hope you will bear with me as I take literary license with a bit of history. The Code of Handsome Lake didn't originate until close to the end of the 1700s, which would place it around forty years after our story takes place. Handsome Lake (1735–1815) was a religious prophet who was born in the town of Caughnawaga on the Genesee River.

When I read of this story of how the white race came to America, a part of Handsome Lake's prophesy, I found it so engaging that I knew it would probably find its way into the story, which, of course, it did.

My thanks to Arthur C. Parker, author of *The Code of Handsome Lake, the Seneca Prophet*, and to Fintan O'Toole, author of *White Savage*, for first bringing my attention to this legend.

Gen Bailey

Remarks from Benjamin Franklin Regarding the American Indian

"Savages we call them, because their Manners differ from ours, which we think the Perfection of Civility. They think the same of theirs."

"The Indian Men when young are Hunters and Warriors; when old, Counsellors; for all their Government is by Counsel of the Sages; there is no Force there are no Prisons, no Officers to compel Obedience, or inflict Punishment.—Hence they generally study Oratory; the best Speaker having the most Influence. The Indian Women till the Ground, dress the Food, nurse and bring up the Children, & preserve & hand down to Posterity the Memory of public Transactions. These Employments of Men and Women are accounted natural & honorable. Having few artificial Wants, they have abundance of Leisure for Improvement by Conversation. Our laborious Manner of Life compar'd with theirs, they esteem slavish & base; and the Learning on which we value ourselves, they regard as frivolous & useless . . ."

"Having frequent Occasions to hold public Councils, they have acquired great Order and Decency in conducting them. The old Men sit in the foremost Ranks, the Warriors in the next, and the Women & Children in the hindmost. The Business of the Women is to take exact Notice of what passes, imprint it in their Memories, for they have no Writing, and communicate it to their Children. They are the Records of the Councils, and they preserve Traditions of the Stipulations in Treaties 100 Years back, which when we compare with our Writings we always find exact. He that would speak rises. The rest observe a profound Silence. When he has finish'd and sits down; they leave him 5 or 6 Minutes to recollect, that if he has omitted any thing he intended to say, or has any thing to add, he may rise again and deliver it. To interrupt another, even in common Conversation, is reckon'd highly indecent. How different this is, from the Conduct of a polite British House of Commons where scarce every person without some confusion, that makes the Speaker hoarse in calling to Order and how different from the Mode of Conversation in many polite Companies of Europe, where if you do not deliver your Sentence with great Rapidity, you are cut off in the middle of it by the Impatients Loquacity of those you converse with, and never suffer'd to finish it—"

"When any of them come into our Towns, our People are apt to croud round them, gaze upon them, & incommode them where they desire to be private; this they esteem great Rudeness, the Effect of & Want of Instruction in the Rules of Civility & good Manners. We have, say they, as much Curiosity as you, and when you come into our Towns, we wish for Opportunities of looking at you; but for this purpose we hide our Selves behind Bushes where you are to pass, and never intrude ourselves into your Company—"

"Their Manner of entering one anothers villages has likewise its Rules. It is reckon'd uncivil in travelling Strangers to enter a Village abruptly, without giving Notice of their Approach. Therefore as soon as they arrive within Hearing, they stop & hollow, remaining there till invited to enter. Two old Men usually come out to them, and lead them in. There is in every Village a vacant Dwelling called the Strangers House. Here they are plac'd, while the old Men go round from Hut to Hut, acquainting the Inhabitants that Strangers are arriv'd who are probably hungry & weary; and every one sends them what he can spare of Victuals & Skins to repose on. When the Strangers are refresh'd, Pipes & Tobacco are brought, and then, but not before, Conversation begins with Enquiries who they are, whither bound, what News, &c, and it usually ends with Offers of Service if the Strangers have occasions of Guides or any Necessaries for continuing their Journey and nothing is exacted for the Entertainment."

Benjamin Franklin, 1782–1783
Source: www.wampumchronicles.com/benfranklin.html

Enter the rich world of historical romance with Berkley Books.

Lynn Kurland

Patricia Potter

Betina Krahn

Jodi Thomas

Anne Gracie

Love is timeless.

penguin.com